BITTER-ASHES-BOOK FOUR

DUCK, DUCK, NOOSE

SARA C ROETHLE

1

I frowned across the table at Marcos, the executioner of my now dead enemy, Aislin. His long, pure white hair hung forward as he looked down at the coffee cup I had placed in front of him. I'd figured a little civility could go a long way, but apparently I'd figured wrong.

He hadn't touched the hot beverage, something that pissed me off more than it should, based solely on the fact I couldn't have any. Alaric had assured me that because I'm Vaettir, caffeine, rough-housing, or even radiation wouldn't be able to hurt my baby, but I couldn't bring myself to drink it. I'd been raised amongst humans, and some practices would stay with me forever.

"Where did you learn to transfer energies?" I demanded for the hundredth time as I shifted in my seat and tugged my soft, gray sweater down over the small bump of my belly.

Marcos simply stared at me.

Alejandro snorted. I turned back to see him leaning

against the stone wall behind me, looking admittedly scrumptious with his long, black hair draped around his strong Native American features. He'd also been one of Aislin's people, but I liked him better. He'd been more than happy to come to my side. Of course, that probably had more to do with the fact that she'd intended to kill him than anything else.

Alejandro had been assigned Marcos guard duty since we'd first arrived back at the Salr originally shown to me by the Morrigan. Alejandro's usual partner was Aila, since we didn't necessarily trust him to be alone with Tallie and Marcos, both formerly Aislin's people. Now that Aislin was dead, they didn't have much reason to betray us, but better safe than sorry.

When Alejandro and Aila needed rest, either Mikael and Tallie, or Sophie and Alaric would take over on guard duty. Since apparently being pregnant made me an invalid, I didn't get to guard anyone. Of course, Faas didn't get to stand guard either, mainly because Marcos, as a true necromancer, was more than a match for his powers as an executioner. Faas was capable of draining a person's energy, which was a scary trait to have, but Marcos had proven his skills at energy manipulation were superior.

Alejandro flipped his hair over his shoulder, showcasing his strong cheekbones and dark eyes. His crimson tee shirt made his skin stand out in rich contrast. "He's not going to tell you anything. He's been Aislin's pet for over a century." He sneered at Marcos. "Probably mourning the loss of his little tyrant queen."

"I mourn the loss of no one," Marcos interjected.

Alejandro and I jumped at the sound of his voice. He

hadn't spoken since we'd brought him to the Salr, and I had begun to think he never would.

I turned and raised an eyebrow at him. He still had a fading bruise on his cheek from my fist, but the rest of his face was like a pale, smooth stone. His expression gave nothing away.

I sighed at his renewed silence. "And here I thought we were about to become friends."

He tilted his head. "We can become *friends*, Phantom Queen, but I will not confide information in front of the traitor." His eyes flicked to Alejandro.

I narrowed my eyes at him. "Then we'll find a different guard."

Marcos shook his head. "We speak alone, or not at all."

"Why?" I pressed, pushing my wavy hair away from my face, only to have it fall forward again.

He pursed his lips. "There are certain things that only *you* will understand. I would not have your opinion instantly swayed by the words of others, before you've had the time to decide yourself."

Well now I was intrigued. "Fine," I snapped.

"Maddy—" Alejandro began, but I cut him off with a sharp look.

He didn't seem happy about it, but went to the door, opened it, and exited the small room. Aila peeked her head in from the hallway after Alejandro passed, likely wondering why I hadn't followed him out.

"We need a moment," I told her.

She raised both eyebrows in surprise high enough that I thought they might touch the hairline of her white-blonde ponytail. "Mikael expressly demanded that you

SARA C. ROETHLE

not be left alone with him." She nodded in Marcos' direction.

"You'll just be right outside the door," I said sweetly.

Aila frowned. "If you come to harm, I'm blaming Alejandro."

"Hey!" Alejandro called from somewhere behind her, but Aila shut the door before I could hear whatever snide remark he likely had for her.

I turned back to Marcos. "Happy?"

He smiled a wicked smile, making me suddenly regret my decision. "You're very trusting for someone who's been narrowly escaping death for the past month," he observed.

I gave him a patient smile in an attempt to hide my anxiety, then aimed my eyes at the bruise on his face. "I think I've already proven I'm not afraid of you."

He nodded in acceptance. "Touché, nor have you any reason to be. To answer your original question, I'm descended from the goddess Hecate. My ability to shift energy wasn't something I learned. It is a talent I've always possessed."

I'd heard of the goddess Hecate, and knew she was associated with necromancy, so it made sense. One thing didn't though. "And why did we need to be alone for you to tell me that?"

"We didn't, but I wasn't sure if you wanted the others to know just what you're planning."

I inhaled sharply. There was no way for him to know. The exact details of my plan had remained between the Morrigan and myself. I'd filled Alaric in on as much as I could, and he knew the gist of my plan, but I'd sworn that certain things I would keep secret.

4

"I've been inside your head, Madeline," he taunted. "Don't play dumb."

I exhaled and did my best to relax. He was referring to when he'd taken the key from me. He'd connected with my energy in order to separate it from the key, but if he caught a glimpse of anything else, it was brief. "What exactly is it you think you know?"

"You're going to regrow Yggdrasil," he stated. "You're going to bridge the gap between the mundane world and the gods. In effect, you'll be releasing magic to affect the lives of mortals."

So maybe he did know my plan. "The only way to defeat the key is to return it to its natural state. It needs to be reunited with the earth, time, and fate. But first, it has to be reunited with *me*."

A knock sounded on the door, then Alejandro poked his head in. "Everything alright?"

"We're fine," I said quickly, praying he hadn't overheard anything. Alaric at least knew I wanted to regrow Ygdrassil, but he didn't know I wanted the key back.

Alejandro shut the door, and I turned back to Marcos.

"Why don't you want them to know?" he questioned.

"They don't trust the Morrigan," I explained. "If they knew the exact plan she came up with, they'd simply think it's her way of returning to this world for another reign of terror."

He smirked. "And is it?"

I frowned. "No, it's not."

He laughed, and finally took a sip of his coffee, though it was likely cold by now. "Are you sure?"

"Her energy lived inside me for a time, as you know. She

had no malicious intent. Now why all of the sudden interest?"

He took another sip of his cooling coffee. "You managed to beat me at my own game. This interest is anything *but* sudden."

I frowned, thinking back to when he'd tried to steal my banshees from me. It hadn't been difficult to break his connection with them, but it scared me none-the-less. Next time I might not be so lucky, and without the key or the Morrigan, the banshees were the only ace in the hole I had left.

I sighed. "Let me rephrase. Why are you suddenly speaking with me so candidly?"

"My goddess has bade me to do so," he replied simply.

I cleared my throat in an attempt to hide my sudden discomfort. "You're talking to me because Hecate told you to?"

He nodded. "Is that so odd? You had your goddess *inside* you."

I took a shaky breath, thinking of Mara. She'd technically been *inside* Marcos too, using his body to kill Aislin. "The Morrigan wasn't exactly a goddess," I explained. "She told me the old gods no longer answer the calls of their children."

"You know, many view Hecate and the Morrigan as the same incarnation of the *dark goddess*," he said conversationally.

I frowned. "But they're not. I *met* the Morrigan, and I highly doubt she's whispering in your ear right now."

He chuckled. "You are correct. My point is, Hecate isn't like the old gods either. She is an incarnation of the dark goddess, just as the Morrigan was, just as others were before her. Kali is another good example. They were all individuals, yet they were composed of the same energy, existing at different times. The Morrigan was a bit of an anomaly because she was reborn from the destruction of Yggdrasil, but the energy is the same. None of the death goddesses can fully leave this realm, as their energy is needed to keep this world in balance."

I eyed Marcos' coffee, seriously wishing I had a cup after that whopper an info-dump. "So if the Morrigan wasn't a true goddess, how am I, as Vaettir, connected to her. Aren't we all connected to the old gods . . . the *real* old gods?"

His smile made me a bit ill. "You are correct. No Vaettir are descended from the Morrigan. As Vaettir, I imagine you are descended from a different death goddess, perhaps Kali. Yet, upon your birth you became a fitting vessel for the Morrigan's energy, which has been reborn time and again since her mortal death. That energy cannot leave this realm. It is sometimes even reborn as human."

Kali? I was getting a headache. "So I'm the reincarnation of the Morrigan's energy, the energy created when Yggdrasil was destroyed, but a descendent of Kali or some other death goddess?"

He nodded. "Someone truly powerful enough to be sought by the key. It would not choose a human."

"Please get to the point," I said tiredly, not wanting to admit that all the things he was talking about were beyond my comprehension.

Marcos rolled his eyes. "Hecate can speak to me because she is a death goddess. She is the earth itself, light and dark, life and death. She never *fully* leaves this world, because she's too much a part of it."

I narrowed my eyes at him. "If all of this is true, why are you not an empath, and why am I not a true necromancer?"

Marcos sighed and began tracing the table's woodgrain with his finger absentmindedly. "Kali, Hecate, the Morrigan, and all other embodiments of the dark goddess were still individual women with their own affinities. Hecate was the daughter of Titans, giving her power over the sea, and she was also a true necromancer, traveling freely to the spirit underworld. The Morrigan, I'm told, was created when Yggdrasil was destroyed. The Norns became the keepers of time and fate. The charm, or the key, as you call it, became the wild magic and chaos that pushes everything forward. The Morrigan was left with all the rest, including emotion. Hence, empathy."

My eyes widened, not because he'd told me something new, but because very few knew that story. Had he gleaned it when he'd taken the key from me, or had Hecate really told him? I bit my lip, realizing another option. *Estus.* He'd known that I was connected to the Morrigan, and knew that she had previously possessed the key.

I glanced at the door behind us, knowing we'd likely have another visit from Alejandro soon, or worse, Alaric or Mikael would realize that I was alone in a room with Marcos.

"While this is all highly informative," I began evenly, wishing I could quiz him for information for hours, "I still don't understand your motivation for speaking with me."

He'd been looking down at his hand, still tracing along the wood grain, but now smiled up at me through a curtain of pure white hair. "Hecate believes in your cause, and would like to assist in your purpose."

I shook my head. "And just like that, you'll give up any allegiance you had to Aislin?"

He smirked. "I've no allegiance to anyone, nor does Hecate. Aislin sought the charm, and so I followed out of convenience."

"Then why aren't you trying to run to Estus' waiting arms right now?" I countered.

Marcos frowned. "I want the charm, not a ruler, and Estus will not be so easily overcome. His power lies in diplomacy, and in making his people adore him. Now that he has what he wants, he will be fortifying his empire. We need to plan carefully."

"We?" I asked.

"You and I," he clarified. "We have the same goals. It's only natural we should work together."

I narrowed my eyes at him. "No offense, but less than a week ago you helped kidnap me. You tied me to a chair, cut open my arm, and stole the key from me. I'm not feeling terribly trusting right now."

He chuckled. "And you would not have done the same to me, had the positions been reversed?"

I smirked. "I don't know, but here you are sitting in a chair without ropes, sipping coffee. I don't remember being offered any coffee when I was at *your* mercy."

He offered a smug smile. "Yes, I suppose you could have attempted to torture this information out of me. Or you could have starved me until I was too weak to deny your bidding."

I smiled sweetly. "Exactly, so please don't compare me to yourself."

He nodded. "Point taken, but the fact still stands, you *need* me to transfer the charm's energy, and you also need a plan to bring us to that point. As you witnessed, the transfer takes time and ritual. We'll need to create a situation where we can separate Estus from his people, in order to subdue him long enough to regain the charm."

I sighed. "And how do you propose we do all of this?"

Marcos' eyes met mine. "We must make you Doyen of the remaining Vaettir not yet under Estus' rule. The best way to conquer an empire, is to build a stronger one."

My jaw fell. There was a knock at the door, then Alaric's head poked in. "What the hell is going on here?" he asked, his attention one hundred percent on me.

I glanced at Marcos, then back to Alaric. "Making new friends?" I said hopefully.

Alaric frowned, then let out an exaggerated sigh. "Of *course* you are, because a pain in the ass Viking and the little nymph Kira that hides in rooms and eavesdrops on conversations aren't enough, let's add our enemy's pet necromancer to the gang."

I remained in my seat and smiled nervously up at him as he came the rest of the way into the room. "Just one big, happy family?" I asked, half-joking.

His expression softened as he looked down at me with a loving smile, though his eyes still held worry. "Madeline, you've somehow acquired an exceedingly dark sense of humor."

I smiled. "I learned from the best."

Marcos watched our interaction curiously.

As if just remembering we had company, Alaric offered me a hand up out of my seat.

I turned to Marcos, unsure of what else to say. "I'll get back to you," I said finally, leaving it at that.

"One last thing," he said, just as I was turning to leave.

Alaric and I turned back to him.

"You've weakened your banshees to a dangerous point. They need a constant source of energy to survive. They need to feed off the dead, and you've denied them all sustenance. Do not let your best form of defense whither into nothing."

I frowned. He was right. I'd spent as little time around the banshees as possible, and I hadn't visited any more graveyards. It wasn't that I was ungrateful for the help they offered, but they scared me. When I was with them at full power, it was almost overwhelming, and I became something I wasn't. I was afraid to feel that again, and even more afraid that next time, maybe I wouldn't come back from it.

I nodded. "I'll keep that in mind, and I will let you know what we decide regarding your proposal."

He smiled, and it for some reason made me nervous. He'd known a whole hell of a lot about my plans, and now I was considering letting him in on even more. I didn't have much of a choice, really. Marcos was an integral part of the process.

So why did I feel like I was stepping off a ledge?

Marcos held his arms wide to encompass the small room. "I'll be waiting, obviously."

He'd be waiting all right, with his dark goddess whispering in his ear all the while.

2

We left Marcos in his room, guarded by Aila and Alejandro, to go speak with Mikael. As we walked, I explained what Marcos and I had discussed, leaving out the implications of what regrowing Yggdrasil might mean.

Holding my hand, Alaric led me down the stony corridor of our Salr. After walking a short way, we took a left into what had become our common room. The room had a large, wooden table, perfect for talking strategy, and a fireplace with two cozy chairs in front of it, perfect for Mikael to have his nightcap while I sipped herbal tea. The fireplace was currently blazing, and Mikael was currently seated at the table with a chess board in front of him.

He looked up at us with his strange, reddish eyes as we entered the room. The firelight flickered off his auburn hair and old-fashioned smoking jacket as he lounged comfortably in his seat. "It's about time," he said tiredly.

I looked down at the half-played game of chess, then

raised an eyebrow at Alaric, surprised he'd willingly play a game with Mikael.

He sighed. "I have to do *something* to pass the time."

Mikael stood, walked around the table, then pulled out an extra chair for me. "Come watch the game," he invited. "The winner gets to make you his bride." He looked over his shoulder and waggled his eyebrows at me.

Alaric dropped my hand as I sat, then took a step toward the board. He pursed his lips, then moved a piece. "Checkmate."

Mikael walked back around the table, then slumped down into his seat. "Not fair," he argued. "I was too distracted by the potential prize. Now that the prize sits before us, I demand a rematch."

Alaric sat beside me and tsked at Mikael. "You really should have learned to cope with defeat by now, since you're at such an *advanced* age."

Mikael shrugged. "It's been a difficult skill to learn, since I so rarely lose."

I took a deep breath and leaned forward, wanting to interrupt the banter before it became threatening. Mikael and Alaric had learned to live with each other, but Alaric still wanted nothing more than to kill Mikael, and Mikael knew it.

"So I just had an interesting conversation with Marcos," I explained, knowing it would get Mikael's attention.

He narrowed his eyes at me, as if divining whether or not I was joking.

"He wants to help us take the key back from Estus," I continued, eyeing him seriously.

He turned his head to the side, then narrowed his eyes a bit more, as if waiting for the punchline.

"He thinks we need to gain a large clan of our own first," I continued. "Now that Estus has what he wants, he will be surrounded by *his* people, moving his plan forward to enact revenge on the humans for forcing the Vaettir into hiding."

"I take it you're not kidding?" Mikael replied blandly.

"I had much the same reaction," Alaric chimed in, patting my hand where it lay on the table.

"I think Marcos is right," I continued, undaunted. "If just our small group goes after Estus, we may never reach him, even with the banshees. The fact that we need to subdue him and not kill him makes our success even more unlikely."

"Or we could just try to kill him," Mikael countered.

I rolled my eyes. "The key is not going to let its host die so easily." I bit my lip, not wanting to admit the next part. "And I think it will come back to me willingly if we corner Estus long enough for Marcos to transfer it. It *did* choose me, after all."

Mikael sighed and leaned back in his chair. "So your entire plan revolves around trusting the sidekick of our newly dead enemy? I must tell you Madeline, that doesn't sound terribly wise."

Alaric cleared his throat, bringing my attention to his face, and the sudden rage that lurked in his expression. "You are *not* allowing the key back inside of you."

"I need it to regrow Yggdrasil," I countered. "There is no other choice."

Alaric huffed, exasperated. In a sharp irritated movement, he pushed his long, black hair behind his ears. "The whole reasoning behind regrowing Yggdrasil was to relieve you of the key. Now that it's no longer within you, we simply need to eliminate the threat it poses."

"What's this about regrowing Yggdrasil?" Mikael interrupted.

I turned angry eyes to him. It wasn't really my anger, but Alaric's emotions overwhelming my own. "Before the key was taken from me, the Morrigan and I were going to regrow Yggdrasil," I explained. "It would return both entities to their natural state."

Mikael burst out laughing.

Both Alaric and I stared at him with our jaws agape.

Once he had calmed himself enough to speak, he explained, "I really never expected to hear *you* of all people, Madeline, blurting out such an insane plan."

I glared at him.

"Exactly," Alaric agreed. "It's absolutely insane. We didn't spend all this time trying to free her from the key for her to just take it back."

Mikael shook his head and laughed again. "You misunderstand. The plan is absolutely brilliant." He turned his shining eyes to me. "Do you realize what will happen if we manage to succeed? With Yggdrasil once again bridging the way for the old gods, true magic will return to these lands."

"Why would we want that?" Alaric snapped. His anger felt like fire ants biting my skin.

Mikael seemed to sober a bit, then started laughing again. "Because it would be fun!"

Alaric sighed and rolled his eyes, then directed his full attention on me. "Madeline, please do not take into account the opinion of this madman." He gestured to Mikael. "There are so many things about this plan that could go wrong. So many things that could bring harm to you or our daughter."

I shook my head. "Our daughter is at the forefront of my thoughts in all of this. Do you truly think that once Estus has built his base of power, he will allow us to live? Even if he chose to forget about us, the key would not. It always comes back for those who manage to rid themselves of it." I glanced at Mikael.

His expression suddenly serious, Mikael nodded. "It will come for us all. Of that, I am sure."

Alaric seemed close to tears, making my heart ache so much more than his anger had. He grabbed my hand and gave it a squeeze. "Are you sure this is the only choice?"

I nodded. "Think of it as keeping our enemies close. If I have the key, it at least won't be trying to kill me."

"She's right," Mikael agreed.

Mikael's overwhelming sadness washed over me. Normally his emotions were entirely shut off from my empathic senses, unless they were incredibly strong. I knew he was likely thinking of Erykah, his wife who'd lost her life to the vengeful key. Guilt was one of the most difficult emotions to quell.

"But," he added, "I do not trust Marcos. We should not formulate our plan around him."

"We *need* him to get the key back," I stated.

"Or you could attempt to learn Marcos' skill," Mikael countered.

I glared at him. "I thought you were supposed to be on my side."

He smiled warmly. "I *am* on your side, hence the suggestion that will keep you away from the necromancer."

Alaric nodded and turned his serious gaze to Mikael. "He's already begun to manipulate her. I found them chatting alone in a room with no guards present."

Mikael frowned at me. "You don't know of what he's capable, Madeline."

Feeling ganged up on, I snapped, "Maybe *you* don't know *of what* I'm capable!"

Not reacting to my anger, Mikael continued, "I know exactly what you're capable of, and yes, you're very scary, but Marcos was able to cut you off from your banshees before. He is a threat, and will always be a threat, even if he is outwardly agreeing to aid us."

"There are always threats in war," I countered. "The trick is in choosing the right ones to accept."

Alaric laughed, and it was so out of context in the situation that I was without words.

He continued to laugh as he shook his head.

"*What*?" I asked, completely stunned by his reaction.

He smiled warmly at me, though underneath that smile I sensed sadness. "Nothing, you've just obviously been spending too much time around the rest of us. *The trick is to choose the right threats to accept*," he paraphrased. "I never thought I'd hear *you* say something like that."

I rolled my eyes, but couldn't help my smile. He had that effect on me. I turned back to Mikael. "Do you want to hear my plan, or not?"

He nodded for me to go on.

"Marcos made an excellent point to me earlier," I began, causing both the men to sigh. Unperturbed, I continued,

"Now that Estus has what he wants, he's going to want to solidify his base of power. He didn't become Doyen by being stupid. He manipulated others into following him, even though he's not as powerful as many other Vaettir."

Alaric raised an eyebrow at me. "I agree, but just out of curiosity, why do you now think he isn't overly powerful? You used to be terrified of him."

I shrugged. "When he and Aislin kidnapped me, they admitted they were slowly dying. They didn't have the power to remain eternally young like some of us." I eyed Mikael and Alaric in turn. "Neither of them had the power to push forth their plan without the key. They needed its protection first."

Both men nodded, and I continued, "It stands to reason that Estus will continue to be cautious. He'll keep his people close to him, swaying them to his cause. Only once success is ensured will he attack humanity, exposing the Vaettir while enacting his vengeance for acts committed long before he was born."

"And so we must kill him sooner rather than later," Alaric interrupted, "cutting off his plan before he has a chance to truly begin."

I shook my head. "You know as well as I that he is already going to be nearly unreachable. If he manages to recruit those who were loyal to Aislin, he will become unstoppable."

"And?" Mikael urged, seeming to already know what I was thinking.

"And the best way to defeat an empire, is to build a greater one," I finished, feeling silly for echoing Marcos' words. I still didn't trust his role in things, but I had to admit, his plan of action trumped anything I had come up with.

I didn't have any chance to elaborate on the plan as a throat cleared in the doorway. We all turned to see Faas and Tabitha enter the room. Tabitha was a surprise, as she had remained in Norway to gather Mikael's people. When we'd first taunted Estus with news that I had the charm, Mikael's people had dispersed to avoid detection, but given recent circumstances, it was time to bring everyone together again.

Tabitha stood a few inches taller than her brother, though that was where the dissimilarities ended. Both possessed white-blond hair, Tabitha's long, while Faas' was shaved on either side, with a long topknot that partially obscured his eyes. Both wore their chosen style of dress, very Viking-esque, though Tabitha had toned down her look during her travels.

Mikael stood to greet them, and the trio began speaking in Old Norsk. Having only learned a few words here and there, I turned to Alaric for a translation.

He explained with a somber expression, "Many of Mikael's people are missing, likely killed by Aislin's clan. Tabitha gathered those she could find and instructed them to come here."

I frowned and turned my gaze to Mikael's back. I'd had no chance to get to know most of his people, save the ones that had traveled with us from the start, but I knew the deaths would affect him. His clan was small, and he viewed many of its members like family. Of course, I had no way of telling just how he felt, because in that moment, he was shielding like a son-of-a-bitch. He always had his shields up to a certain extent, but I'd come to realize whenever I felt absolutely *nothing* from him, was when he was feeling the most.

Mikael said a few more words to Faas and Tabitha, then the siblings left the room as he came to stand before us. He looked down at me sadly. "It seems I will be providing you with a much smaller head start on your empire than I'd originally planned."

I met his sad eyes. "I'm sorry, maybe some of them will still show up."

"Maybe," he agreed, though I could tell by his tone he was simply humoring me.

He walked around the table and resumed his seat. "I've already sent out a few scouts to find any who wish to leave Aislin's old clan, but we'll need to enlist the aid of Alejandro, Tallie, and Marcos to convince those more loyal to their dead Doyen."

Right to business then, I thought, wanting to offer some form of comfort to Mikael, but knowing he wouldn't appreciate it. He needed to deal with things in his own way. "I don't think Marcos will be of much use in that aspect. I got the impression from Alejandro that many are not terribly fond of him."

Alaric snorted. "I don't blame them."

Mikael smiled. "Fear can be a wonderful motivator, and I'm afraid it's likely our best tactic." He met my eyes with a wry look. "You Madeline, have become a bit scary."

I shook my head. "The banshees are scary, not me."

Mikael shrugged. "Be that as it may, we're much more likely to gain an empire with the *Phantom Queen* at the forefront. With that image in mind, Marcos will be a useful addition."

"I thought the *Viking King* was going to be at the forefront," I said, only half joking. Our original deal had been for Mikael to lead after we'd defeated Aislin and Estus. He, for one, would at least know what he was doing.

He bowed his head slightly in acknowledgement. "I can share a throne if you can."

Alaric scoffed. "You're proposing that you and she share the role of Doyen?" he asked, his gaze firmly on Mikael.

Mikael nodded, then turned to me as he offered his explanation. "I may have lost many of my people, but not all, and I hold sway with the independent clans here in Ireland. Not only that, but my diplomatic tactics will be a necessary backer to your . . . scariness. My other added value is my age. Many of the more ancient among us will not willingly follow someone as young as you. With me as part of the package, we will gain more powerful allies, not just those afraid of phantoms."

"So how does Marcos fit in?" I asked curiously.

"He will be your commanding general, or *Merkismathr*," he explained, "Though he will be this in name only. We're obviously not going to let him command anything. Regardless, he was *Merkismathr* to Aislin, so it will be a believable role."

"What if I want Alaric to be my merki-whatsit?" I asked, knowing I was going to botch the pronunciation of the word no matter how hard I tried.

Mikael shook his head. "Pretty though he may be, stealing Aislin's second in command will give you more clout. It's a matter of image, nothing more."

I nodded in understanding. "So we build up our ranks, then take the key back before Estus can make his move."

Mikael nodded. "With any luck, we'll cast enough doubt in the hearts of those who remain with Estus to avoid much of a fight."

Alaric sighed. "Or they'll fight, and we'll launch the equivalent of World War III, with the key on one side, and a phantom army on the other. The humans who manage to survive will attempt to hunt us down, much as they did in the past, only this time, it won't be small scale witch hunts."

I frowned at him. "Thanks a lot, Negative Nancy."

"Either way," Mikael interjected, "a large, strong army is our best chance of survival. I agree with Madeline. The key *will* force Estus to come back for her, even if Estus himself doesn't care about her death. I will not have those I care about slaughtered once again, simply because I underestimated the key's thirst for vengeance."

I shook my head. "It's not about vengeance. It's about chaos. It cannot leave those it has touched to live out their lives in harmony. It goes against what the key is at its core."

Mikael shrugged. "Either way, the results are the same. We need to be ready for it, which means recruiting as many powerful Vaettir as possible." He eyed me steadily. "It also means you need to rebuild your army. Your banshees have begun to fade to mere specters."

I nodded. "I know, but—"

"You're scared," Mikael finished for me. "But we brought you back to yourself before. We can do it again."

I looked to Alaric, needing reassurance.

He took both my hands in his and gave them a squeeze. "You know how I feel about the banshees, but Mikael is right. They will protect you, and I cannot argue against anything that increases your chances of survival. I believe without the Morrigan or the key taking up space in your mind, you'll have more control over them this time. Not only that, but your powers have grown stronger, as you exhibited when you kept the banshees from Marcos. To steal your words once more, you must choose which threats are worth accepting."

I nodded, then took a deep, shaky breath. "So we recruit all we can, and I will strengthen the banshees."

With a sad expression, Alaric bowed his head in acceptance, just as Mikael nodded his own assent.

We were all agreed. We had a plan . . . kind of.

3

W e didn't have time to solidify our plans, as an argument broke out somewhere down the hall. Sophie's voice was prominent, shouting above the rest. Her anger hit me like a ton of bricks, even from the distance, though underneath her fiery rage was heartache. There was only one person I could think of that would cause that sort of response in Sophie. Well two, really, but James was dead.

I turned nervous eyes to Mikael as we all stood. "Is there any chance some of Aislin's people could have found us?"

Alaric took a step toward me and placed his hand on my arm, suddenly concerned. "What are you thinking?"

The yelling grew louder for a moment, then cut off abruptly. The sound of high-heeled boots clacked the rest of the way down the hall, quickly approaching us.

I shivered. "There's only one person that could elicit

this sort of response from Sophie," I explained, but was cut off as she appeared in the doorway.

Her long, black hair hung loose down to her waist, framing a silk, crimson tank top and black jeans. Her dark eyes were red-rimmed and puffy, though no tears fell down her pale cheeks.

She startled for a moment as she realized she already had our full attention, then her face set into determined lines. "We have *visitors*," she explained.

"Maya?" I breathed, still overwhelmed by Sophie's emotions.

She glared at me, though I wasn't the source of her anger. "Among others," she explained. "They've brought a message. Apparently, they want to join us, and want to bring many of Aislin's other people with them."

That explained Sophie's anger. Sophie had risked her life for Maya, and Maya had not only betrayed her, but later came back and tried to kill her. There was one thing I didn't understand though. "How did they find us?"

Alaric lifted a hand to his chin in thought. "Tallie or Alejandro could have at some point contacted them. Though we've done our best to never leave either of them alone."

Sophie turned her glare to Mikael. "They could have followed Tabitha and the others. It wouldn't have been difficult."

"But they just got here," I argued. It seemed a little fast to have everyone arrive.

Mikael smiled. "I told you I was sending out scouts to see if any of Aislin's people were willing to defect to our side. This must be our first shipment."

I turned wide eyes to him, utterly flummoxed. "*What*? I thought you were just feeling things out, not inviting everyone over for a party."

He continued to smile. "My spies infiltrated Aislin's remaining clans in Scandinavia, just to test the waters, and see where they all stood. Any who offhandedly expressed that they would follow me were first asked to leave Aislin's Salr. Once they were alone, and could be easily killed should they betray my spies, they were invited to come here." He turned to Sophie. "Although, it seems we have not given them a warm welcome."

I frowned. "So you had them drawn away from the group before giving them an offer. What would have happened if they tried to run back to the Salr to divulge our location to the others?"

He pushed his red hair away from his face and looked at me like I was being extremely silly.

"Right," I replied, getting the gist. "If there was any chance of betrayal, the new recruits would have been killed."

"The others can join us," Sophie snapped, "but not Maya."

Mikael shook his head. "It would not be a very good welcome to kill one of our new members, and we cannot send her away to spread word of our location."

Sophie glared at him, then turned her gaze first to me, then to Alaric. Unfortunately, none of us could agree to her terms. Mikael was right. We were on shaky ground as it was, and we needed to take what we could get.

With a grunt of frustration, Sophie turned on her heel and marched back out of the room.

I turned back to Alaric and Mikael.

"We should probably go see to our new guests," Mikael stated.

Alaric and I sighed in unison. I didn't particularly want to see Maya either, and I knew he likely felt the same. We'd *all* risked our lives to save her, and she'd played us. She'd been held prisoner in Estus' dungeon, but had refuted claims that she'd joined Aislin's clan. We'd busted her out, and she'd been lying all along. As soon as we'd joined Mikael's clan, she became our enemy.

Mikael headed for the door. Alaric and I gave each other tired looks, then followed him out of the room toward the entrance of the Salr. There was no sign of Sophie in the hall. Alaric glanced over to meet my eyes, clearly conveying his worry. We'd need to check on her later to make sure she wasn't devising anything that would upset our plans. Scratch that. *He'd* need to check on her. Sophie was scary when she was mad.

Mikael reached the entry room, then touched his fingers to the solid wall. Seconds later, he was pulled through until he disappeared entirely. Alaric and I went next, and soon we were all above ground, standing in the middle of a circle of large stones, surrounded by loamy green earth. In front of us stood Maya, along with three other people I didn't recognize, and one who looked vaguely familiar.

The familiar one, a tall man with long, blond hair woven into a tight braid, stepped forward. He bowed his head to Mikael, then started speaking in Old Norsk. He must have been one of Mikael's spies, judging by the companionable tone of their conversation. A red-haired woman stepped forward from the small waiting crowd to join in on the conversation.

Maya waited patiently with the others, eyeing me with a small, secretive smile on her face.

I glared at her.

Finished with his conversation, Mikael turned his gaze to me. "Most of Aislin's people have turned to Estus," he explained. "These few were personally spited by him, and so chose to branch away from their clan. Others may follow once they are made aware of their defection."

I glanced at each of the new recruits. Maya, plus a man and another woman. The woman was around my height, 5'9", with ample curves and dark brown hair cut into a short bob. The man was short, with an athletic build, dark skin, and short, curly hair. Maya could have been his sister with her small frame, flawless black skin, and curly hair nearly reaching her shoulders.

I already knew why Maya hated Estus. He'd had her tortured for days on end, and at one point she'd even lost a foot . . . though it had been miraculously replaced. I'd be interested to learn the stories of the other two. I could even throw in my own story of the time Estus had me tortured, though mine was far less gruesome than Maya's.

Maya's dark eyes met mine as she continued to smile. "This is Dominic," she nodded to the man, "and Rose," she gestured to the woman. "We're willing to name you our Doyen, if it means we'll get to be a part of Estus' downfall."

I believed her. I might not have liked Maya, and she probably didn't like me, but we both hated Estus more.

I looked back to Mikael for guidance.

He shrugged. "It's a start."

Alaric sighed. "Sophie is *not* going to like this."

"I'll stay away from Sophie," Maya cut in quickly. "She has every reason to hate me. I won't get in her way."

I nodded. It was as good as we were going to get.

A sudden gust of chilly air hit us, and I looked up to see the banshees closing in. They were always waiting for me to surface, unable to enter the Salr themselves. Since I'd let their power dwindle, they'd been reduced to insubstantial phantoms, more like traditional ghosts that couldn't really harm anyone. I really needed to recharge them. It had been stupid of me to wait so long.

Even so, all the newcomers looked up nervously as the banshees approached. Since it was daytime, their forms were mostly transparent, making it difficult to view them with any detail, but they were still scary.

"So it's true," Maya observed. She shifted her gaze away from the banshees overhead. "You're the new Phantom Queen. Maybe we stand a chance after all."

I smirked. "You decided to join us, thinking we had no chance of surviving?"

She raised an eyebrow at me. "Don't tell me you wouldn't do the same, if you were in my shoes."

I shrugged. She was right. In fact, I was already doing the same, going up against Estus in a fight I wasn't sure I could win.

I wrapped my arms around myself to ward off the cold, but it did little good. "Let's go back down," I decided. "I'd like to speak to Marcos further."

I was suddenly hit with a wave of nervousness, though it wasn't my own.

"Marcos is here?" the woman, Rose, questioned, her blue eyes wide with fear.

I nodded, realizing I was sensing her nerves, and maybe a bit from Maya and Dominic.

"He joined us after Aislin was killed," I explained. I didn't feel the need to add that Marcos was the one who killed her, though he'd been possessed by the Morrigan at the time.

"Well shit," Maya muttered. She glanced up at the banshees again. "If you're going for the scary vibe, you totally nailed it."

"I'll take that as a compliment," I replied, then turned away from them to re-enter the Salr.

Mikael joined us as Alaric and I began to lower into the earth. I glanced back to see Mikael's people take up posts on either side of the new recruits. It appeared they would remain under guard, which was fine with me.

I closed my eyes, overcome with a strange, sinking feeling, then suddenly we were back underground, facing a long, stone corridor.

"We should find Sophie," Alaric said immediately.

I nodded, then looked to Mikael.

"I'll show the newbies around," he assured, just as said newbies emerged from the wall behind him.

Alaric put his hand at the small of my back and guided me out of the entryway to walk down the corridor. Our room, which was the same room I'd stayed in when Mara was still alive, was down the hall on the right, several doors past our common room.

Sophie's room was right across the hall from ours. We walked side by side until we reached her closed door. I looked to Alaric as he reached for the knob, his dark eyes holding concern.

"Why do I have the feeling she's not going to be in there?" he asked quizzically.

I nodded my agreement as I placed a comforting hand on his arm. "I have the same feeling."

Without another word, he opened the door. The room was empty.

We both walked forward through the doorway, then approached the bed in the center of the large room. Upon the black bedspread lay a note.

Without even needing to read it, Alaric sighed. "She ran away, not wanting to face Maya."

I nodded, but picked up the note for confirmation. Alaric and his sister had spent five hundred years together, so I trusted his assertation, but maybe the note would tell us whether or not she was coming back.

My eyes scanned the note quickly, then I looked up to meet Alaric's waiting gaze. "It says, *If you don't kill her, I will.*"

"Well shit," Alaric muttered.

I pursed my lips in thought. "Would it really be that bad?"

Alaric frowned at me. "If it's your goal to become Doyen, you must plan your next few moves wisely. Our new additions are the keystones of any plan we could hope to form. Their presence is what's going to help us recruit any of AisliIn's remaining people to our cause."

"We couldn't just kill Maya, and keep the others?" I asked hopefully, already knowing the answer.

He smiled down at me. We both knew we couldn't kill

her. "I'll track Sophie down before she can do anything stupid," he promised.

"Won't she already be expecting that though?"

Alaric would try to track his sister down by scent, but she would naturally know that would be his approach after reading her note. I had no doubt she would do her best to remain one step ahead of him, until an opportunity to kill Maya presented itself.

He sighed. "Yes, but I see no other plan of action. I'll simply have to track her faster than she can run away."

A sick feeling of foreboding permeated my gut. "What if she tries to lead you somewhere far away? She's probably already thinking you won't want to leave me alone with our new recruits. It would stand to reason she would run too far for you to follow, hoping to lose you, so that she might return undetected."

He shrugged. "In that case, she'd be correct in her assumptions. I don't like leaving you at all, and will not search for her to the ends of the earth. If she still eludes me by nightfall, I will return without her, and we will keep Maya under guard at all times. Still, I would prefer to end this quietly. If I can speak to her, perhaps I can talk some sense into her."

I folded the note and put it in my back pocket, not wanting to leave it in the room for anyone else to find. "You know how she is when it comes to Maya," I commented. "I have a feeling she might be harder to convince than you're giving her credit for."

He sighed, then pulled me into the circle of his arms. "I know, but I still have to try."

I wrapped my arms around his lower back, resting my

cheek against his chest, right below his neck. His heartbeat thumped gently in my ear. "I know. Please be careful. After all that has happened, I'm going to be a nervous wreck the entire time you're gone."

He turned his face and kissed the side of my head. "I won't do anything dangerous, and I'll be back before you know it."

We pulled away from each other enough to press our lips together in a gentle kiss, then I looked up into his dark eyes. "If you don't return by nightfall, I'm sending out a search party."

"Deal," he replied. "As long as you're not part of that search party."

I frowned.

"*And* I ask that you remain with Mikael at all times until I return," he added.

I blinked up at him in surprise.

He sighed. "I know he'll protect you. That is all I currently care about."

I nodded, still surprised, as he took my hand and led me out of the room. I didn't appreciate the implication that I couldn't protect myself, but given all that had happened, I couldn't really blame him for being worried.

He kept my hand in his as we ventured out in search of Mikael. I still had a feeling of dread in my gut, but knew it would do little good to voice my concerns. Alaric hadn't survived for over five hundred years by being lucky. He could take care of himself, but it was like the concept of being a good driver. You wouldn't cause an accident yourself, but there are always plenty of other assholes on the road, waiting to T-bone you at a red light.

4

We found Mikael in the common room with the new recruits. Aila had joined him, which meant someone else had been tasked with Marcos guard duty. Everyone turned to stare as Alaric and I entered.

My eyes met Mikael's. "A moment please?" I questioned.

He stood without a word, leaving Aila to watch over Maya and the others. Normally, leaving one person to guard three didn't seem like a good idea, but I had little doubt Aila could handle herself, and everyone else for that matter. As we left the room, she crossed her bare, well muscled arms and glared down at Maya, Rose, and Dominic, daring them to make a move. I wasn't at the correct angle to see everyone else's reactions, but I could picture them all staring hard at the table to avoid her gaze.

Mikael walked with us down the hall, out of hearing

range of the others, then turned and waited for an explanation. His amber eyes held slight worry, already expecting the next catastrophe.

"Sophie is missing," Alaric explained quickly. "She intends to kill Maya, and I intend to stop her. I'd appreciate it if you would keep Madeline by your side."

I crossed my arms and pouted, once again not liking the idea that I needed protection, but I kept my mouth shut. Time was of the essence, and we'd already wasted enough of it.

Mikael nodded, his face expressionless, which seemed to be good enough for Alaric. He turned to me and wrapped me up in his arms, then gave me a quick goodbye kiss.

"I love you," he whispered as he pulled away.

"I love you too," I replied.

He turned away from me, then hurried down the hall, as if another touch or glance would change his mind and cause him to stay. I understood completely. I felt the same way.

"What I wouldn't give to have a woman watch me like that," Mikael mused.

I tore my eyes away from Alaric's back as he disappeared around a corner to narrow them at Mikael. "Maybe if you didn't tease us so much, our looks toward you would be a little nicer."

He smirked. "But what would be the fun in that?"

I shook my head and laughed. "We should get back to the new recruits."

Despite my words, I leaned to the side to peek past

Mikael, unable to resist one last glance down the hall, even though I knew I wouldn't see Alaric there.

Mikael sighed, but didn't move back toward the common room. "We'll take care of them later," he explained at my questioning expression.

I furrowed my brow. "I need a distraction, and getting the new recruits settled seems as good a one as any."

He rolled his eyes at me. "We've been plotting and planning all morning. Especially *you*. Let's go above ground and get some fresh air."

I glanced over my shoulder in the direction of the common room. "We probably shouldn't leave Aila alone with them for too long," I countered.

He snorted. "Are you worried about her?"

I laughed, though it was strained. "Not at all, I'm worried about *them*."

Mikael chuckled. He moved his hand to the small of my back, then began guiding me down the hall. "Let's get you a coat, then we'll send someone else to protect the new recruits from Aila."

"We should at least speak more with Marcos," I argued as he hustled me down the hall.

He shook his head. "You need to relax."

"You've already assured me that my baby is basically indestructible, so I really don't *need* to relax."

"I'm not doing this for the sake of your baby," he explained as we reached my room. "Your powers are more based around your mental abilities and emotions, as opposed to physical skills. You need to rest your mind if you hope to be at your best."

We entered my room. I waited by the door while he retrieved my black winter coat from where I'd left it at the foot of the bed.

I sighed and leaned my back against the wall. "There is no way I'm going to be able to relax my mind while Alaric is out looking for Sophie."

Mikael tsked at me. "Your little kitty cat will be fine. He's a survivor, and he won't do anything that would risk him not being able to return to you."

I raised my eyebrows at him as he came to stand in front of me, offering me my coat. "My, that was almost comforting."

When I didn't take my coat from him, he moved to my side, grabbed my shoulder to pull me away from the wall, then wrapped the coat around me.

With a resigned sigh, I stood on my own and put the coat on properly, then met his amber eyes. "Okay," I conceded. "We'll go for a nice, *relaxing* stroll. Then we'll get back to planning."

"You're such a workaholic," he quipped, then led the way out of my room.

I followed him dejectedly as he walked down the hall. At one point, we came across the tall blond man with the braid who'd accompanied Maya and the others. Mikael gave him orders regarding the newbies to relay to Faas. That settled, we finished our journey down the hall to the Salr's entrance. We both touched the wall side by side. I felt a tugging sensation on my hand as I was pulled into the earth, followed by a moment of panic where I couldn't breathe, then we were both above ground, unharmed.

Mikael began walking toward the coast. I followed, glancing around for Alaric, though I knew he was probably long gone. Hopefully not *too* long gone. If Sophie led him too far away, I was going to be pissed.

The ocean breeze coated my lungs with damp, salty air as we reached the beach and walked down the sandy bank. My low heeled boots sank into the sand, making my steps cumbersome, though I had to admit it was nice being back outside. The chilly wind whipped at my hair, blowing it away from my face. Suddenly glad for the coat Mikael had forced upon me, I crossed my arms to keep in the heat. In just his normal Viking garb, Mikael should've been cold, but he showed no signs of it. I briefly wondered if he felt the cold, but just didn't show it, or if it truly didn't affect him at all.

My thoughts were interrupted as Mikael looked over his shoulder and asked, "What do you plan to do once all this is over?"

I glanced at him in surprise, wondering at the abrupt question. "I-I hadn't really thought that far ahead," I stammered

He continued strolling along, his hands tucked casually behind his back, turning his head slightly to throw his words at me. "So we'll regrow Yggdrasil, then just deal with the consequences as they come?"

I shrugged, feeling suddenly uncomfortable as I trotted to catch up to his side. A sudden chill ran up my spine. I glanced over my shoulder to see the banshees following behind us. Their dark shapes swirled in the wind with dancelike movements. I'd learned that only those with innate magic, which all Vaettir possessed, could see them, so I didn't have to worry about any humans happening upon us. Instead, I just marveled at their existence, while feeling guilty for depleting them so much. They were tortured souls, trapped within the boundaries of the earth, and I had a feeling I hadn't made their existence any better.

"What of your child?" Mikael pressed, either not noticing as I kept glancing back at the banshees, or else refusing to acknowledge them.

I shrugged again and turned forward as we continued to walk. "I'm doing this all to ensure my child's survival," I explained. "Once everything is over, then I will continue to plan things accordingly."

"That's exactly why I ask," he explained. "We are forming a clan, based on the concept of you and I as rulers. If we are successful in our endeavors, we will still be in that position after Estus has been defeated. At that point, it may be difficult to disentangle yourself from the affairs of the Vaettir, if that is your wish."

I seriously considered what he'd said. He was implying that if I accepted the role of Doyen now, I might be stuck with it forever. I didn't want to be stuck with it forever. All I wanted was to raise my child with Alaric in a safe, loving environment, free of supernatural forces out to kill me.

"Can't I just hand the full position off to you when the time comes?" I asked hopefully.

He shrugged. "Perhaps, but it will cause an unpre-dictable amount of chaos. Though many of our followers will gladly accept me as Doyen, others will only join us because of you, the new Phantom Queen. If you step down, it could trigger a civil war, and we'll already be dealing with the aftereffects of releasing magic into the world."

"Yeah," I said distantly. "I was avoiding thinking about that part."

He stopped walking and gazed out at the ocean. I halted beside him, now warm from the body heat generated by my movement. The Irish coast was beautiful, reminding me of the Pacific Northwest where I'd grown up, but also very different. The greens behind us were more vibrant, and the ocean seemed to hold darker hues, more mysterious in its depths.

"The first rule of any scheme," he began, "is to consider every possible outcome. We must be prepared for certain outcomes *before* they happen. If we truly manage to regrow Yggdrasil, we must be prepared for the fallout. Humans will undoubtedly be made aware of our existence, and they will suddenly be living in an entirely new world. As we've learned in the past, they do not react well to those who are different from them. Ignorance often leads to hate."

With a sigh, I took a seat in the sand. Moisture immediately soaked into my jeans and the hem of my gray sweater, peeking out from underneath my coat. I cringed a little, then said, "I understand all of that, but what other choice do we have?" I gazed at the cloudy, gray sky, not wanting to meet his eyes.

He sat beside me, close enough that his shoulder touched mine companionably. "If the only way to defeat the key is to use it to regrow Yggdrasil, then there is no other choice. I only want you to be aware that your life afterward might not be just how you would picture it."

I turned to meet his eyes. "What do you think I should do?"

He smiled softly, then moved his gaze back out to the ocean. "I think you should consider staying in power. At least that way, you will be in control of what happens to you."

"I thought you wanted to rule alone," I prodded.

He shrugged. "It's a staggering amount of responsibility. I could take the hit of not being the omnipotent ruler, if it meant I'd have a little help."

I watched the waves as they crashed on the shore. "I can't decide if remaining in power would put my child in more danger, or less."

He laughed softly. "We are all in danger no matter what. The extra power cannot hurt, and I'll always do my best to protect you."

I turned to him, raising my eyebrow at that last part. "And why is that? That you'll protect me," I clarified.

"Honestly?" he asked, turning to meet my gaze.

I nodded.

He gazed up at the sky. "When you first arrived at my Salr, back in Norway, you reminded me of Erykah. Not the woman she'd become, but who she was when we first met, before the world turned her into the hardened woman you experienced. Her telepathy used to drive her crazy. She would constantly pick up stray thoughts, and be overly concerned with everyone else's problems."

I could see where Erykah and I would share some similarities, but I doubted that was the full story. I took a deep breath, unsure if what I had to ask him next was stepping over the line.

"And what about your daughter?" I asked softly.

He turned back to me and smiled, though his eyes held sadness. He was constantly shielding, so I couldn't sense his emotions, but I was pretty sure I knew most of what he was feeling in that moment.

"You didn't happen to empath me, did you?" he asked, half jokingly.

I laughed. "No, it was just a guess. You told me before that you wouldn't let anything happen to my child. I sensed you were trying to make up for what might have happened to your daughter, but you've never really told me."

He took a deep breath and let it out. "Her death was my fault," he explained. "She was only a child," he muttered, as if finding it difficult to speak.

I waited in silence, wanting to reach out to him, but not knowing if he'd appreciate it.

"I've always had many enemies," he explained, turning his gaze up to the sky, "and back then it was no different. I was overly confident, and I left her and Erykah unguarded. I returned to find Erykah beaten half to death, and our daughter dead. Erykah blamed me. That was the end of our relationship. It was many years later that she became involved with the key," he continued. "She found it on a dead man. She was still filled with grief, after all that time, and the key took advantage of that." He glanced at me. "I'm sure you can understand what it was like for her, more than anyone else."

I nodded. "It tries to make you feel like you can't survive without it. When you're barely surviving to begin with, it's not a difficult manipulation to achieve."

Mikael smiled softly. "Yet you somehow managed to

form a partnership with it, rather than becoming its slave." There was no accusation in his tone, just simple observation.

I shrugged. "Only because of the Morrigan, though I suspect my relationship with the key was different from the start, given that I—" I hesitated, recalling what Marcos had said, "have her energy," I finished. "It's why the key chose me. It wants to fulfill its purpose, even if it doesn't quite understand what that purpose is."

"And here I thought it only wanted to cause chaos," he said sarcastically, though good-naturedly.

I shrugged. "It *is* chaos, but chaos isn't necessarily bad. Without chaos, there is no harmony. The key has been separated from the things that are meant to temper it. It's not evil, it's just existing the only way it knows how."

Mikael smirked. "And when did you get so profound?"

I smiled and looked out at the sun slowly making its way across the sky. How long had Alaric been gone now? It couldn't have been more than an hour, but it felt like days. "The Morrigan had a lot to teach me. She wanted me to learn from her mistakes, and I'm doing my best to not disappoint."

He laughed. "If it makes you feel any better, I don't think you're capable of disappointing her. Just by simply being who and what you are, you will accomplish great things."

I shoved his shoulder playfully. "And when did you get so profound?" I asked mockingly.

He rolled his eyes. "Do you want to hear the rest of my story, or not?"

I nodded. "Yes, please continue."

We both turned our gazes back to the sea as he continued, "The key fed upon Erykah's grief. I had long since killed those directly responsible for beating her and murdering our daughter, but she decided their entire clan must die, even those who had nothing to do with it. She began to form an army. Hearing word of this, I returned to our village to find there was little left of the woman I'd known."

I shivered at the thought. Such a thing could have just as easily happened to me.

"But the old Erykah was still in there, she was just hidden," he continued. "She was doing her best to defy the key, but didn't have the tools she needed. When I met with her to try talking some sense into her, she attacked me. She used the key's power to read everything in my mind. I thought she was trying to hurt me, but in reality she was figuring out how I maintained my shields. With her new knowledge of how I shield, she was able to block out the key enough to part herself from it, but she could not bring herself to destroy it. She threw it into the sea, hoping it would sink to the bottom, never to return." He sighed. "And you know the rest."

"It came back and killed her," I muttered. "Just like it will do to us."

Mikael didn't reply. I watched him as his eyes scanned the water. The banshees had left us alone after the initial sighting, but I knew they would come immediately if I called them. Even without the banshees, the Salr, filled with allies, wasn't far. We were safe, but something about the moment made me feel vulnerable.

"We should get back," Mikael announced.

I nodded, and we both stood. We walked side-by-side back down the coast, both deeply entrenched in our own thoughts. Hopefully Alaric would return soon, and we could get back to planning. There'd been a reason I had been avoiding relaxation. It left too much time to think. I didn't want to think. I wanted to *act*. Trusting my gut in the moment had gotten me this far, I'd be a fool to stop now.

5

Alaric cursed his sister as he ran across the loamy green ground. The cool breeze blew his long, black hair away from his face as he propelled himself forward, faster than any normal man should be able to run. Her scent was still strong in the air, giving him hope. She was traveling on foot, which meant he stood a chance of catching her.

He was running northward, in the direction of the abandoned cellar where Estus and Aislin and had taken Madeline when they kidnapped her. Sophie had been there before, but she had no reason to return, so the direction was likely coincidental.

He only wished he knew what Sophie planned. Did she intend to travel far away to someplace he could not track her, only to come back when they least expected it? Or, did she only hope to elude him long enough to return to the Salr before him? He thought the latter unlikely, given she'd left a note. The only reason to warn them of her plan was if she intended to be gone for a while, and didn't want to be found. If she simply disappeared, she would know that he, believing she was in danger, would commence a full scale search for her. As it was, he thought it much more important to get back to Madeline in a timely manner, than to apprehend his sister.

He came to an abrupt halt as a strange smell filtered through his nostrils, mingling with that of his sister. He recognized the scent, but couldn't quite place it. Sensing a presence behind him, he quickly turned around, half expecting to find Sophie. What he hadn't expected was a Norn staring down at him from her great height with her strange-shaped, uptilted eyes. The curling horns of a ram adorned either side of her head, though they were partially covered by a dark green cloak. She held one long arm out to him, ending in the paw of a wolf.

He had learned previously that the Norns did not communicate with normal speech, but with telepathy, which became much more clear with touch. Understanding what the Norn wanted, he stepped forward, placing himself within reach. The wolf paw touched down on his shoulder. His mind flooded with chaotic thoughts.

First he saw banshees swirling in the sky within his mind, laden with a feeling of questioning. The Norn wanted to know where they had come from.

He instantly thought of Madeline before he could debate on whether or not to tell the Norn the truth. As soon as he thought of her, the Norn understood. The images raced on inside his head.

Next he saw images of the banshees terrorizing the countryside, but he got the impression it was an image of the past, likely the last time the Morrigan had summoned them. The Norn was worried. As a weaver of fate, she felt the new presence of the banshees simply should not be. Madeline had broken very basic rules to summon them, rules that held the world as it was together.

He shook his head and tried to convey that Madeline had little choice in the matter. The Morrigan had influenced her actions. Now that Madeline was left without any extra defenses, she needed the banshees.

At the mention of the Morrigan, the Norn took a sudden step back. A look of perplexion crossed her strange face. She obviously had not been aware the Morrigan had returned to the earth at all. Recovering, she placed her paw once more upon his shoulder.

She showed him scenes from a great battle, with many dead. The banshees collected their souls, adding to their immortal army. At first, he thought it was another scene from the past, but the Norn corrected him. This was a possible future. A future she would not allow to take place, nor would her sisters.

At the sudden threat, Alaric stepped away from her, prepared to run. If they thought this new future involved Madeline, what might they do to stop her? He didn't fully understand the Norn's magic, but knew they were capable of sending people back in time. Any creatures capable of such a thing could likely cause great destruction.

He was about to flee, when several more Norns appeared around him, stepping forward from where they'd been concealed behind the surrounding trees. One held Sophie tightly in its grasp, threatening to stab her with its eagle-like talons.

Sophie struggled against her, then went still in surprise as she noticed Alaric. Quickly recovering from her shock, she began to struggle all the more.

"Alaric, run!" she urged, her face red with exertion from fighting against the Norn's grasp.

Even with Sophie's preternatural strength, the Norn didn't seem to be struggling to hold her.

Alaric's eyes darted from Norn to Norn as they began to close in on him. Though none touched him, he was given the image in his mind that if he ran, they would kill Sophie. But if he stayed, would they harm Madeline? He glared at all of them, still thinking of Madeline's safety.

Reading his thoughts, one Norn shook her head. He sighed as more images flashed through his mind. They feared the Phantom Queen, but did not want to harm her. They would use him and his sister as bargaining tools to sway her from her plan. The banshees must be returned to the earth, never to be summoned again.

"If she returns the banshees, she'll stand no chance against the key," Alaric argued out loud.

That seemed to give the Norns pause, but moments later, their panic re-flooded his brain. They were scared, and it was causing them to act rashly. His mind flashed with images of a woman with long, red hair, standing tall while surveying a field of corpses. Though she was in her original body that he'd never physically met, he recognized the Morrigan, looking over the dead with a small smile on her face. The Norns feared the same thing happening to Madeline. At that moment, with the scene in his mind, he couldn't help but fear it too.

Now you see, one spoke into his mind.

"Was that the Morrigan?" Sophie asked out loud. She'd stopped struggling, and instead hung limply in the Norn's grip.

Alaric shook his head, not in reply to Sophie's question, but in reply to the Norn's proposal. "I understand the risks, but Madeline is not the Morrigan. She won't make the same mistakes."

The Norn's collective mental sigh enveloped him.

There is only one end to this situation, a voice stated in his head. *She must put them back, or she must be killed.*

Alaric's pulse sped as he debated what to do. Would they kill Sophie if he ran, or would they just use her as a bargaining chip? He couldn't decide if Madeline and Sophie would be better off with him in the Norn's possession, or with him by Madeline's side to relay what the Norns had said.

He scanned the Norns. "One of you also told her that the only way for her to part herself from the key was to die, or to put its energy into our child," he countered. "I really don't think you have as firm a grasp on the future as you claim."

It is true, the voice began, *that she has thwarted fate many times. Her very creation thwarted fate. None were to possess the power of Yggdrasil. Yet, we cannot risk certain ends.*

"Or, you could help us achieve the correct end," he countered. "We can regrow Yggdrasil and restore things to the way they were."

"I vote for that idea," Sophie added sarcastically.

Alaric glared at her, letting her know she wasn't helping the situation.

The Norns seemed genuinely surprised. *You would suggest we work together?*

At that moment, he was reminded of how the Norns came to be as they were now. They were originally part of Yggdrasil, the World Tree, and had created the Vaettir in the image of the old gods, because they were lonely, and wanted children. Then, the Vaettir destroyed Yggdrasil, turning the Norns into what they were now, separating them from the key, and from the energy that composed the Morrigan, or so Madeline had explained to him. Once Yggdrasil was gone, the Vaettir had sentenced the Norns to a life of solitude. The Vaettir would not live amongst them, nor would they listen to their foretellings. He smiled faintly. The Norns were probably surprised that he was listening to their opinions at all, let alone offering to work with them.

After thinking it over, Alaric nodded in reply to the question. "We'll need you in the end regardless," he stated. "We might as well work together from the beginning."

The Norns nodded their antlered heads in unison. *Balance will be restored*, they all agreed.

Alaric had a brief moment of relief, then the voice added, *But the banshees must still be laid to rest.*

He sighed. "Let me talk to Madeline. I'll tell her what you've said, and that you're willing to help us."

No, the voice said. *If you leave us, she will have no reason to comply. We have been betrayed by your people many times.*

He glanced at Sophie, who shrugged, then turned back to the Norns in front of him. "What do you propose?"

You will come with us, the voice in his mind stated. *A messenger will be sent to Madeline.*

"If you harm her," he began, ready to launch into a fight to the death right then and there.

We will send a message, nothing more, the voice explained. *You will both remain with us until an agreement can be made.*

He quickly sorted through his options. He could run, but he'd have to leave Sophie, and it might cause the Norns to attack Madeline, or he could stay, and perhaps a non-violent agreement could be made. His choice was clear, but it pained him that he'd be unable to return to Madeline like he'd promised. She was probably already worried, and he knew for a fact if he didn't return by nightfall, a search party would be sent.

"Fine," he stated through gritted teeth. "Send your messenger. I will not run."

The Norns nodded in unison as Sophie let out a tired sigh.

Alaric glared at her. "This is all your fault, you know."

She snorted. "It's your fault for agreeing to let Maya join us."

Alaric rolled his eyes. No matter how many years they lived, Sophie would always be his *little* sister, and he would always need to protect her, no matter how much she infuriated him.

I LEANED BACK against the cushy chair, taking no comfort in the warm fire in front of me, or the steaming mug in my hands.

"He should have been back by now," I stated.

Mikael sighed from his seat a few feet away. The fire's

reflection danced across the glass of amber whiskey in his hand. "A search party has been sent. I'm sure Tallie has *sniffed* him out by now," he said tiredly. "Her tracking skills are beyond even Alaric and Sophie's. If there's any trouble, Aila and Frode will handle it."

Frode was the blond braid man who'd accompanied Maya and the others. Both he and Aila had joined in the search for Alaric. I'd tried to go myself, but had been met with a resounding *no* from the entire group.

I pouted, thinking back to that moment as I stared into the fire. Even Frode, who I didn't really know, seemed to fully comprehend the situation. He'd assured me they would bring Alaric back in one piece. I'd told him not to make promises he might not be able to keep.

I placed my hand on the slight bump of my belly. "For some reason," I began, "I feel like I'd know it if he'd come to any harm. Like I'd somehow *sense* it. Is that ridiculous?"

I watched Mikael out of the corner of my eye as he smiled softly. "I knew when Erykah died, though I was an entire ocean away. She was in my dreams that night."

Gripping my mug with both hands, I gently swirled the tea around within the vessel. "You're making me want to go to sleep, just so I'll know. It feels wrong that I'm not out there looking for him."

Mikael chuckled. "I'm sure he would do his best to kill me upon his return if I let you run off into the woods in search of him. You still have many enemies, and it would do no one any good if you died running off to save him, especially when he may not be in any danger."

I sighed and took a sip of my chamomile tea. The scent and taste were normally soothing to me, but at that moment, nothing could compete with my anxiety. "If he wasn't in danger, he would have returned by now."

"You place a great deal of faith in him," he observed.

"Yes, I do," I answered instantly.

He stood with his whiskey in his left hand, then offered me his right. "It's late. Let's get you to bed."

"I'm not going to be able to sleep," I argued, staring up at him.

"Then I'll sing you a lullaby," he joked, "just as you did for me back when you needed to learn to shield, and wanted to enter my mind while I slept."

I took his hand and rose to my feet, careful not to slosh my hot tea. "First," I began, "you were drunk, and I was just trying to get you to shut up. Second, that situation didn't end very well for either of us. I thought you were going to kill me after the key forced its way into your memories."

He arched an eyebrow at me with my hand still in his. "Were we successful in teaching you how to shield, or not?"

I sighed. "Well yes, but—"

He raised his whiskey-filled hand to silence me. "Then perhaps we'll be successful at getting you to sleep."

I slumped my shoulders in defeat, knowing there was no way I was going to be able to sleep. Still, I was grateful he was at least attempting to take care of me. I almost felt bad. Mainly because if Alaric was gone for a few hours more, and I was still awake, I'd hit Mikael over the head if I had to so I could use my banshees to help me search for him. Alaric would do the same for me. That's what being partners was all about.

6

Alaric leaned his back against the wall in the candlelit cellar where Aislin had met her end. There was still a bloodstain in the middle of the floor, though her corpse had been disposed of by Mikael's people. Against the opposite wall sat the chair where Madeline had been tied up for Marcos to remove the key from her.

He clenched his jaw in irritation. He and Sophie had been sitting in the cellar with the Norns standing guard for hours now, leaving Madeline alone in the Salr with several of Aislin's people, including Marcos, and there was nothing he could do about it. He stifled a sigh. She wasn't entirely alone. Mikael was watching over her, but it did little to comfort him. He hoped Mikael would be able to stop her from running off to search for him. A Norn messenger was on the way. Hopefully Madeline would soon know that he was safe, and wouldn't do anything foolish.

Still, there would be conflict once she was told the

banshees must be returned to the earth. Alaric wasn't even sure she knew *how* to return them, even if she eventually agreed to the Norn's terms. He imagined she didn't, else she might have considered it already. When she was around their power for too long, she became slightly intoxicated with it, and he knew that it scared her. She'd allowed the banshees to grow weak because she was afraid of giving them fresh power. Yet, the fact still remained that using the banshees was their best chance of cornering Estus.

Sophie let out a long sigh. He'd been ignoring her since they'd arrived at the cellar, annoyed with her selfishness when so much was at stake.

"I'm sorry," she muttered.

He glanced to his left where she sat leaning against the wall, her slender body draped in a curtain of dark hair. "Huh, what was that?" he replied sarcastically. "I couldn't quite hear you?"

"I'm *sorry*," she said sharply. "I let my emotions get the better of me. I wasn't thinking clearly."

Alaric rolled his eyes at her. "This seems to be a theme with you regarding Maya."

Even at just the brief mention of Maya's names, Sophie's expression hardened. "If Madeline not only used and betrayed you, then tried to kill you, you'd feel the same."

He met her dark eyes and the ferocity that was always there, just below the surface. "You really love her that much?"

At that, Sophie seemed to deflate. "I *did*. When she left Estus' Salr the first time, I thought she was doing it to get away from him, and that she truly regretted leaving me behind. I held out hope. Then, when Estus recaptured her and had her tortured, I thought maybe if I saved her, those hopes could come true. I thought maybe she'd held that same idea in her heart." She took a deep, shaky breath, then slumped against the wall. "Then we escaped Estus' Salr. I left you and Madeline behind to fend for yourselves, all for Maya. As soon as we were safe in the outside world, she admitted she was Aislin's spy, and she left me. You have no idea how that felt."

He raised an eyebrow at her. "Kind of like being abandoned by your own sister after risking your life to help with her idiotic plan?"

She glared at him. "I knew you would be fine. You always are."

That last bit stung, though he wouldn't admit it out loud. He *had* survived many dire situations, but the idea that he was *expected* to survive those situations without help made him feel the slightest bit lonely. It was part of why he felt so close to Madeline. She would always do her best to save him, just as he would do for her. Neither of them had to deal with their problems alone. It was that bond that worried him now, knowing that Madeline would do whatever it took to rescue him.

Sophie eyed him curiously as he thought things over. The Norns left to guard them were still as statues, not acknowledging their conversation, or even their existence.

"I suppose I can understand your actions," he eventually conceded. "Though you've still been a royal pain in the ass."

She smiled. "Isn't that what little sisters are supposed to do?"

He laughed. "Tabitha doesn't seem to give Faas quite as much grief."

Sophie shoved his shoulder playfully. "You obviously haven't been paying attention. They're always arguing when they think no one is listening."

He smirked. "And *you've* been paying attention? I was under the impression that you only paid attention to *yourself*."

"Hah *hah*," she replied sarcastically. "You're one to throw stones. All you see is Madeline."

He rolled his eyes. "If that were true, I wouldn't be sitting in an old cellar with my little sister, leaving Madeline in the care of *Mikael*."

Her eyes widened in mock surprise. "Woah, sorry, maybe you care about me a little *too* much."

There was something in the way she said the last remark that made him sense there was more to her attitude than she was letting on. His tone turned serious. "I do, you know. I'm aware that things have been centered around Madeline, and I'm sorry if that made you feel alone. We never even properly talked about James' death."

"There was nothing to talk about," she snapped instantly.

"You cried," he countered. "You never cry. The only other time I've seen you cry in the past ten years was when Maya tried to kill you."

She frowned. "I simply felt responsible. I had said some," she hesitated, "*things* to him that made him angry. He provoked Madeline and the banshees because of me."

He eyed her patiently, waiting for her to give him the

real explanation. He knew his sister well enough to know that she hadn't been *that* upset over a little guilt.

"*Fine*," she snapped, turning her gaze away from him and down to her lap. "James was still in love with me," she said quickly. "I thought—" she bit her lip, then began again, "I thought that perhaps he felt toward me what I felt toward Maya. He was an evil person, and didn't really deserve my sympathy, but I couldn't help relating to how he felt. When Maya tried to kill me, I just couldn't understand it, because even after everything, I hadn't wanted to kill James, and I knew he would have never tried to harm me. I suppose when James died, I saw too much of myself in him, dying because of the one he loved, who could not love him back."

Alaric took a deep breath, then let it out. Her explanation had been a lot more than he'd expected.

She continued, "These feelings have been especially hard to cope with while seeing you and Madeline together, returning each other's love equally." As if realizing she'd admitted an uncharacteristic amount of weakness, she took on a joking expression and added, "It's positively vomit-inducing really, the way you two go all moon-eyed around each other."

Suddenly Alaric felt guilty. He hadn't considered the idea that his relationship had only made things harder on Sophie after her terrible luck in love. "You know," he observed, "Aila goes a little bit moon-eyed when she's around *you*."

Sophie smiled with a distant expression. "I know, but Aila has even more trouble showing her emotions than you or I," she laughed.

Alaric grinned. "She fits right in."

Sophie turned her gaze back to him. "Just one big, dysfunctional family."

He smiled, but it was hard to quiet his sudden anxiety. After a moment's silence, he added, "Yes, a family, of sorts. Hopefully we're capable of saving it."

Sophie glanced at the Norns, then back to Alaric. "I trust Madeline to lead with her heart, and Mikael to be more pragmatic. They make a good team. It's up to them now, much more than it is to us."

Alaric rubbed at his tired eyes. Sophie was right. As much as he wanted to be capable of saving the day, everything was currently up to Madeline and Mikael. Even he could admit they made a good team. Too bad he'd still have to kill Mikael after all this was over. Some crimes simply could not be forgiven, at least not by him.

MIKAEL and I sat in the grass outside the Salr as the first rays of sunlight crept over the horizon. I hadn't slept a wink, and he hadn't either, refusing to rest no matter how many times I'd promised I wouldn't leave. He knew because of our oath that I couldn't really lie to him, but still, he'd remained by my side.

"I'm sure they'll be back soon," he assured as we both gazed off into the distance.

I had a flannel blanket wrapped around me, but felt chilled to the bone. Not only was Alaric yet to return, but there'd been no sign of Tallie, Aila, or Frode either.

I perked up as I noticed movement in a far off copse of trees, but whatever it was seemed too big to be Alaric or one of the others. I squinted my eyes, straining to see whatever it was.

"Is that . . . " Mikael trailed off, sounding surprised.

"A Norn," I finished for him.

The tall shape had emerged from the tree line to reveal its antlered head, though at the distance I could make out few other details. I only knew it was a Norn because no other creature shared that particular shape. Its humanoid body was nearly seven feet tall, and its antlers, like those of a whitetail deer, added a good two feet on top of that.

Without a word, Mikael and I both stood to begin walking toward the Norn as she continued to make her way in our direction. I left my blanket on the ground, not wanting to be huddled in its hindering warmth should conflict occur. The Norn was alone, as far I could tell, but I couldn't help glancing warily around us as we walked. I suddenly felt vulnerable being out in the open. The banshees had hung back out of sight, too weak to do anything but watch.

"What do you think she wants?" I whispered to Mikael as we plodded along, our boots kicking up the morning dew from the grass.

He shook his head, his eyes remaining on the Norn, still a good distance off. "I haven't seen any Norns since we went back in time," he whispered. "I wasn't even sure there were any left after the deaths of those I knew."

We stopped talking as the Norn drew close enough to hear us. She took a few more long strides, then stood before us, towering over even Mikael, which few managed to do.

The children of Bastet are with my sisters, a voice echoed through my mind. *I've come to bargain with you for their lives.*

I suddenly felt like I couldn't breathe. She had Alaric and Sophie? "What do you mean, *you've come to bargain for their lives*?" I asked.

We require that you return your phantoms to the earth, she explained. *Then we will all work together to meet your goals.*

I glanced at Mikael, who looked confused. "I take it you're hearing a voice in your head right now?" he questioned.

I nodded, realizing the Norn had been *speaking* only to me. "They're holding Alaric and Sophie hostage," I explained around the lump in my throat. "They want me to send the banshees back into the earth."

"Well we can't do that," Mikael replied blandly. He turned to the Norn. "Kidnapping two of our people against their will, then attempting to bargain with their lives, is a direct call to war," he stated boldly. "If you harm them. We will slaughter all of your kind."

After a moment of shock, I began tugging on Mikael's arm frantically, trying to keep him from speaking further. What the hell was he doing?

The Norn's thin lips curved downward into a perplexed frown.

We cannot risk the phantom's existence, the voice argued. *The threat is too great.*

Apparently now involved in the internal conversation, Mikael replied, "And we cannot risk the key coming back to kill us all. If we fail, Estus will march on all of humanity. It will be worldwide war. Millions will be slaughtered. Surely the banshees do not pose a greater risk than that?"

We will prevent that fate without the phantoms, the Norn argued.

Her panic was almost overwhelming. I felt like I could barely breathe around it. The Norns usually didn't involve themselves in the affairs of humans or Vaettir, and I wasn't sure why they'd chosen now to start, unless they were truly worried the world as they knew it might end.

You hope to regrow Yggdrasil, the Norn explained in answer to my thoughts. *To restore balance. We share in that goal. We can help you achieve it. The dead are not a necessary factor.*

I blinked up at her, surprised. "You do realize that regrowing Yggdrasil would require you giving up your current forms?" I questioned.

The Norns had been a part of Yggdrasil, symbolizing fate. If we were to regrow the World Tree as it was, the remaining Norns would have to return to their original forms within the tree, effectively ending their independent lives.

She bowed her antlered head. *We were never meant to be this way. When we are not ignored, we are killed. We wish to return to Yggdrasil, where we can once again weave the strings of fate.*

I took a deep, shaky breath, but Mikael spoke first. "In that case, it seems *we* are the ones holding all the cards. You will return Alaric and Sophie to us, then you will aid us in any way we deem necessary, if you ever hope to be returned to your previous form."

The Norn stared at him blankly.

I stared at him too, jaw agape. He'd somehow turned the entire situation around on the Norn.

I will discuss this with my sisters, she finally replied.

Just as I sighed in relief, Mikael snapped, "*No,* you will answer for them. Do we have a deal, or not?"

The Norn narrowed her eyes in sudden anger, though her gaze turned to me, instead of Mikael. *I hope that you do not prove us right. The phantoms should never have been raised again. They nearly destroyed the world before the Morrigan destroyed herself.*

"Do we have a deal?" Mikael asked again calmly.

She pursed her thin lips in distaste, then nodded her head.

"Good," he said simply. "Now lead us to our lost associates."

The Norn nodded again.

I looked to Mikael once more in utter shock. "You know, I have never been more grateful for your existence than I am right now."

He waved me off with a smile. "Oh I bet you say that to all the guys."

I shook my head in awe of Mikael's diplomacy, suddenly exceedingly pleased he would be my co-Doyen. If I'd handled that conversation, my banshees would already be gone, and I'd be doing whatever else the Norn might ask of me. It just went to show that you should never feel powerless in any given situation. When your opponent has given you few choices, you simply had to give them even less.

We had just begun to follow the Norn into the woods, when Tallie, Aila, and Frode appeared ahead of us. Tallie stared in awe at the Norn for several seconds before giving her a wide berth to approach us. Frode and Aila seemed unfazed as they moved to stand beside Mikael.

Tallie smoothed her fingers over her shiny black pony-tail, glancing at me nervously, her delicate features creased with worry. "We couldn't find them," she explained. Her eyes shifted to the Norn again. "What is that?" she whispered.

"It's a Norn," I whispered back.

Tallie's eyes widened. "Holy shit."

"My sentiments exactly," I replied. "Though she's actually leading us to Alaric and Sophie."

I could sense sudden great relief coming from Tallie's petite form, though on the outside she just nodded somberly, having failed in her task. Seeming to rally, she tugged her leather coat straight, ready to re-enter the woods for round two.

"We should get going," Mikael advised. He looked to Aila and Frode, both standing tall and super blond beside him, then to Tallie. "The three of you will come with us, just in case."

Everyone nodded as the Norn waited patiently.

"Why does the Norn have Sophie and Alaric?" I heard Frode whisper to Mikael as we all turned and began walking.

"She hoped to use them as bargaining chips," Mikael explained. "She thought she might force us to adhere to her wishes."

Mikael and Frode laughed. It was one of those exceedingly macho moments that were often highly irritating to those not involved. I watched as Aila and Tallie gave each other knowing looks, though I was left out of the exchange. Normally, I might have felt shunned, but right then, all I wanted to do was make sure Alaric was okay.

Aila and Tallie could have their girl's moment without me.

As we walked on for over an hour, I began to recognize our surroundings, though I had only walked that route once before, and I'd been traveling in the other direction at the time. Still, it seemed like we were walking in the direction of the old cellar where I'd been held after Aislin and Estus had kidnapped me. It was a logical guess, since there wasn't much else to be found in the long expanse of woodland ahead of us, that I knew of. It was still too soon to tell for sure though, as the cellar was many miles off.

The Norn stumbled, then hunched over, holding a paw to her head.

I ran to her side, not fast enough to beat Mikael and Tallie there. Her eyes were shut, and she panted as if in pain. I reached a hand out to touch her arm, rubbing my palm across the scratchy fabric of her shapeless clothing, but she didn't seem to notice.

Something's wrong, a voice echoed in my head along with a searing wave of pain.

Panic shot through me, mingling with the pain to make me feel ill. Had something happened to her sisters? If they were with Alaric and Sophie ...

"Where are they?" Mikael demanded, obviously coming to the same conclusion.

A moment later, my suspicions were confirmed. Images of the cellar flashed through my mind. Before I could react, Mikael had moved to the other side of the Norn to hoist me into his arms, carrying me like a small child. It would have been easier for him to throw me over his shoulders, but that would put uncomfortable pressure on my baby bump.

I wrapped my arms around his neck and he began to run, leaving the Norn behind.

Tallie shot ahead of us, faster than Mikael, Aila, or Frode could run. She was as fast as Alaric, maybe even faster. Mikael had known I wouldn't be able to keep up, even with the slowest amongst us.

Wanting nothing more than to break free of Mikael's grasp to run on my own, I fought the tears streaming down my face. It felt like we weren't running fast enough. I'd always been a terrible judge of distance, but if I remembered correctly, the cellar was still six or seven miles away. We wouldn't make it in time to stop whatever was happening.

Still, Mikael ran on as Frode and Aila kept pace on either side of us. I kept my arms wrapped tightly around his neck, wanting to make carrying me as easy as possible. For a normal man, running at such a pace with a 5 foot 9 woman in his arms would have been nearly impossible, but Mikael was no normal man.

Feeling helpless, I sent my thoughts out to the banshees, but only received a weak echo in reply. I had deprived them of their strength, and now it was coming back to bite me. There was nothing I could do but cling to Mikael and hope we wouldn't be too late.

7

By the time we reached the cellar, I felt completely numb. We still had no idea what had happened, but something had befallen the Norn's sisters, and it had been bad enough to immobilize her.

Tallie had already gone down into the cellar, and now re-emerged, an unreadable look on her face. Mikael approached her, still holding me tightly in his arms.

She shook her head.

The response was all I needed. I struggled, but Mikael's arms tightened around me, refusing to let go. "Maddy, wait," he pleaded.

Though I had little to spare, I concentrated and shot a small burst of energy at him. His arms loosened in surprise, and I suddenly fell to the ground, hitting my tailbone on the rocky earth.

Not taking a moment to recover, I scrambled away from him. I wasn't sure what I was thinking, but I had to get down into that cellar. Alaric couldn't be hurt. He couldn't be.

I avoided Aila as she made a grab for me. They were all trying to keep me from seeing whatever was in that cellar.

Aila started to lunge at me again, but Mikael darted in and stopped her, even though he'd tried to stop me himself a moment before. I ran to the open door of the cellar, lying flush with the ground, then hurried down the old, concrete stairs, my heart beating so loudly in my ears that I couldn't even hear my own footsteps.

Candles still burned around the room, though many had been blown out, and some flames had been drowned in blood. I stood frozen at the base of the stairs, surveying the massacre. The entire room was drenched in blood. Over the chair I'd once been tied to, which had been knocked onto its side, lay the hunched form of a Norn, dead. Her sisters were scattered about the room, not one of them living.

I jumped as I realized Mikael was standing right behind me.

"They're not here," I mumbled as relief mingled with the numbing shock that had taken over my body. "Alaric and Sophie aren't here," I stated more firmly.

My knees suddenly collapsed, but Mikael caught me, lifting me back into his arms. Frode descended the stairs behind us, then walked further into the room. He approached the Norn draped across the chair, and a moment later, I realized why. One of her arms was pinned under her chest against the side of the chair. Her forearm stuck out at an odd angle, the elbow bent so the avian talons were above the torso. In her upright claws rested a white envelope. It was square, like the invitation to a wedding or party. Frode retrieved it, then returned to us.

"Can you stand?" Mikael whispered into my ear.

I nodded, and he let me down, though he kept a bracing arm around my waist. Normally I would have protested, but at that moment, I needed the extra support.

I took the offered envelope from Frode, knowing without a doubt that it was meant for me. I opened it, then pulled a square of card stock from within. I squinted down at the paper, but could hardly see the words with the dim lighting in the room. Realizing my predicament, Mikael moved so we were both bathed in the sunlight streaming through the open cellar door.

The neatly scrawled text read:

To Madeline Ville,
You are cordially invited to the inauguration ball of Estus Mac An Tsagairt, as he ascends the throne of the Vaettir. The event will be held in his home, February 22nd, at 10 in the evening.

I stared down at the page, rereading the text multiple times. It said nothing about Alaric and Sophie, but it didn't need to. The message was implied. I would attend the *inauguration ball* if I ever wanted to see them alive again.

"That's in four days," Mikael stated, reading the note over my shoulder.

"We need to catch a plane," I replied.

I still felt entirely numb. I knew everything would catch up with me any moment, but all I could think about that second was getting the hell out of Ireland.

"I had already begun preparations for leaving the country," he explained. "I wanted us to be capable of departing at a moment's notice."

As gratitude overwhelmed me, everything else began to sink in. I swayed on my feet again, and Mikael caught me and pulled me into a hug. "We'll find them, and we'll save them," he whispered against my hair. "That's a promise."

I could hear Frode backing away up the stairs to join the others, leaving us alone in the gory room. I held tightly onto Mikael, feeling unable to move just yet.

"He's not dead, right?" I questioned weakly as fresh tears began to fall, unable to convince myself that I would ever see Alaric again.

"He's not dead," he assured. "I swear to you, you would know it if he were."

I nodded, scratching my cheek against his linen shirt, then pulled away. "We need to gather the others from the Salr," I said, pulling myself together. "I want to be on a plane before the day is through."

"Consider it done," he replied with a nod.

I took one final glance around the macabre room, then ascended the concrete stairs.

Aila, Frode, and Tallie all waited silently above.

Tallie stepped forward, but kept her gaze on the ground. "I'm sorry, I just saw the scene and was horrified. I didn't consider you'd think Alaric had been killed."

While her initial reaction after seeing the room had given me the scare of a lifetime, I couldn't blame her. The room was a horrifying sight for anyone, even one of the Vaettir.

"Don't worry about it," I said distantly, gazing into the

woods around us for any sign that the Norn's murderers might still be near. At that thought, I asked, "Can you sense any energy nearby?"

She shook her head, tossing her black ponytail from side to side. "I can't sense anyone within ten miles of us, probably more."

"But you couldn't sense Alaric earlier either," I countered, "and this place is within ten miles of the Salr."

She glanced over her shoulder at the still open cellar door. "The cellar must somehow be warded," she explained. "When we were first tracking Alaric and Sophie, I couldn't get a feel for them, nor did I sense the Norns. It's probably why the Norns chose this place to hold them, though their plan backfired in a horrible way." She frowned, deep in thought. "Did Estus do this?"

I nodded. "This was his way of inviting us to his inauguration. He took Alaric and Sophie to ensure we'd show up. He might not have killed the Norns himself, but it was on his orders. If only we'd gotten here thirty minutes sooner."

"Speaking of Norns," Mikael cut in, "we should check on the one we left behind. She may now be our singular hope in bringing our plans to fruition."

I gasped. I'd forgotten all about her. We needed the Norns to regrow Yggdrasil. *Fate* was part of the equation we couldn't leave out. Was that why those who guarded Alaric and Sophie had been slaughtered? I'd simply thought it was a message, letting me know just what could happen to the man I loved if I didn't obey, but maybe there was more to it. Maybe Estus knew what I planned, and was trying to stop me.

Without asking permission, Mikael picked me up in his

arms again. He ran in the direction we'd come as everyone else moved to follow him. I couldn't help feeling like we should be scouring the woods for Alaric and Sophie, just in case, but if Tallie couldn't sense them from outside the cellar, they were long gone.

Tallie darted ahead of us through the trees, once again amazing me with her speed. If she wanted, she could turn into a wolf and move even faster, though transformation took a lot of her energy.

As the gentle rhythm of Mikael's graceful steps washed over me, I began to plan. I couldn't think about the possible outcomes of what lay before us. I couldn't think about what was happening to Alaric and Sophie right in that moment. I could only think about what I could *do*.

Mikael had claimed that travel arrangements wouldn't be an issue. It was a long flight from Ireland to Spokane, Washington, so the sooner we left, the better. There wasn't much for us to pack up at the Salr, except for the extra people. Many of our small group were accustomed to carrying weapons, which would be another concern, since we would be going through airport security. Everyone might just have to acquire new weapons once we reached the states, but finding quality weaponry could take time, and time we did not have.

We only had four days to make it to the *ball* to save Alaric and Sophie, but that begged the question, why did Estus want me there?

"What do you think he's planning?" I asked out loud.

Only breathing slightly harder from exertion, Mikael kept his eyes on the path ahead of him as he answered, "I've been thinking about that too, and I'm really not sure.

Perhaps he's hoping to distract you from forming an army long enough for him to enact his plan, or maybe he's hoping to force you into joining him, using Alaric and Sophie as leverage."

I frowned, then tensed as Mikael leapt over a well-rotted log.

"Or perhaps it's just a trap," Frode chimed in as he sped up to reach Mikael's side, "and Estus will kill us all as soon as we arrive."

"Then we'll have to arrive *en force*," Mikael countered. "Many of Aislin's people are in the States. If we can contact enough of them, perhaps they will rally to our cause."

I kept quiet, retreating into my own thoughts. I didn't care if it was a trap. I was going regardless. I *would* save Alaric and Sophie. There was no other choice.

My resolve strengthened, I wrapped my arms more tightly around Mikael's shoulders, glad he was willing to walk into a situation with me that might mean all our deaths. He might have been an ancient, power-hungry, manipulative Viking, but he was also my friend. I needed all of the friends I could get.

MIKAEL LET me down to my feet as we reached the Norn. Tallie already stood by her side, looking uncomfortable. The Norn sat in the dirt with her long legs pulled up to her chest, draped in her shapeless clothing. Her antlered head was bowed over her knees as she wept.

Her sorrow hit me like a ton of bricks, and it was all I could do to force myself to approach.

"I tried to speak to her," Tallie explained, "but I don't think she's heard a single word."

The Norn let out a heart rending sob, but did not lift her head to acknowledge that she wasn't alone. I knelt by her side as tears formed in my eyes. They came easily, since I already had plenty of things to cry about, even without the Norn's emotions affecting me.

I touched her shoulder, but she didn't seem to notice. Normally you'd say someone's name to get their attention, but I didn't know hers. I wasn't sure if the Norns even used names. I'd sure never been given one to call any of them by.

Not knowing what else to do, I knelt down beside her and wrapped my arms around her shoulders. I hugged her, because sometimes, that's the only comfort one person can really offer another. The comfort of another body, holding them close, sharing in their pain.

She let out another sob, then leaned her weight against me.

I am the only one left, a weak voice whispered in my mind. *All of my sister's have left me. I cannot bear this burden alone.*

"There's still hope," I soothed. "We can still return you to your true form. Maybe then, you'll be closer to your lost sisters."

She finally lifted her head to look at me. Her strange, uptilted eyes were swollen and red-rimmed from her tears. The Norns had always seemed so *different* to me, not like humans or Vaettir, but in that moment, she seemed just like all the rest of us. Lost and alone, longing for safety and love.

You will truly regrow Yggdrasil? she questioned, as if needing reassurance.

I nodded. "That's been my plan all along."

Frode cleared his throat, then leaned toward Mikael and whispered, "I'm guessing there's a whole other side to this conversation I'm not hearing?"

"Yes," Mikael answered simply, then moved to kneel before the Norn, though he turned his eyes to me. "Will she join us?"

I nodded, my arms still loosely wrapped around her shoulders. "I think so."

We will need the Morrigan, the voice said in my head. *We cannot regrow Yggdrasil without her energy. We need fate, chaos, emotion, life and death. All parts must be present.*

I frowned. Mara, the Morrigan, had left the world once again, after temporarily possessing Marcos. Her energy had been too weakened to remain. Logically I knew we'd need her energy to bring our goals to fruition, but I was hoping we'd either find a way around it, or another solution would present itself. I might even be able to use *my* energy, but I wasn't sure what such a sacrifice would entail.

Reading my thoughts, the Norn answered, *We can bring the Morrigan's energy back, if only in a small way. If you bring her to once again reside inside you, she may be able to remain until the time comes to regrow the tree. We'll need the help of the necromancer.*

"Marcos?" I questioned. "How do you know about him?"

Suddenly her sorrow turned to anger, hot enough to scald. *He fed off the energy of my sisters in the past. I can sense him, just as I can sense you. It is why we feared the banshees.*

Executioners and other denizens of death are instinctually programmed to stay away from each other, and if they come together, they compete until one is killed. You have somehow gathered three in one space, including yourself. It is unnatural, and terrifying.

I frowned as I thought over what she'd said. In the beginning, Faas had been downright bitter toward me, but we'd eventually become friends. Marcos didn't seem to feel a need to compete with me, as long as I helped him achieve Hecate's goals.

It is all because of you, the Norn explained in reply to my thoughts. *You are the earth and all that it encompasses. You are a uniting force, bending the laws of nature to your will.*

Mikael smiled suddenly, obviously still hearing everything I was. "So what you're saying," he began, as he glanced between me and the Norn, "is that we have a chance."

The Norn seemed surprised. She was silent for several seconds, then answered, *Yes. There are powers at your disposal to rival those of the charm, but the cycle of fate is slowly unravelling. I truly cannot say what will happen.*

Mikael winked at her. "Don't worry, I've always been very lucky. You'll be reunited with your sisters in no time."

The Norn didn't seem to know what to say to that. No one did. What remained of Fate was quite literally on our side, perhaps with a little added luck, we might actually succeed. The world was basically depending on us. No pressure, or anything.

8

Once the Norn had recovered, we returned to the Salr to share the news, and to get everyone ready to go. Mikael had stayed outside to make calls on his cell to arrange our travel. He'd ordered Frode and Aila to remain by my side while I spread the news and packed my things. Tallie vowed to protect me too, but Mikael didn't seem to believe her.

I came through the entrance first. Faas was there, waiting just inside the Salr for our return, looking sullen with his white-blond topknot of hair hanging forward into his eyes. Like me, Faas was more magically imposing than physically, as we were both executioners. We were even the same height.

He heaved a sigh of relief, then looked past me as Aila, Frode, and Tallie appeared. Next came the Norn. She crouched as she entered, then stood to her full height, antlers nearly reaching the ceiling.

Faas took a step back, wide-eyed.

Once he'd recovered, he turned his gaze back to me. "Is that what I think it is?"

"*She's* a Norn," I explained. "She's on our side.

He nodded, instantly accepting my explanation, then glanced at the dirt wall as if expecting more people to come through. He brought his eyes back to me. "Mikael?"

"Up above, making plans," I explained. "Alaric and Sophie have been taken by Estus. We all need to get on a plane to the States to rescue them."

I could feel anxiety wafting off him like a bitter perfume, but he took me at my word without asking for further explanation. "Might I ask . . . " he trailed off as his eyes flicked to the Norn.

"Later," I answered as I walked past him. "Help me spread word to everyone that it's time to leave. Make sure someone escorts Maya and the others up, while keeping a close eye on them."

Faas fell into step beside me. "Consider it done. What about Marcos?"

"I'll talk to him. There are some things we need to discuss before we leave." I held up a hand to cut him off as he began to speak, knowing he was going to reject the idea of me speaking to Marcos on my own. "Frode and Aila will remain with me," I added.

Faas sighed, then nodded. "I'll get everyone ready, but don't get too comfortable around Marcos."

"If you think I stand any chance of being *comfortable* with anything right now," I replied, "you are sorely mistaken."

He put a hand on my shoulder to halt my progression, surprising me since he was not the physically affectionate type. "We'll get him back," he assured, his pale eyes earnest.

I didn't have to ask to whom he referred. Everyone knew Alaric would be at the forefront of my mind. I nodded, holding back tears as they suddenly attacked me, then turned away to continue on with my mission.

Faas walked off in the other direction without another word, as Frode and Aila fell into step on either side of me. I felt like a dwarf between their tall, muscled frames, but I couldn't say that I minded. Extra protection was rarely a bad thing, even if it could be annoying.

We continued down the hall silently until we reached the room where Marcos was being held. Outside the door stood Alejandro and Tabitha, casually chatting. Alejandro had somehow managed to fit in much better with Mikael's people than Tallie had, though I sensed Tallie's *need* to fit in was greater. Alejandro didn't really care. He was just happy as long as no one was trying to kill him. Unfortunately, his happiness would probably end once we reached the States.

"It's time to go," I announced.

Tabitha looked to Aila for confirmation, which irked me, but I couldn't really blame her. Mikael was her leader, not me, even if we were planning on ruling together.

Alejandro simply nodded, accepting my orders. "Alaric and Sophie?" he questioned.

I shook my head.

He frowned, and I could sense Tabitha's worry, but neither spoke.

"Aila and Frode will aid me with Marcos," I explained, not wanting to discuss *anything* else further. "Find Faas and help him gather the others."

Tabitha and Alejandro both nodded, then left us. I was glad once they were gone. Aila would never push me to talk about anything emotional, and I had a feeling Frode wouldn't either, though I'd only just met him the previous day. Alejandro and Tabitha were different.

I opened the door and the three of us entered the room. Marcos was sitting on the floor with his back against the stone wall. His long, white hair hid his expression. He remained motionless, not acknowledging our arrival.

"Rushing to Estus' Salr is a mistake," he stated.

"How did you . . . " I trailed off, wondering how he knew our plan before we'd told it to anyone.

He moved his head a fraction to peer through his hair and meet my eyes. "You know just who whispers in my ear," he replied vaguely.

I glanced to Aila, then to Frode on either side of me. He was claiming Hecate had told him of our plan, and I had no choice but to believe him. There was no other way for him to know.

"Mistake or no, we're going," I replied.

He stood and took a graceful step toward us. His shape-less black clothing made his pale face seem ghostly, and his spiderweb-like hair only added to the effect. "Well this should at least prove interesting," he commented with a small smile on his gaunt face.

"Who says you're going?" Aila remarked snidely.

"He is," I answered before there could be any arguments. "He's part of the plan."

Aila didn't reply, but I could sense her unhappiness. No one seemed to like Marcos, myself included.

He spread his arms wide, encompassing the rest of the

room. "Seeing as I have no possessions, I suppose I'm ready to go."

I nodded, then turned to leave the room, expecting everyone to follow.

Mikael found us just as we re-entered the hall, his cell phone still in his hand. "Everything is arranged. We'll fly out of Dublin in three hours, so we need to get moving."

I nodded, suppressing tears, glad we wouldn't have to wait around much. As long as I was moving toward our agenda, I could keep myself together. If I had to wait, I wasn't sure if I could keep myself from breaking down. Wallowing would do Alaric no good. Action would. Guess which one I was in favor of.

"I need to pack my things," I breathed.

Mikael looked past me to Aila, Frode, and Marcos, then turned his gaze back to me. "Several cars should arrive on the main road to pick us up shortly. Aila and Frode will remain with you while you pack. *I'll* take Marcos."

I glanced behind me as everyone nodded. Marcos seemed calm with a small, secretive smile on his face.

"You have a problem with that?" I questioned, hoping he wasn't about to give us trouble.

"Not at all," he replied politely. "In fact, I'm quite interested to see how this whole new endeavor will work out."

Taking him at his word, I turned back to Mikael and gave him a final nod. "I'll see you above ground shortly."

He nodded in reply, then walked past me and took hold of Marcos' arm, guiding him back down the hall away from the rest of us.

I watched them go, wondering if Mikael would be a match for Marcos should Marcos decide to rebel. I shook my head. Mikael only took well calculated risks. If he felt fine taking sole custody of Marcos, it meant he wasn't worried about it, so I shouldn't be either.

Aila cleared her throat, drawing my attention to her. "We should get moving. You aren't the only one who has things to pack."

Forcing myself back into the current moment, I nodded, then turned to head back toward my room, deep in thought. I didn't get far. I nearly jumped out of my skin as I almost walked right into Kira.

She looked up at me with her large, green eyes, accented by the bangs of her forest green hair. Her delicate face held concern. "What's going on?" she asked softly. "I heard someone say that you were leaving."

I bit my lip and mentally cursed myself. In all the chaos I'd forgotten about Kira. I'd originally found her living alone in the Salr, but she'd been more than happy to have the extra company that came with my presence. She'd grown accustomed to having extra people around, and now here I was, about to leave her behind without a word.

"Alaric's been kidnapped," I explained, tilting my head to look down at her diminutive form. "We have to fly to the U.S. to get him back."

Her eyes widened, then she looked down at her feet.

"What is it?" I pressed, anxious to get on with things.

She mumbled something that I couldn't quite hear.

With an impatient huff, I knelt in front of her. "I'm sorry, but I'm kind of in a rush, please just tell me what you have to say."

She met my eyes. "I'd like to go with you," she stated clearly. "I'd like to find my sister, if I can."

A promise I'd made came to mind. A promise to reunite Kira with her sister Sivi, even if Sivi might not be the sister Kira remembered.

I took a deep breath. "She may still be allied with our enemy," I explained. Sivi felt no loyalty to Estus, but she still lived in his Salr under his rule, or at least, she had the last time I'd seen her. "But you can come with us if you want. Just please don't get your hopes up."

Kira nodded excitedly. "I'll pack my things," she replied quickly. "*Please* don't leave without me."

I stood. "Meet us above ground. Cars will be arriving soon to take us to the airport."

She nodded again, then darted past me toward her room further down the hall.

Aila fell into step beside me as I began to walk in the other direction, while Frode trailed behind us. Aila didn't speak, but there was a small smile on her face.

"*What*?" I asked tiredly.

She shook her head and continued to smile. "You're just a big softy, aren't you?"

I snorted. "Says the woman that puts out seed for the birds every single morning."

She frowned.

"I get up early," I said with a wink. "But don't worry, your secret is safe with me."

She sighed heavily as Frode chuckled behind us. I was feeling better. Soon I'd be on a plane, and we'd be one step closer to getting Alaric and Sophie back. Fate had already put me through hell. Surely she wouldn't be cruel enough to take Alaric away from me after everything we'd endured? I bit my lip as I thought of the Norns, and the negative things they'd done along with the positive. I really shouldn't have been putting so much faith in fate. She could be a real bitch.

ALARIC GROANED as he sat up and brushed himself off. Why was he lying in the dirt? He glanced around at his surroundings. He was in a forest, but the smells were strange and the air felt thin. Suddenly remembering everything, he hopped to his feet, searching frantically for Sophie. He soon spotted her a few yards away, lying still at the base of a massive tree.

His heart in his throat, he rushed toward her, then crouched by her still form, placing his hand on her shoulder.

She rolled over with a groan, then looked up at him through slitted eyes. "Wha—" she began to question.

"Estus," he breathed.

Estus, accompanied by several others, had found them in the cellar. They'd fought, and many of the Norns were killed. The last thing he could remember was Estus chanting words he didn't understand, then everything had gone black.

"Why aren't we dead?" Sophie questioned as she sat up, brushing the dirt from her black clothing.

He shook his head, then again observed their surroundings. They weren't anywhere near the Salr in Ireland, of that he was sure. The trees were different, as were the smells.

He stood and offered Sophie a hand up. She took it, and they began walking.

"Why would he just leave us in a forest?" Sophie questioned. "I don't understand. I can't seem to remember what happened."

Alaric fought against a sickening feeling of foreboding in his gut. The entire experience had felt somewhat familiar, but it couldn't be what he was thinking. It was impossible.

"Let's just search for signs of civilization," he replied. "Then we can at least ask where we are."

"We have to still be in Ireland, right?" she asked, glancing up at the trees surrounding them. "We couldn't have been unconscious for long enough to board a plane or boat."

"I don't think we were unconscious for long at all," he muttered as he continued walking.

The air was cold and moist, carrying the scent of woodsmoke with it.

"A fire," Sophie observed. "We should follow the scent."

He nodded in agreement, deciding it best to keep his fears to himself. They continued on in silence as the smell of woodsmoke grew stronger.

Eventually they found a rocky path. Alaric tried to quiet his thoughts, but they persisted. The cellar where they'd been held was only seven or eight miles from the Salr where Madeline waited. Would Estus head there next? Would he attack Madeline and the others, just as he had the Norns?

He frowned. If Estus' only intent was to kill, he and Sophie would be dead. No, he just wanted them out of the way, but why? What difference did his presence make in anything Estus might have planned for Madeline ... unless he hoped to use them as bargaining chips, just as the Norns had planned.

A small home came into view with rough stone walls and a thatched roof. Smoke wafted out of a stone chimney sprouting out of the structure's center.

Sophie began to rush forward, but Alaric caught her arm.

"Wait," he urged.

Instead of continuing down the path, he walked into the trees where it would be easier to hide. Sophie followed after him, not asking questions. He made a wide circle toward the house, dreading actually reaching it. If the structural elements of the home weren't enough, he was sure whomever dwelled inside would verify his fears. Still, he couldn't just wait around, hiding from his fate.

He had almost reached the side of the house with Sophie still close behind him, when the front door opened with a loud creak of wood.

Alaric and Sophie watched, concealed within the trees, as a man exited with a rough-looking ax slung over one shoulder. He wore a ratty tunic and threadbare breeches, definitely not modern day attire.

"Fuck," Alaric muttered, using his arm to push his sister back away from the home.

"But wha—" she whispered.

Alaric shook his head and hurried her away. The woodcutter had turned to look in their direction, but hadn't spotted them yet. With a final glance at the man, Alaric turned and ran, tugging Sophie along beside him.

After running a mile or so, he finally halted.

"What the hell is going on?" Sophie panted.

He shook his head. How was this even possible? Estus did not have that sort of power . . . unless he'd used the key. *Or*, unless the key had used him.

"We've been sent back in time," he explained.

Sophie's eyes widened. She'd seen the woodcutter just as he had, but he understood it was a difficult conclusion to jump to. He was only able to fathom it since he'd travelled back before with Madeline and Mikael.

"But why?" she gasped, glancing frantically at the woods around them. "*How?*"

He leaned against a nearby tree, feeling utterly defeated. "Estus is probably using us to force Madeline into doing something she doesn't want to do. Maybe he wants her to send back the banshees, or maybe he needs her to participate in his plans."

Sophie slumped to the ground to sit amongst the dead pine needles and grass. She looked up at him like a child would, hoping their parent was about to tell them that they were safe, and none of the monsters were real. Unfortunately all of the monsters were real, and one of them was effectively holding them hostage in the past.

"How do we get back?" she asked finally.

"We don't," Alaric answered. "We only were able to return before with the help of a Norn, and the energy of Yggdrasil, which only Madeline could touch."

Tears trickled down Sophie's face.

He sat in the dirt across from her. "Estus kept us alive for a reason. I'm guessing he'll give Madeline the offer to bring us back, but only if she adheres to his wishes."

Sophie put her elbows on her knees and buried her head in her hands. "He'll just use her to get what he wants, then he'll leave us here forever."

"Probably," Alaric replied honestly.

Would he never get to see Madeline again? Would he not be there when his daughter finally came into the world? A single tear slipped down his cheek.

"Why the long faces?" a voice asked from behind them.

Alaric leapt to his feet. He hadn't heard anyone approach, nor had he smelled them. He turned, then looked the woman who'd spoken up and down, from her long, curly red hair, to her sparkling blue eyes.

Her pink lips curved into a smile. She wasn't in the body he'd met, but he'd recognize that smug smile anywhere. "Hello Alaric," she purred. "Fancy seeing you here."

"Is that . . . " Sophie trailed off, still seated in the dirt.

"The Morrigan," Alaric replied, feeling almost as shocked as he had when he'd realized they'd traveled back in time.

The Morrigan smiled, and it chilled him to the bone. He hadn't liked her in spirit form, and he was getting the feeling the real deal was going to be much, *much* worse.

9

"How did you find us?" Alaric demanded.

The Morrigan smoothed her hands over her long, green velvet dress. "I am the earth," she explained. "I sensed a massive, magical disruption, tearing time apart."

Sophie finally rose to her feet. "How do you even know who we are? We don't even truly exist in this time. You won't actually meet us until the distant future."

The Morrigan smirked. "If you think time is truly linear, you are mistaken, and if you think I'm held by the bonds of time, you're even more wrong. My spirit exists in all times at once."

"But if that were true," Alaric countered, "the you in this time would know your future, and you'd be able to save yourself from your fate."

The Morrigan chuckled. "I am not the me in this time. She will still make the same mistakes. I am the energy that will be left over, the energy you met in the future, only I can exist more solidly in this time because my original form is still bound to the earth."

"That makes no sense," Sophie argued.

"Don't try to understand it," the Morrigan replied. "It's as incomprehensible as fate. It exists, but not entirely within the bounds of known reality."

Alaric let out a loud sigh, already annoyed with the Morrigan, though her presence also gave him a measure of hope.

He took a step toward her. "All of that aside, why have you come for us?"

Her smile suddenly leaked away, leaving her blue eyes intense. "You honestly think I would leave the father of Madeline's child to rot in the past? I may not like you, but I would never do such a thing to her."

"So you can send us back?" Sophie asked hopefully.

The Morrigan frowned. "Not quite, but the real me could."

"Then . . . " Alaric trailed off, waiting for her to get to the point.

"Well," the Morrigan explained. "We can find her and ask, but she's a bit . . . vengeful at the moment. She may be difficult to convince."

"If she's our only chance, then we have to try," he stated.

The Morrigan answered him with a sharp nod. "Yes, we must." She turned to Sophie. "We should probably send you in first. She's likely to kill Alaric on the spot just for being a man."

Sophie bit her lip, but nodded. "So how do we find her?"

The Morrigan rolled her eyes like Sophie had asked a

very silly question. "We walk, of course," she explained, then turned on her heel and marched away.

With a huff of exasperation, Alaric hurried after her, followed by Sophie. He let out a sigh as he jogged to catch up. Madeline just *had* to be descended from the Morrigan. Alaric would have taken any other goddess, or creature resembling a goddess, over the egotistical, red-headed woman marching off ahead of him.

"A PRIVATE JET?" I questioned in disbelief.

Mikael looked smug as he nodded. He hadn't said anything about a private jet all the way to the airport. Then we'd arrived, and had been directed to our own, private boarding area.

The rest of our people waited around us. Frode and Aila were still keeping an eye on Marcos, while Faas, Tabitha, and the red-haired woman that had arrived at the Salr when Frode first showed up, all watched over Maya, Rose, and Dominic. Alejandro seemed to be doing his best to hit on Tabitha, while Tallie sat off in a corner by herself. Kira stood a few feet away from me, looking around the boarding area in awe. Her mismatched, oversize clothes and green hair actually blended in well with the human populace. She looked like any other preteen trying to fit in with her peers. The fact that she was traveling with a bunch of dangerous looking adults was besides the point.

Unfortunately, being dangerous looking wouldn't get us far. Really, our party was pretty pathetic. Sure Mikael, Frode, and Aila were physically imposing, but the rest of us were a bit lackluster when it came to the intimidation factor. Okay, Marcos got by on sheer creepiness, but most of us weren't exactly tough.

"So why haven't we used this jet previously?" I pressed, turning my attention back to Mikael as we stood side-by-side, surveying the rest of our group.

He'd changed into street clothes to fit in with the crowd, though the tight, hunter green tee-shirt contrasting with his long auburn hair made him stand out more in my opinion, not less. Of course, being 6'5" and built like the Viking he actually was, he was bound to stand out no matter what.

He scoffed. "Do you have any idea what a pain in the ass it is to make flight arrangements, even with your own jet? It's not worth it when only a few people are flying. The only reason we're good to go now is because I started planning this trip when we first arrived in Ireland."

I rolled my eyes at him. "How on earth could you have known we'd need to go back to the States at some point?"

"Well that's where your story began, isn't it? In any great adventure, you must at some point end up back where you began."

I furrowed my brow as I tried to determine whether or not he was serious.

He chuckled at my expression. "*Or*, knowing that Estus maintained his main base of operation in the States, I thought it likely that we'd need to travel there eventually."

"Ah," I replied, "that makes a little more sense."

A stewardess appeared from within the long corridor leading to the plane. She gestured for us to begin boarding, and that was it. Apparently you didn't get the full steward experience when you flew private. It was a decent trade off though, since we'd gotten to keep most of our weapons in our luggage. Blades only though. Luckily, most of the Vaettir weren't fond of guns. If you had to use a gun, it meant you were weak. Physical prowess was needed to be successful with blades. I wasn't accustomed to either, though Alaric had taught me basic fighting skills.

Everyone automatically waited while Mikael and I boarded the plane first, which felt weird on so many levels. Was I seriously somehow supposed to transition into the role of these people's leader? Not to mention that we hoped to recruit many, many more members.

I shook my head as we stepped into the narrow corridor and made our way toward the plane. We'd probably all be dead in a few days. No need to worry about a future that might never come. I clutched my belly nervously as I thought of Alaric. Though death was likely imminent, I had plenty of reasons to fight. We all did.

Even the Norn was willing to fight with us, though she wasn't willing to fly with us. She had her own means of travel that I was sure I wouldn't comprehend. Hopefully it wouldn't take her long to find us again, but she had some time. We had to find Alaric and Sophie and figure out a way to trap Estus before we could move on to the task of regrowing Yggdrasil.

We reached the end of the corridor and entered the jet, which was smaller than I'd expected. Our entire party would barely fit.

Seeming unconcerned about, well, anything, Mikael walked past the cockpit and small bathroom, then sat in one of the large, cozy seats in the main cabin. He patted the chair next to him as he grinned up at me.

The aircraft was obviously designed with luxury in mind, with the seats clustered to face each other around central tables. More like you were just hanging out at a restaurant than flying somewhere. I sat with a sigh, then moved my brown canvas purse to my lap. It was filled with snacks. Growing an entire other person was hungry work.

The rest of our companions slowly filtered into the plane behind us. I turned to observe them, once again thinking about what a strange little clan we made. Marcos ended up in a seat next to Tallie, who widened her eyes in fear and scooted as far away from him as her armrest would allow. He seemed unperturbed. Everyone else did their best to choose seats away from Marcos, but in the end, there simply weren't enough seats to be choosy. Alejandro and Tabitha ended up across from Marcos and Tallie. I was glad to see Tallie relax at their presence, if only a fraction.

The seats across from us had been avoided too, though I guessed it was likely they'd just already been spoken for, as we ended up sitting across from Faas and Aila. Aila was never far from Mikael's side, and lately, Faas didn't seem to want to be away from mine.

Mikael asked the stewardess, a woman who appeared to be in her late fifties, to bring him a glass of bourbon on ice before the plane could even take off. I looked over at him to make a snide remark, then realized he looked almost scared.

My jaw dropped in surprise as I stared at him.

He glared at me. "I don't like flying."

Faas remained utterly silent at the admission, while a small smile curved Aila's lips. I had a feeling she'd already known about his fear.

I turned back to Mikael with a grin. "You know, I'm never going to be able to let you live this one down."

He scowled. "Well, once we crash and die in a fiery explosion that we have no chance of surviving, you can mock me in Hell."

I laughed, feeling almost cheerful for the first time since Alaric had been taken . . . almost. "So it's a control issue?" I questioned. "You don't like the idea that you can't talk or fight your way out of a plane crash."

He continued to glare at me as the stewardess returned with his bourbon. He took the glass from her, then downed it in a single swallow, the ice cubes bracing against his upper lip. He handed the glass back to her. "Another, please."

I was about to make a comment, then the plane began to move down the tarmac, and Mikael gripped the armrests so tightly I didn't have the heart to make fun of him. Still, I enjoyed seeing him like that. I was used to his defenses being utterly impenetrable. It was nice to not feel like the weak, scared one for once.

The plane rumbled into motion, not giving the stewardess time to return with a second glass of bourbon.

As we took off, I sighed, then placed my hand on top of Mikael's. "Think happy thoughts of alcohol, money, and women with loose morals," I joked.

Though he looked a little pale, he managed to leer at me. "How about I think happy thoughts of fine wine, and *you*, on a bed with satin sheets."

I made a sound of disgust and removed my hand, though the exchange seemed to have made Mikael feel less scared, just as it made me feel less morose. Friendship worked in odd ways.

Aila watched the entire exchange with her small smile still in place, then leaned back in her seat and relaxed as the plane gained elevation. Before long, we reached altitude and leveled off.

The stewardess finally was able to return with Mikael's bourbon, and asked if anyone else needed anything. I ended up with a cup of decaf coffee and a pastry, because my cravings never ceased no matter what else was going on.

I lifted my pastry, prepared to take a bite, then dropped it back to my plate as my stomach did a little flip flop. I scowled at the offending pastry. It had sounded so good when I'd ordered it. Turning my attention away from my food, I announced, "We should discuss our plan for when we arrive in Washington."

"Storm the castle and retrieve the kitty cats," Mikael stated. "Plain and simple."

"There's nothing simple about it," I argued. "Estus will be well prepared for an attack, and we're not exactly . . . " I trailed off as I glanced around the rest of the cabin.

"Well equipped?" Faas offered.

"Okay," Mikael corrected, then turned his head to meet my eyes. "First we'll visit some graveyards to give your army a bit of juice, *then* we'll storm the castle."

I sighed. "Except my army can't enter any Salr."

"Yes," Mikael replied, "but we only need to enter long enough to pull Alaric and Sophie out. I don't imagine we'll be able to corner Estus on this visit, but dealing him a major blow will make all his followers question their allegiance to him. That is our real intent," he explained. "Oh, and to rescue your kitties," he added.

Faas nodded along with what Mikael was saying. "I agree. This is not about *winning*. It's about weakening Estus' fortifications to grow our own forces. We simply need to retrieve Alaric and Sophie, and make a good show."

"And we need to survive," Aila added. "Though we'd likely stand better chances just sneaking in to rescue Alaric and Sophie."

Mikael shook his head. "Estus will *definitely* be expecting that, just as he'll be expecting us to aim for defeating him. Our best strategy is to focus on a more minor victory so that we might solidify our own power base in preparation for a true attack. *But*," he added, turning toward me, "I still believe having your phantoms at their best is a necessary back up plan. They will make a clean retreat more likely, and lessen the chances of Estus sending troops after us into the outside world."

I bit my lip. I knew strengthening my banshees was necessary. If I'd done it sooner, I could have possibly saved some of the Norns, and maybe could have even prevented Alaric and Sophie from being kidnapped, but frankly, I was still scared. The Norns had been right about one thing. The power of the banshees was intoxicating. It was a little too easy to get swept away.

"You're strong enough to do it," Faas said suddenly.

I looked up to see him staring directly at me, as if he'd read my thoughts.

He smiled softly and flipped his blond hair out of his eyes. "Your worry is quite clear," he explained.

I glanced around the cabin at our other passengers.

Some of them I had grown to trust, but others, I wasn't willing to show them any weakness. Faas was being vague on purpose. He wanted to reassure me, but without letting everyone else know that I desperately needed reassuring.

I nodded, accepting his encouragement, though not really believing it. Was I strong enough?

"There's one more thing," Mikael added, drawing my attention back to him. "We're still going to be outnumbered within the Salr. While I plan to have people in place to create distractions should the need arise, we need to go in with as much power as necessary. That means you and Faas should both be . . . well fed."

I glanced at Marcos, who was minding his own business across the hall, looking out the window. I leaned close to Mikael's side and whispered, "What about him?" I nodded in Marcos' direction.

"I don't think we want him to possess any more power than necessary," Mikael whispered back.

I frowned. "But if he's truly on our side, wouldn't having him at full power be really helpful in our . . . showing of power?"

I glanced again at Marcos. We were keeping our voices down, and as far as I knew he didn't have supernatural hearing . . . although I didn't really know much about him. Honestly, it didn't much matter if he heard us. He already knew we didn't trust him, else we wouldn't have felt the need to keep guards on him twenty-four-seven.

"What is your opinion?" Mikael whispered in my ear.

Faas and Aila both watched our near silent conversation. Aila didn't seem to mind not being included, but Faas was scowling as he glanced between us and Marcos.

I thought back to my conversation with Marcos, and all he'd divulged about Hecate and what her plans were. As far as I knew, we had the same end goal, but conversely, he might be capable of achieving that goal without *my* help, especially if Hecate was truly willing to lend her energy. Although, I had a feeling she was only powerful enough in this world to exist in more of an advisory capacity. If she had powers like Mara, the Morrigan, possessed after we'd summoned her, Marcos would have never followed Aislin, nor would he have allowed us to take him prisoner.

That memory led me back to the fact that Marcos had been the one to remove the key from me, to place it inside Estus and Aislin. Even if we didn't trust him, we *needed* him, and we'd have to give him access to power at some point.

My mind made up, I turned and placed my mouth near Mikael's ear and replied, "I think if we have to trust him at some point, we may as well start now."

He nodded, accepting my judgement.

"Although," I continued, still keeping my voice down, "that does beg the question of how we intend to acquire extra power. I can't drain energy like Faas, nor am I a true necromancer like Marcos, so I can't gain energy from the long dead. I kind of need some fresh kills."

Mikael seemed to think for a moment. "Can you not gain energy from your banshees? If you allow them to recharge with the energy of the long dead, then you could recharge from them."

Damn, he was right, and that once again led back to my need for the banshees to gain power. It was just like trusting Marcos. I'd have to do it sooner or later, so I might as well do it sooner when we could really benefit from it.

"Okay," I breathed, feeling nervous. "So first stop, a big old cemetery."

Mikael grinned. "A fitting beginning to lead to Estus' end," he snickered.

All I could do was sigh and hope he was right. Estus had to die. If we succeeded in our plan, he'd become fertilizer for the roots of Yggdrasil, and wouldn't get to experience the unleashing of magic and the old gods into the mortal world. His end would only mean the beginning to more chaos, but I'd take permanent chaos over living in a world where Estus reigned supreme any day of the week.

10

I opened my eyes slowly, then jolted awake when I realized we were no longer in the air. Light streamed in through the windows, but gave no clue to the time of day. At one point we'd landed to refuel, but I'd barely woken up to note where we were or what day it was. Now we'd touched down for a second time, which meant we were in Washington State.

"Rise and shine, morning glory," Alejandro said as he grinned down at me. His long, dark hair was still tousled from sleep, but he either didn't notice it, or didn't care.

Frode stood beside him, without a strand out of place in his blond braid, hanging over his shoulder like a dead snake.

I glanced at the seat beside me. It was empty.

"Where's Mikael?" I grumbled as I lifted my hands to rub my tired eyes.

"He and Aila are getting everyone's weapons out of storage," Alejandro explained. "He wants us armed and ready the moment we step off the plane."

I nodded, then forced myself to stand.

Everyone else still milled about the cabin around us, waiting for Mikael and Aila to return. Faas had left his seat to join his sister in conversation. Maya, Rose, and Dominic stood near the back of the plane, arms crossed and not talking to anyone.

I turned my attention back to Alejandro and Frode. "I'm guessing you two are supposed to stay with me until Mikael returns?"

They both nodded.

"Well then hopefully waiting outside of the bathroom door is good enough," I commented, then hurried past them toward the flimsy, plastic door of the restroom.

I'd always thought the having to pee a lot thing only happened later in a pregnancy, but recently when I had to pee, I had to go *right then.*

By the time I exited the tiny bathroom, Mikael and Aila had returned. After handing everyone their respective weapons, Mikael approached me with two large, sheathed blades in hand, each almost as long as my forearms. The sheaths had metal clips on the backs, made for sliding over a belt.

I looked at the blades in his hands in question. "You know I'm just as likely to fall and stab myself with one of those as I am to actually stab someone else."

"Humor me," he stated with a smile, then slid a sheath onto my belt near each of my hips.

I felt odd with the heavy blades on me, like I was going to whack things with my hips as I walked by. "Aren't we supposed to wait until we leave the airport to bust out the weapons?"

"We're at a small, private airport," he explained, "not commercial."

Finished handing out her portion of the weapons, Aila came to stand at Mikael's side. She lifted a cell phone up in front of her face. "There are three graveyards near here," she informed us. "Does it matter which one we visit?"

I shrugged. "It matters more what time it is. It's easier for the banshees to gather energy when it's dark."

Aila glanced at the phone again, then dropped it to her side. "Five forty-one pm."

I cursed under my breath. If we had to wait until evening to gather power, that meant we'd be losing another day. Since we'd flown through the night, that meant Estus' *ball* was only three days away. I was hoping we might pop in early, leaving him less time to prepare whatever he was planning.

"We have time," Mikael assured in response to my sour look.

I sighed. "Estus could be torturing Alaric and Sophie as we speak. I'm sure time is passing much differently for them."

Mikael put a hand on my shoulder, then turned me to walk down the aisle ahead of him, toward the exit. I reached the open door and was nearly blown back by the cold wind. I snugged my short, black coat a little tighter around me, then walked outside onto the platform. Instead of a narrow corridor to lead us into a building, we just had a stairway mounted on a small vehicle that was meant to drive from plane to plane to release the passengers.

I made my way out onto the stairs, holding tight to the railing as the wind whipped my loose hair around my head. Mikael and Aila followed shortly after me as the others filtered out of the plane. The surrounding tarmac was mostly empty, save a group of people waiting below us, and several huge, black SUVs.

"Umm, Mikael?" I questioned as I came to a stop, halting everyone's progress behind me.

He leaned forward over my shoulder. "They're with us," he assured.

I nodded, then continued down the steps, feeling uneasy about the prospect of even more people joining our ranks, though that was our goal. I guess I just didn't expect Mikael to already have so many people in place.

The group at the end of the stairs was composed of four men and a woman. Three of the men and the woman were unloading things from the bottom of the plane. The man not aiding the others waited by the bottom step. He was of asian decent, tall and slender, though obviously in good shape. His short, black hair was styled with gel that held against the strong winter winds. He wore one of those casual white suits, a bit loose and made of thin fabric, that looked good on very few men, but he pulled it off quite nicely.

He offered me a hand as I reached the last step, which I dutifully ignored. My boots clacked as they hit the tarmac, followed by Mikael and Aila, then everyone else. I moved to the side, making way.

"Silver," Mikael said to the man as he moved to stand at my side, "you would dare attempt to touch the Phantom Queen?" There was sarcasm in his tone, but also a hint of seriousness. It was a tone that said, *you didn't really do anything wrong, but still, back off.*

I watched the exchange silently, wondering where a man got a name like *Silver*, then moved away as Faas beckoned me to follow him.

Faas leaned close to my shoulder as we moved away. "Silver runs Mikael's affairs here in the States," he whispered. Since we were about the same height, the gesture was a lot more comfortable than when Mikael did it. "He made our travel and lodging arrangements."

I glanced over my shoulder to take another look at Silver and Mikael's ongoing exchange, surprised Mikael would put that much trust in anyone other than Aila.

At my perplexed expression, Faas explained, "Silver is even older than Mikael. They've known each other a *very* long time."

My jaw dropped as we turned around to wait side by side. Mikael was over a thousand years old, so that made Silver, well, *ancient*. I suddenly regretted that I'd snubbed his hand. My regret wasn't necessarily logical, it just felt a little odd to snub someone who'd seen so much more than I had. He'd lived through the Crusades, the Renaissance . . . *everything*, and I'd just snubbed him. I tilted my head in thought. Mikael had lived through all of the same events, but he was a different story. He pretty much begged for regular snubbing.

Tabitha came to stand on my other side as Faas and I continued to observe Mikael and Silver.

"I'm starving," she announced, seeming a bit bored with the entire scenario.

At her words, my stomach growled, and both siblings simultaneously looked down at it.

Faas tsked at me. "Madeline, you know keeping up your physical energy is a necessity to maintain your magical energies."

I rolled my eyes at him, cheated of making a catty remark as Mikael and Silver approached us. Behind them, I noticed most of the others carrying luggage to the SUVs.

Mikael stopped in front of us, addressing Faas. "You'll ride with us, along with Marcos," he instructed. "We'll need to begin our planning. We'll first head to the hotel, then we'll leave for the cemetery at nightfall."

I sighed, wishing nightfall were closer. "Why a hotel? Are there no vacant Salr near here?"

Mikael tsked at me. "Staying at a hotel will make us more difficult to find. All of the Salr are likely being watched by Estus' people."

Faas glanced to where Marcos stood, guarded by Frode and Aila. "You truly intend to include him in our plans?"

Mikael's expression turned cold. "You truly intend to question your Doyen?"

Instantly cowed, Faas bowed his head in acquiescence, then marched past me to do as Mikael had bade him.

Mikael turned his attention back to me. "Madeline, this is Silver," he introduced, gesturing to the man beside him. "One of my oldest colleagues."

This time when Silver offered his hand, I took it.

He gave my hand a gentle shake, then withdrew. "She tastes like death, and the earth," he commented, glancing to Mikael. "I can sense nothing else."

I frowned, not sure if I'd just been oddly insulted.

Mikael turned his gaze to me. "Silver is a very different kind of empath," he explained. "Whereas you sense emotions, he senses a person's true nature and intentions . . . among other things."

I *really* didn't like that the first thing he'd sensed about me was death, but I kept my mouth shut. I followed beside Mikael as Silver led the way to the nearest SUV. Faas joined us as we reached the vehicle, along with Marcos, Aila, and Frode.

Frode offered to drive, while Aila took the front passenger seat. The rest of us piled into the back to *plan*. I ended up sandwiched between Mikael and Faas in the middle row of seats, while Marcos and Silver sat behind us.

As Frode started the ignition and steered the vehicle to follow the line of other SUVs, which had all begun to move, Faas and Mikael turned around partially in their seats. The leather creaked with their movements as Frode turned the heat on full blast. I frowned and looked down at my lap, realizing I was the only one who had put on my seatbelt.

With a huff, I turned in my seat as far as the belt would allow, making my knees touch with Mikael's. From the awkward position I could see Marcos, but would have to either crane my neck uncomfortably to see Silver, or turn the other way entirely, pushing my knees up against Faas' instead.

"I've sent word to the smaller clans," Silver explained while Frode pulled the SUV out onto a tree-lined highway. "We should have a decent force by morning."

The sight of the tall redwoods put me at ease. The Pacific Northwest would always be home, even if most of my time spent there was either in solitude, or fighting for my life.

Mikael nodded. "More will be coming from Ireland and Europe," he explained, ignoring everyone except Silver. "We've recruited a few of Aislin's people, and hope to use their presence to sway more to our side."

There was a moment of silence where I imagined Silver nodding, though I couldn't see him.

Mikael turned to me, and his expression softened. "You need to eat something before we visit the cemetery. I want you at your best when you return the banshees to full power. Faas will remain by your side at all times, just in case."

I turned around in the other direction to face Faas, putting my back to Mikael.

"I will be able to weaken you, if need be," he assured.

"That will not be necessary," a cool voice stated from behind us.

I turned my body back to Mikael to turn my head toward Marcos.

Mikael mirrored me, his expression cold. "And why is that?" he asked, not quite masking his sudden irritation.

Marcos smiled. "Madeline is the Phantom Queen. I assure you, she has the power to live up to her name."

"That's the point," Mikael countered. "She could easily live up to that name, but she is much more than that. She mustn't forget herself."

Marcos nodded. "If that is your worry, I will gladly aid her."

"No," Faas snapped, just as I replied, "How?"

Ignoring Faas, Marcos answered with his eyes on me,

"You could give me partial control of the banshees. My talents are aligned with the old dead, while yours are more in tune with death itself." He glanced behind me at Faas. "You could aid her as well, and not by draining away her power. Phantoms are composed of lingering energy. You could serve to weaken her force, or to make it much, much stronger."

I suddenly felt ten times more nervous. "This seems like a really bad idea."

I turned back to Mikael to find him deep in thought.

I stared at him. "Don't tell me you're actually considering having the three of us work together? Aren't you the one who didn't want to give Marcos any power?"

He nodded. "Yes, but we must assess the risks and possible gains. If what he's saying is true, we could quite possibly use the banshees to save *many* lives. If the three of you could join forces, and give the banshees unrivaled power, few would dare stand against us."

I let out a shaky breath. "There are so many *buts* and *what ifs* inherent in that statement that I don't even know where to start."

"It is unnatural," Silver interrupted. "There are rules. If such a force came into being, fate would destroy it."

Before I could ask just what he meant about fate destroying things, Mikael countered, "Fate is already all but destroyed. Madeline's existence goes against fate itself. The Morrigan was no goddess, yet here her energy sits." He gestured to me. "And she has somehow ended up in the presence of both Faas and Marcos, who are both willing to aid her. If such a union simply could not exist, we would never have gotten this far."

"We cannot trust him," Faas snapped. He sounded as shocked as I was that Mikael was actually considering Marcos' suggestion. "He will steal the banshees and kill us all."

Mikael turned calm eyes to me. "No," he said evenly, "he will not. Madeline could easily beat him if she tried."

My jaw dropped. "Why this sudden change of heart?"

He smiled softly and turned in Silver's direction. "You said Madeline tasted of death and the earth," he explained. He turned back to me. "You are many things. I thought perhaps your true nature was associated with emotion since your empathy is so strong, but Silver only tasted those two things." He glanced at Silver again. "What do you sense from Marcos?"

There was a moment of silence, then Silver answered. "Very little. I sense power, and a taste of the grave. He is empowered by those who linger, long after their bodies have turned to dust. His emotions are almost non-existent. I also sense that he is goddess-touched."

My eyes widened. Did he mean Hecate?

"Now what about Faas?" Mikael asked.

"Energy," Silver answered instantly. "He is the balance between life and death. The energy that animates, and that eventually leaves the body cold."

"But with Madeline," Mikael continued, "you simply tasted death, and the earth."

I whipped around so I could see Silver's face as he answered, "Yes. She is not the lingering spirits, nor is she the energy she has the power to release. She is death itself. The very thing that holds the fabric of the world together, and allows life to exist, even briefly. She is the earth, insomuch as it is a part of the endless cycle of life and death."

I still wasn't sure what Mikael was getting at, but it was making my heart flutter nervously. He put a hand on my shoulder, then slowly turned me to face him, pulling my attention away from Silver.

"Madeline," he began, waiting for me to fully meet his eyes. "Your powers have confused me from the start, but I think I finally understand. It's really quite simple, and I should have figured it out as soon as we learned you were descended from the Morrigan. The rest of us are mere children of the traits we embody. I am skilled at manipulation, but I am not manipulation itself. Alaric is skilled at war, but he is not war. He is simply a man with certain inclinations and skills. You are not a woman blessed with the gift of death. You *are* death. You are the missing piece in the puzzle that the Morrigan had previously composed. You are like the key, or the Norns. A pure element of nature. Truly, you cannot even be considered Vaettir."

My mouth went dry. When I was able to speak, I questioned, "And you got all of this from Silver saying I tasted like death?"

He shrugged, seeming somewhat abashed. "First, there was your becoming one with the key. In all the years I chased after the charm, never once did it meld with its holder. Then, you did the same with the Morrigan. Within the bonds of our physical forms and reality, it didn't make sense. These were no temporary possessions. You all existed in the same form at once, sharing control. Your energies melded. When Silver said you tasted only of death and earth, it finally made sense. You are pure energy in mortal form, just as the key was pure energy placed inside of an object, and the Norns are pure energy inside their odd, mortal forms. Those energies can meld together should they choose, because they are not barred by the restraints that hold the rest of us in place."

I shook my head over and over. None of it made sense. I was just like everyone else.

"Madeline," he continued. "I think you never knew your parents, because perhaps you never had any. I think you were created in the same way the key was."

The SUV came to a screeching halt as a deer darted across the highway, throwing us all slightly forward.

"Sorry," Frode mumbled.

The deer bounded out of sight and we regained momentum, just as all our minds seemed to catch back up to the moment at once.

"That's impossible," Faas argued. "She's an executioner. She is one of the Vaettir."

Before anyone else could argue, Marcos stated, "He's right."

We all turned to him.

"Mikael is right," he clarified. "I do not know about your parents. I suspect you were born as a normal Vaettir child, but it's as I've already told you. You are a vessel for energies as old as time itself. It is why my goddess has bade me follow you."

I licked my lips as I tried to choose my words. "But Hecate is the same as the Morrigan. Wouldn't that make me like you?"

He shook his head, showing no signs of being upset that I'd just revealed his secret. "I told you, Hecate and the

Morrigan were different women, with the same associations. Hecate was created as a goddess, the Morrigan as something else entirely. Your existence did not make sense to us. The Vaettir were created by the Norns in the image of the old gods, but the Norns did not create anyone to embody the Morrigan's energy."

I felt like I was going to throw up. "I need to talk to the Norn."

Marcos chuckled. "She will have little to tell you. They do not understand your existence either, because they do not fully understand their own."

"This is all beside the point," Mikael cut in.

I turned wide eyes to him. "Beside what point? We're talking about the idea that I might not have even been born like a normal person."

He smiled to soften the blow his words had dealt me. "And as important as that may be," he continued, "my point now is that I do not think Marcos is any match for you. I do not think we have to fear giving him power. *And*," he continued before I could interrupt, "it brings about another interesting idea. If the key never melded with one of its former carriers because they were not like *you*, then what has happened now that it's been placed inside Estus? When the Morrigan was inside you, your energies melded, but when she was within Sophie, it was a possession where Sophie was entirely taken over."

I had to swallow a few times to get enough saliva in my mouth to speak. "You're saying that the key might have possessed Estus, just like the Morrigan did with Sophie. They can't share the space."

Mikael nodded sharply. "It's only a theory, but if the key

has taken full control, we are no longer dealing with Estus. We are dealing with chaos itself."

The SUV came to a stop again, and we all peered forward to see why. We were in the middle of a one lane, scenic highway, bordered on both sides by massive redwoods. Two of the other SUVs were stopped in front of us, then one behind. For a moment I thought maybe the lead driver had just stopped for another deer, or some other animal, then I saw *them*.

I knew instantly they were Vaettir by the predatory way they walked, slowly surrounding all the vehicles. As if realizing these were not friendly forces, the lead vehicle slammed on the gas. A man dressed in jeans and a biker jacket went flying up over the roof of the SUV, only to hit the next one as it careened after the first. Frode had just started to push on the gas, when both SUVs came to another halt. The short distance we'd traveled revealed a roadblock composed of a massive pick up truck and another SUV.

"Do we turn around?" Frode asked as the new arrivals neared our vehicle.

"Not going to happen," Silver replied.

I glanced behind us to see several more vehicles had moved to block our retreat.

My heart raced. I waited for someone else in the vehicle to decide what to do. If chaos really had taken charge, we were about to get a taste of it.

11

Mikael quickly undid my seatbelt, which I appreciated since I'd entirely forgotten about it. Some of the Vaettir who'd stopped us came to stand on either side of our vehicle. A man and a woman stood on the left, near the passenger door, and four more women on the side with the sliding door that admitted passengers to the back rows of seats. I vaguely recognized a few of them from my time spent in Estus' Salr.

"They're Estus' people," I whispered, stating the obvious.

Mikael removed the knife sheathed at my left hip and placed it in my hand. "As soon as we clear a path, *run*," he explained quietly. He turned to glance at everyone else in the vehicle. "Faas and Frode, stay with Madeline. Everyone else make sure she has a clear line of escape into the woods."

"What about those in the other vehicles?" I asked in a

panic, thinking of Tabitha, Kira, and everyone else I didn't want to get hurt.

"They'll follow our lead," Mikael replied.

Before I could answer, Aila threw open the passenger door and leapt out feet first, fast enough to completely trample the woman closest to her.

I slung my purse across my shoulders and crouched, ready to propel myself out of the vehicle as everyone exploded into motion.

Faas slid open the passenger door. One of the other women lunged for him. He lifted a hand toward her and she slid to the ground, either unconscious or dead as he drained her energy away, then used it to blast back the other two women. Once the way was momentarily clear, he grabbed my free hand and pulled me out of the vehicle. Everyone flooded out behind us.

I tried to look back, but almost fell as Faas forcefully dragged me forward, blasting away any that attempted to hinder us.

"Run, Madeline," he demanded, his voice a harsh pant.

Realizing I'd help everyone more by running away, I matched Faas' pace, with a tight grip on my blade. We made for the tree line. Another man leapt forward to bar our way. I instinctively slashed at him with the knife. He evaded my swipe, then Frode appeared beside us.

Tiny shards of ice splashed my face harmlessly as a pale blue, shimmery stream shot forth from Frode's open hand to the man who'd blocked our way. He fell screaming as his chest became encased in ice.

I blinked in shock at Frode for about two seconds, then Faas tugged me forward again.

The three of us ran, leaving the sounds of fighting behind. My purse thunked annoyingly at my hip with every stride, while I held the knife out in front of me, terrified I'd fall and stab myself, but not willing to give it up.

A million thoughts raced through my mind as we leapt over fallen logs and scrambled through the underbrush. Neither Faas nor I were very fast, but Frode couldn't very well carry both of us, so we stuck to our *human* pace.

Eventually my lungs began to burn, and sweat dripped into my eyes despite the cold, but I pushed onward. Some of the Vaettir could track by scent, so we wanted to quickly gain as much distance as possible.

I stumbled, sending pain shooting up through my knee, then almost immediately stumbled again, then stopped trying to run. Faas and Frode halted on either side of me as I tried to catch my breath. I took a second to slip the knife in my hand back into its sheath, then took a spinning glance at the woods around us. Everything was still, but that meant little. We could be attacked at any moment.

Faas looked a question at me, and I nodded. I hadn't quite caught my breath, but we needed to keep moving. The three of us turned as one, then continued to run, though my legs protested every step.

We ran far enough that I was staggering with every step. Faas and Frode continued forward effortlessly. Given our human-like frailty, Faas should have been as tired as I, but he also worked hard to stay in shape in an attempt to keep up with the more physically skilled members of the clan, like Frode. I was out of shape, and it showed.

Unable to go on any longer, I halted, then hunched over with my hands on my knees as I tried to regain my breath.

Faas and Frode flanked me, looking around in all directions for either signs of pursuit, or signs that anyone on our side had made it out alive.

My thoughts instantly turned to Mikael. We'd been outnumbered by Estus' people, but he hadn't survived over a thousand years by sheer wits alone. He was a warrior with lifetimes of experience. He *had* to be okay, or so I kept telling myself.

Just as I was finally able to catch my breath and stand straight, the sound of several pairs of feet came crashing toward us. I put my hand on one of the knives at my belt, then Tallie and Alejandro appeared. Instantly spotting us, Tallie changed her direction and made a beeline our way, Alejandro hot on her heels.

"Where is everyone else?" I demanded as they reached us.

Tallie pushed slightly sweaty black hair away from her face. Her dark eyes held worry, like she was a puppy ready to get kicked. "I don't know," she admitted. "Mikael ordered us to find you to make sure you'd escaped. We should keep moving."

"But—" I began.

"She's right," Faas interrupted. "Madeline, if something happens to you, all hope is lost. We cannot stand up against the key without you."

"Well, shit," I grumbled, knowing he was right.

"Let's go," he prompted. "Mikael will be fine. Few would hold any chance of standing against him."

I nodded at his assurance, then began walking, unable to force my legs to run.

Alejandro fell into step beside me, grumbling, "Of

course they had to choose the middle of the woods to attack. They couldn't have forced our escape somewhere near a city . . . "

Not picking up on his sarcasm, Frode explained, "This attack was well planned. If there are trackers amongst them, they'll be on our trail by now. I don't know these woods, but it would stand to reason that civilization is quite far off."

"So we just keep walking, not knowing where we're going?" I questioned.

Frode nodded sharply. "Either that, or we loop back around in an attempt to catch those who may be hunting us. Though in doing so, we'd be taking a greater risk."

"I vote for that," I said instantly.

I halted suddenly, noticing someone casually leaning against a tree ahead of us. His white hair shielded his face, though I imagined it held a smug smile.

"How the hell did you get ahead of us?" I forced my steps toward Marcos.

He shrugged, then pushed away from the tree to meet us halfway.

Out of the corner of my eye, I noticed Tallie had maneuvered herself behind me, as if I would protect her from Marcos.

Faas glared at Marcos, but stated, "We need to keep moving. Our previous plan still applies. If we can find the nearest graveyard, we'll be relatively safe with the banshees back at full power."

I nodded, knowing he was right, but hating the idea of leaving everyone else behind. Should worst come to worst, I knew where Estus' Salr was. With our power recharged, we could attempt to rescue Alaric, Sophie, and whomever else might now be held prisoner, on our own. Marcos and Faas were both formidable when they were at full power. Frode and Alejandro made good muscle. I was yet to witness Alejandro's powers, but he was descended from Xolotl, the Aztec god of thunder, so I had a feeling he could be pretty scary if need be. Tallie was more useful as a tracker, but who knew when turning into a wolf might come in handy?

"Let's go," I sighed finally, regretting it as soon as I'd said it.

We all began walking with Marcos leading the way. I had no idea where he was going, but any direction was good, as long as it took us farther from the ambush site. Dry pine needles and loose branches crunched underneath our boots, sounding ear-shatteringly loud in the quiet forest. I kept waiting for someone to pop out and attack us, but the attack never came.

As the hours dwindled on and night fell, I increasingly regretted our decision to move on without the others. We would have to stop and rest at some point, but we had no food or bedding. I hated to imagine what the cold, stinging air would feel like without the added heat of movement. Even worse, I felt uncomfortable sleeping at all with my current company.

I trusted Faas, and to an extent I trusted Frode, since Mikael had entrusted him with my *care*. I really didn't think Tallie would try to harm me, and Alejandro had become something that almost resembled a friend, but, and this was a really big *but*, I didn't trust any of them not to hand me over if their lives depended on it. If Estus' people found us, and it was either sacrifice Madeline or you're all dead meat, I was toast. Without my banshees or some fresh corpses to *release*, I couldn't even defend myself should such a situation occur.

It would be better if we managed to reach a town or city, I thought, as we stumbled along in the dark. I'd had the wherewithal to sling my purse across my shoulders when we ran, and it bounced around against my hip now irritatingly. I had cash, my fake IDs, a tube of chapstick, and . . . my jaw dropped. I had a purse full of snacks and I'd only just realized it. I also had a phone. I could try calling Mikael.

As if sensing the nearby presence of snacks, Tallie's stomach growled loudly.

I stopped walking and unzipped my bag. Tallie and Faas stopped instantly beside me, but Marcos, Alejandro, and Frode all walked a few more steps before realizing we'd halted.

I produced a granola bar and handed it to Tallie. Then pulled out trail mix, dried apricots, and a package of slightly smushed, miniature chocolate donuts.

"Gee mom, why didn't you tell us you brought snacks," Alejandro quipped as he came to stand before me.

I held out the trail mix to him. He could have the apricots too if he wanted, but the donuts were *mine*.

A branch breaking somewhere behind me caught my attention. We all turned to see a small figure limping toward us. I shoved the donuts back into my purse and placed a hand over my knife. A few near-silent moments later, the moonlight revealed Maya. She leaned heavily on her right leg, as if the left had been badly injured. I knew it must have been a severe break or muscle tear, because Maya didn't feel pain. A twisted ankle or knee wouldn't cause her to limp as badly as she was.

"No offense, but you're probably the last person I wanted to see."

She smiled, coming to stand in front of me. "None taken. Personally, I'm just glad to be alive right now. I can handle being unwanted."

"What happened?" I demanded.

She'd obviously seen more of the fight than any of us, so maybe she knew where Mikael and the others were, or if they were even still alive.

"Estus' people were there to take us prisoner, not kill us," she explained, "though they weren't going gently about it. I took off while the fighting was still going on. Some on our side had been incapacitated, many on Estus' side had been killed. I didn't hang around to see how it all ended."

"Mikael?" I pressed.

She smirked. "Last I saw, he was decapitating a man. Didn't seem like he planned to leave until the fight was over."

I cursed quietly under my breath. If Mikael had stayed for the entire fight, he was either dead, taken prisoner, or he was looking for us. I prayed the latter was the case, but if it was, he should have found us by now. He could run without tiring many more miles than we'd walked. Of course, I had no idea about his tracking skills. Perhaps he was just lost in the woods like the rest of us.

Once again remembering my phone, I retrieved it from my purse and fumbled for the button to turn it on. Mikael had given it to me after I'd been stolen away by the Morrigan, but I hadn't had a chance to use it since, so I wasn't quite comfortable with all of its functions. Most Vaettir weren't into technology, but Mikael was an exception. He had a phone, and so did Aila, though I didn't have her number, only Mikael's.

The screen lit up to reveal I had no service. I groaned and held down the power button until the phone shut back off.

"Let's go," I sighed, pulling my donuts back out of my purse and replacing them with the phone.

"Where's my snack?" Frode protested.

I took a moment to toss him the apricots, then kept walking. "Be nice and share," I chided when he shoved half the bag of apricots in his mouth at once.

"This is the worst camping trip ever," he whined.

"You're all crazy," I heard Tallie mutter under her breath, her mouth full of granola bar.

I wasn't about to argue with her.

THE MORRIGAN, Alaric, and Sophie had walked through the night, though Alaric barely felt tired. His focus was only on their end goal, not on food or rest. Sophie was a different story.

"I'm *starving*," she groaned.

Alaric glared at her. "Feel free to scamper off and catch a deer."

She made a look like she tasted something sour. "There's no need to be rude, Grumpy Gus."

He sighed. He knew taking his frustration out on

Sophie would do little good, but it was difficult to hold back. It was her fault he'd been separated from Madeline, even if she'd had no way to foresee Estus sending them into the past.

He took a steadying breath as they tromped over broken branches and pine needles, then forced out, "I'm sorry. We're in this together. We shouldn't be fighting."

He knew deep down Sophie was terrified. Though she didn't have a partner and unborn child to return too, she would still be losing her life if they remained trapped in the past.

"Morrigan," Alaric called out patiently to the woman marching roughly twenty feet ahead of them, "how much farther?"

She stopped, then turned and waited for them to catch up with a wry look on her face. "You may call me Mara," she explained. "Morrigan is such a formal title. And to answer your question, we should reach the current Morrigan's fortress within a few more hours."

"And explain to me again, what will we do once we arrive?"

Mara smirked. "Sophie will approach the Morrigan, armed with information only I would know. She will convince her of your plight, and she will use her power to send you back to the correct time."

"She, err, I mean you, have that kind of power?" Sophie questioned, coming to a standstill beside Alaric.

Mara nodded. "You met me long after I'd lost my mortal form, and most of my power. In this time, the Morrigan has the charm, what you refer to as the key. It was the key's power that sent you here, and that power can send you back."

So Estus *had* used the key's power to send them back, Alaric thought. Or else the key was entirely in control, and had sent them back itself. "If the key sent us here," he began, "then how will we convince it to send us back?"

Mara grinned like the proverbial crocodile. "You are assuming the current Morrigan has no control over the key. In truth, we were partners. We both came from Yggdrasil. Together we represented two thirds of the power contained within the World Tree."

Sophie took a small step back in surprise. "On second thought, I'm not really sure I want to meet . . . you."

Mara's smile widened. "Yes, I'm quite scary."

Sophie groaned.

Alaric shared her sentiments. He'd only heard a few stories of the original Phantom Queen, but they were enough to give anyone nightmares. He'd already seen Madeline use the banshees to kill, and he had a feeling the original Morrigan would kill a man first, and ask questions never.

"Let's go," Mara said happily, then turned away and started walking again.

Alaric briefly considered running in the other direction, but knew he had no choice but to follow. If it was death, or remaining in the past forever, longing for a reunion with Madeline that would never come, he would gladly end things right there.

12

I sat, leaning my back against the rough bark of a tree with my knees pulled up to my chest, as the damp ground soaked through the seat of my jeans.

We'd walked until I could walk no more. If I'd been the only one to give up, someone probably would have carried me, but Faas was just as tired as I was, and Maya's injury seemed to worsen the longer we trudged on. All of my snacks were gone, and everyone had spiraled downward into a depressed fugue.

"I see I've joined the correct side," Maya muttered sarcastically as she rested against the next tree over, her injured leg sprawled out at an awkward angle.

I glared at her, though with only the dim moonlight, she was hard to see. "Why *did* you join us? The last time I saw you, you were loyal enough to Aislin that you tried to kill Sophie."

"Aislin is dead," she stated simply.

"So what," I pressed, "you'll give me that same sort of loyalty until I die?"

Maya was silent for several seconds.

"Aislin saved her life," Alejandro explained from my other side. "More than once," he added. "Oh, and she gave her back her foot."

"Oh yeah," I mused. "I've been wondering about that."

James had tortured Maya to the point of cutting off her foot, mutilating her hands, and cauterizing the wounds. Yet the next time we saw her, she had was perfectly whole.

Maya sighed loudly. "Aislin's true magic was in healing," she explained, "though she rarely used it unless it directly benefitted her in some way."

"Sounds about right," I replied, remembering what type of woman Aislin had been. She and her brother were like two peas in a pod.

"Maya was born with a disorder," Alejandro continued, despite Maya's annoyed grunt. "Her power was poison. She could kill others with a touch, but it was also slowly killing *her*."

I turned to raise an eyebrow at him, though in the darkness it was hard to tell if he noticed.

"She's descended from the goddess Mefitis," he explained, "who was basically just the personification of the poisonous gasses that seeped from fissures in the earth."

"How do you know all this?" I interrupted.

"I'm much older than I look," he replied.

Maya let out a long sigh, then picked up the explanation. "I was able to survive my childhood, but the poison was slowly killing me," she said tiredly. "Aislin *healed* my affliction, thus, I owed her my life."

"So if poison was your power," I began curiously, "then why don't you feel pain?"

"That was a side effect," Maya replied. "Poison was not only my power. It was what *composed* me. Neutralizing it took away many other things, including empathy and my ability to feel pain."

I nodded, understanding enough of what she'd explained to comprehend why she'd been so loyal to Aislin. "So you became Aislin's spy out of gratitude?"

"And because Aislin constantly threatened to return her poison," Alejandro added.

"Ah, now that sounds more like Aislin," I replied, "but that still doesn't explain why you decided to join me instead of Estus."

Maya laughed bitterly. "With Aislin dead, I was finally free of the threat of my poison, but I am not free of being Vaettir. I still needed to choose a clan. You saw what Estus did to me. Do you blame me for not choosing him?"

I shook my head, though she probably didn't see it. "But you also knew we had good reason to reject you."

"Even if you killed me, it would be better than living my life in fear of Estus. My entire existence has been *fear*, and I'm tired. If you killed me, it would at least mean an end to everything. I know the kind of person you are. You would release my soul, granting me peace. Estus would keep my heart in a box."

"Now you see why Tallie and I were more than happy to join you," Alejandro chimed in. "You may stand a good chance of calling many to your cause out of fear, but your true appeal lies in you actually caring what happens to those around you."

"Even if it means positioning yourself against the near unstoppable force that is Estus?" I questioned.

Alejandro laughed. "As far as I'm concerned, *you're* an unstoppable force. You had both Estus and Aislin gunning for you, and you're somehow not only still alive, but still fighting."

"Gee, you're going to make me blush," I replied sarcastically, then laughed.

Alejandro laughed too. "Any day I can make a lady blush is a good day."

"If you're all quite finished," Faas interrupted. "We should start moving again."

I sighed, unsure if I even had the willpower to stand.

Marcos, who'd remained silent during our conversations, suddenly appeared before me, extending his hand.

I looked at his long, thin fingers for a moment, then took his hand. If he was on my side, then he was on my side, and I had to either trust him, or kill him. I was going with trust, though it pained me.

I swayed on my feet slightly as I stood, then managed to steady myself. I was glad I'd gotten plenty of sleep on the plane. Without that, there was no way I would have still been moving.

As Alejandro walked past us to help Maya up, Frode came to stand on my other side.

He leaned close to my shoulder. "Allow me to aid you," he whispered.

I looked a question at him, able to clearly see his expression with how near he was.

"He's asking permission to touch you," Faas explained. "You don't seem able to walk any farther."

"Oh," I muttered. "Sure."

Frode swooped me up in his arms. I wrapped an arm around the back of his neck, surprised to find that I didn't even feel awkward about it. I'd been carried around so much since we first started running from Estus, I'd come to accept it as a necessity. I needed the help.

After a short argument, Maya allowed Alejandro to carry her. Faas refused help offered by Tallie, and began to trudge ahead on his own.

The rest of us followed. Though Marcos remained near Frode and I, it was clear he walked on his *own*. Not truly a part of the group.

Eventually the sounds of traffic could be heard, still aways off. As far as I could tell we'd kept to one direction, so it had to be a new highway, not the one we'd left. On one hand, it could be a good thing. A highway meant a path to civilization. On the other hand, we weren't likely to get a ride with how many of us there were, and how some of us looked. Plus, walking along a road would make us easier to find, either by Estus, or by our own people. It was a toss up.

Still, we really didn't have any other choices. We continued walking.

Soon headlights came into view, flashing through the trees, and much to our surprise, the light of homes. It seemed we were nearing a small town, stationed next to a highway.

"Oh thank the gods," Alejandro muttered. "We can get some food."

I snorted from my perch in Frode's arms. "We're

running for our lives, separated from our companions, and your first though is *food*?"

"A man must have his priorities," he joked, though his voice was drowned in and out by the sound of the sparse, late night traffic on the highway.

Frode let me down to my feet. "Check your phone," he advised. "Maybe you'll have service now."

I retrieved my cell phone from my purse and turned it back on. Sure enough, I had service, though it was sketchy. I instantly dialed Mikael's cell number and held the phone up to my ear.

A moment later, I lowered it with a huff. "Straight to voicemail." I didn't have Aila's number, and none of the other Vaettir deigned to carry phones.

"Let's check out the town," Frode advised.

No one argued. As soon as there was a lull in traffic, Frode swept me back up in his arms and we hurried across the highway, toward the nearby lights of civilization. Even though I'd given Alejandro a hard time for thinking only of food, I had to admit, it was also at the forefront of my mind. I felt weak and shaky. I needed food and sleep. Hopefully the town could provide accommodations for both. Heck, maybe they'd even have a graveyard. A one stop shop for all of our physical and metaphysical needs.

We passed by a gas station and a few dark storefronts, then turned away from the highway toward what seemed like the main stretch of town. I noticed a sign that said *Welcome to Littleburg*. The name was fitting for the tiny town. I had just begun to fret that they wouldn't even have a hotel or any open restaurants, when a neon motel sign came into view.

We continued down the quiet street as the occasional car flashed past us. I watched Marcos as he walked, thinking he looked horribly out of place in the quaint town. He belonged in a hidden dungeon, or perhaps on the streets of a big city, with his long white hair and all black clothing. He was so tall and thin that he looked like some sort of phantom, his pale skin and acrimonious expression only adding to the effect.

"We should ask at the inn if there are any graveyards nearby," I stated, breaking the silence.

"You need to rest," Faas answered instantly.

"We need to recharge so we're able to defend ourselves," I countered.

"You need to be at full strength to control the banshees," he countered right back.

"Remember what Mikael said," Frode stated vaguely.

Faas grunted in reply.

I appreciated that they weren't divulging Mikael's speculations to those who weren't in the SUV with us. I hadn't even had time to really think about it all. Still, I was with Frode. I could handle going straight to the graveyard, or so I kept telling myself.

"So graveyard first," I said, making sure everyone was on the same page.

"Then food," Alejandro added.

"Then *rest*," Tallie groaned.

I thought about my phone again, wishing I had anyone else's numbers besides Mikael. Wishing any one else even had a phone. It seemed impossible to move our plan forward with such a small group, but I was more worried about the others even being alive. Maya had said Estus' people were there to take everyone prisoner, not to kill them, but that didn't mean deaths weren't possible. There were many amongst our group who would not go gently into the good night.

My thoughts turned to Alaric, and the fact that the *ball* was only three, no two, considering it was past midnight, days away. I couldn't help but speculate that perhaps I'd been allowed to escape on purpose. Maybe the main goal of the ambush was to weaken my entourage. To make me face Estus without any backup. If only I knew what he was planning.

If he'd been fully consumed by the key . . . well, I hated to think why the key might want me alone. Our energies were meant to be one, along with the Norns, at least according to Mikael, but the key was also chaos. It wouldn't have balance on its mind. It would have destruction.

We reached the front of the motel. It was two stories high, with a squat, central lobby. There were probably only around forty rooms, most vacant judging by the near-empty parking lot. Frode let me back down to my feet, but remained near my side to make sure I didn't fall over, then we all waited outside while Alejandro entered the lobby. We watched through the front window as he laughed and flirted with the lone woman at the front desk. Several minutes passed before he returned outside to us.

"The cemetery is two miles away," he explained as he came to stand before Frode and I. "They also have plenty of vacancies, and will give us a twenty percent discount." He waggled his eyebrows at me.

"At last," I said dramatically. "Your lascivious nature has proven useful for something."

He laughed, then pointed us in the direction of the cemetery. Back I went into Frode's muscular arms, and we all began to walk once more.

My heart was beating faster than my lack of exertion should have allowed. Soon I would do all I could to recharge my banshees. Marcos would gather power too. I glanced at him again, internally praying he wouldn't betray us. In a fair, metaphysical fight, I could probably take him, but he was still scary. The memory of him flinging aside twenty warriors at a time with energy stolen from the Norns was still too fresh in my mind, as was the memory of him removing the key from me. Still, if he was truly on our side, that amount of power could prove invaluable.

If we truly only had this small group to take down Estus, we were going to need the power. Faas, Marcos, and I would have to form the perfect trifecta of death.

It was terrifying, but that's what we were going for. Hopefully it would be more terrifying for everyone else than it would be for us. Summoning an army of death brought a whole new meaning to facing your fears.

ALARIC STARED at the distant castle. He stood at the top of a small hill with Mara and Sophie, giving them a clear view of the still far off structure. It was about midday, though with the heavy cloud cover, it was difficult to tell. As he stared, deep in thought, a single ray of sunlight peeked through the clouds to shine on the dark stone of the castle, its menacing walls impossibly high. From what he could make out, the castle was square shaped, with four towers, twenty feet taller than the side walls, composing the corners. Narrow windows, barely visible at this distance, interrupted the perfect stone walls.

A dense forest spanned several miles in all directions around the castle. Alaric attempted to plot out their course, but the trees were so closely spaced, little could be seen. They'd simply have to make their way in the general direction of the castle and hope for the best.

"Why do I get the feeling this isn't a normal forest?" Sophie asked from behind him, startling him out of his thoughts.

"Because it's not," Mara answered from his other side. "You must remember, I was quite feared in this time, but I was also despised. I took many precautions to keep my enemies from reaching me."

Alaric stroked his chin in thought as he continued to stare at the castle. "What sort of precautions?"

He turned in time to see Mara shrug. "Magic beasts, poisonous traps, reanimated corpses . . . that sort of thing."

"You couldn't have mentioned any of this sooner?" Sophie gasped.

Mara rolled her eyes. "My defenses shouldn't be much trouble for two children of Bastet. If you cannot defeat them, you are not deserving of your lineage."

A low growl trickled out of Sophie's throat.

"We have no weapons," Alaric muttered, ignoring his sister's ire, "so I'd say our best chance is stealth. We'll fight where we must," he turned to Mara, "but avoiding as many traps as possible will help us reach Madeline more quickly."

"Yes," Mara agreed, her tone suddenly serious. "I hate to

admit that Madeline might need help, but she's in an . . . uncomfortable situation."

He turned to fully face Mara. How had she known just what situation Madeline was in? "You can *see* her?"

Mara sighed. "Only from afar, and only when she's raising enough power to thin the veil between worlds."

He raised his eyebrows in surprise. "She's powerful enough to thin the veil between worlds?"

Mara smirked. "She's a denizen of death. Thinning the veil is what she does."

"Where is she now?" Alaric demanded.

She narrowed her eyes at him. "I told you, I can only catch glimpses when she raises power, which she hasn't in a while. The last time I sensed her fully was when she tried to use the banshees to rescue you, but they were too weak to do any good." She shook her head. "Silly girl," she muttered.

"She's afraid of them," he explained. "I don't blame her for weakening them."

Mara's expression suddenly turned fierce. "You would have her live in fear?" she snapped.

"I would have her *live*," he snapped back. "Fear exists for a reason. It keeps us alive."

She turned her gaze back to the forest. "Are you afraid now?"

"Yes," he answered simply.

Mara and Sophie both turned surprised expressions toward him.

"I do not fear my death," he explained, "but I would be a liar if I said I didn't fear never meeting my child, and never seeing Madeline again." He turned to Sophie. "And it would be foolish for you to assume that I do not fear *your* death, and the idea that I might not be able to protect you from it."

Sophie smiled softly, making the entire admission of fear worth it. He wasn't sure he'd ever admitted to fear before that moment, not in his entire life. Perhaps even after five hundred years, a man could still change.

"Well isn't that touching," Mara mocked from behind Alaric's back. "Can we please just get this over with?"

He turned and raised an eyebrow at her, then gestured to the forest ahead. "Lead the way."

Mara smirked, but started forward without another word.

Alaric followed after her, with Sophie trailing behind him. Yes, even after five hundred years a man could change, and he could still find new experiences. Like finding his soulmate, becoming a father, and traveling into a real life enchanted forest, complete with magic beasts, poisonous traps, and perhaps even a zombie or two.

13

The graveyard was small, just like the town, but it was also fairly old, at least in part. The little town must have been there for a very long time, because some of the graves dated back to the late 1800s.

Faas and Marcos stood on either side of me, while everyone else stood back near the small, neighborhood street leading to the cemetery. I shifted my feet in the damp grass, feeling anxious. There were no houses right along the border of the cemetery, but the neighborhood wasn't far off. I wouldn't be surprised if someone ended up calling the police on us for loitering in the cemetery at night.

With a single thought, I called the banshees to me, but they were barely wisps of energy now. I'd depleted them into almost nothing. It was time to fix that.

Marcos took my hand, startling me.

"I can help," he said at my wide-eyed look.

Faas put a hand on my shoulder. "I'll be here if things

get out of control," he assured, then his hand dropped as he took a few steps back.

I nodded lightly to him, then turned my gaze to the shadowy graves. We stood in the center of the graveyard. The older graves lay before us, and the newer ones behind us. I could sense them to an extent, but it was nothing like the waves of power I'd ridden when I summoned the banshees with the Morrigan's help. Ritual had been needed then, sealed by the death of the Morrigan's body. If the banshees faded entirely, I'd need that same ritual again. As it was, I might still have a chance of restoring them.

Marcos gave my hand a squeeze, then suddenly power washed over me. I could feel each and every grave. Many of them just felt like empty shells, their energy long since moved on, but some spirits still lingered. A portion of the energy that previously inhabited the corpses remained tied to the earth, unable to let go.

"What are you doing?" I gasped.

"Connecting you," he explained simply. "Think of me as a metaphysical switchboard."

White forms began to swirl around us. Marcos was drawing the energy in, and he was giving it to me. He hadn't lied when he said he was willing to help.

Giving in to the odd sensation, I focused my will onto the banshees. I was filling up with energy, similar to what happened when I released the soul from one of the Vaettir, but somehow different. These weren't souls, but residual memories and shards of personalities who'd long since perished in reality.

I took all of that strange energy and focused it on the banshees. They responded instantly, starved for power.

I heard Frode mutter, "Holy shit," from somewhere behind us as the banshees began to take form. He'd come to Ireland after I'd allowed them to be depleted, so he'd never seen them at full power.

Their almost invisible forms slowly filled out until a dozen or so cloaked women hovered before us. Their slightly transparent faces were eerie, but still showed that they had been individuals in life. Different women with different experiences. All unable to move on.

I continued to pour energy into them as more shapes formed behind them. Other phantoms, some with large wings, others more animalistic with glowing red eyes, came into being, though they weren't fully corporeal. When looking right at them, it was hard to make out distinct shapes, but occasionally you'd catch a solid glimpse out of the corner of your eye.

The banshees all bowed their heads. "We are here, my Queen," they stated as one.

"Thank the gods," I muttered as my body flooded with relief. It had worked, and I felt completely in control.

The banshees turned to Marcos, his hand still in mine, as they added, "and my King."

Well shit. I pulled my hand away as I turned on him. "You tricked me," I accused.

He smirked, not at all afraid of the ire in my expression. "They simply acknowledge the energy that helps to sustain them. I assure you, they will listen to your orders over mine."

A hand grabbed me from behind and pulled me farther away from Marcos. Faas' face was suddenly right beside

SARA C. ROETHLE

mine as he held me close. "But they will listen to only you if she dies," he spat venomously.

Marcos tilted his head to the side, spilling pure white hair over his shoulder. "I have no intention of harming her, if that is what you are implying. The phantoms are anchored to the earth by *her* ritual. If Madeline dies, that ritual would need to be performed once more. I do not have the correct tools to complete it."

My heart was thundering in my ears at the sudden shock of realizing Marcos' level of power, but I wasn't overly afraid. I could *feel* my connection to the banshees. They were still mine. They just now used a portion of Marcos' power to give themselves form. In fact, they felt more powerful than ever.

"You strengthened them," I said to Marcos in surprise.

He nodded. "My powers work well with yours. I'm able to support you with the extra sources of energy that only I have access to."

"But why?" I asked, still not fully understanding. "Why would you share so much of your power?"

He seemed perplexed. "I already told you, Madeline. Our goals are the same."

"Huh," was the only reply I had for him.

Faas finally let me go, then moved to stand at my side as the others warily approached. The banshees remained immobile, silently waiting for orders as the other phantoms swirled around them.

"So . . . time for food?" Alejandro asked as he approached us.

Maya looked up at the phantoms warily. "We should be careful. Anyone who can sense energy will sense *this*."

146

"She's right," Tallie added, positioning herself so that we were all between the phantoms and her. "I would be able to track this amount of energy, no problem."

I turned my gaze back to the banshees. I could use them to travel, and I was guessing they would probably take Marcos along for the ride too, but not everyone else. If Estus' people found us, we'd have to fight, not flee. A sudden idea struck me.

"Good," I muttered to myself.

"What?" Tallie asked.

"I said *good*," I stated a little louder. "Let them find us. I want them all to see what they're dealing with, then we'll see how many are still willing to stand at Estus' side."

Marcos smiled wickedly.

"But first," Alejandro interjected, raising a finger into the air, "*food.*"

I nodded, though food wasn't even a secondary thought for me at that moment. Perhaps tertiary or quaternary. Alejandro was right though, we needed to eat. Especially Faas and I. If we let our physical forms grow weak, our metaphysical powers would be weakened too.

The sky around us had just begun to grow light. We'd been out for an entire night. It was winter, so for the light to be starting to show meant it was probably around seven. The sun wouldn't fully rise until nine. I'd turned my phone back off, wanting to conserve its battery, so I didn't check it to verify the time.

Instead, I squinted at the early morning sun and yawned. "Let's look for a breakfast place, then we'll try to get a few hours of sleep before we storm the castle."

Alejandro raised an eyebrow at me. "So you truly plan

to invade Estus' Salr with only this small group?" He moved his hand in a sweeping gesture, encompassing our companions.

I glanced up at the banshees, still visible, but less tangible in the early morning light. "We're not actually storming the castle," I joked, turning my gaze back to Alejandro. "We were invited."

He smirked. "Something tells me that invitation didn't include a host of phantoms."

I grinned. "Well it also didn't warn us about the advance attack, so I'm not too worried about being rude. Payback is a bitch."

"And Estus has a lot coming to him," Maya stated coldly from where she stood behind me.

I nodded, then silently led the way as we left the cemetery, for the first time almost glad that Maya was with us. Besides me, she was the only person present who had real reason to hate Estus, and she was willing to sacrifice her life if it meant she could help take him down. Estus had bullied and tortured far too many people over his long life. It was about damn time some of his victims came back to bite him.

Did karma apply to sadistic Doyen's inhabited by pure chaos? We were about to find out.

THEY'D BEEN WALKING through the shadowy forest for roughly an hour when Mara suddenly staggered. Alaric had to catch her arm to keep her from falling.

"What's wrong?" he demanded, thinking perhaps she'd happened upon one of her own traps.

She held a hand to her eyes for several seconds, then brushed her red hair out of her face and stood straight.

Sophie moved toward Alaric's side, forming a three person circle as they waited for Mara to explain herself.

Mara glanced back and forth between the two of them. "Madeline did . . . something," she explained. "It was something big, considering I felt it without even trying to look in on her."

"How is that even possible?" Sophie inquired. "That you felt her without trying, I mean."

Mara shook her head, still seeming disoriented. Alaric had the sudden urge to shake her until the answers rattled loose, but resisted.

"We are composed of the same energy," she explained. "It's not like the connection you have with your goddess, where you were simply made by the Norns in her image. Madeline and I are both mortal embodiments of the same energy. She is simply a newer, less concentrated version of what I once was."

"What did she do?" Alaric interrupted, caring less about *how* Mara had sensed Madeline, and more about *what* she had sensed.

She shook her head again, as if trying to work something out in her mind. "I believe she has restored the banshees, but something is wrong with the energy. It's different, and more powerful."

Alaric wanted to ask more, but something behind Mara caught his eye. His jaw dropped. "What was it you said about magical beasts again?"

Mara's eyes widened, then she looked over her shoulder, spotting the creature merely twenty feet away. "Well," she began, her voice quavering, "I didn't say much, but I should probably explain now. They're basically unstoppable, pure embodiments of nature's energy."

He stared at the creature as it watched them from within the shadows created by the dense trees. It was massive, around fifteen feet tall. It stood mostly on its hind legs, but leaned forward on heavy arms, like a great ape, only its skin was made of what looked like gnarled tree bark, hanging with loose moss and vines. Its head boasted a wide maw, and beady, glowing red eyes, with two small slits for nostrils. Its shoulders were wider than Alaric was tall.

"You can't control it?" he whispered, keeping his gaze firmly on the unmoving creature.

"No," Mara whispered back. "It is under control of the current Morrigan."

"But *you're* the Morrigan," Sophie rasped.

Mara shook her head minutely. "No, I am simply a cumulation of that same energy. Little more than a ghost, really. I have no power in this time."

"Shit," Sophie replied. "Should we run?"

The beast took a few steps forward, its massive knuckles pounding into the ground as it took on an aggressive stance. It let out an ear shattering roar.

"Yep," Mara said with a cringe. "We should definitely run."

Alaric didn't need her to say it twice. He turned and shoved his sister ahead of him. She darted forward, needing no extra encouragement. They ran as the beast charged them, the heavy impact of its gait echoing throughout the forest around them.

Alaric wove his way through the trees in the direction of the castle, keeping an eye on Sophie and Mara as they ran. The creature toppled trees as it gave chase, too wide to fit through many of the narrow openings. They all had to dive out of the way more than once as the falling trees narrowly missed them.

Not only had Mara claimed the creature was unstoppable, neither he nor Sophie had any weapons. They were both capable of partial shape changes that could provide them with razor sharp teeth and claws, but he had a feeling their attacks would do little good against the creature's tough bark. They needed a magic user to defeat the creature. He almost laughed as he ran, thinking how perfect James would have been for the job with his fire powers, but those days were over. He was dead.

His mind quickly sorted through any other options. They could climb a tree, but the creature had already proven itself capable of felling several trees without hardly trying. They could continue to run, neither he nor Sophie would tire any time soon, even with the full night of walking, but the only possible salvation was the Morrigan's castle. If he went storming in there along with the women, he would be cooked. The only options left were to somehow outrun the creature enough that it would lose their trail, which at the moment, seemed unlikely, or to somehow trick it.

The sound of water running in the distance brought to mind another idea. If the creature couldn't swim, perhaps they could escape it, or even drown it. Of course, that was assuming whatever body of water they might find would be deep enough, or wide enough, to impede the magical beast.

"What types of waterways are near here!" Alaric shouted as they ran.

Mara, with her green velvet dress hiked up around her knees for ease of movement, leapt over a fallen log like a gazelle, then answered, "There are several streams that lead into a lake! What are you thinking?"

He was glad she didn't sound the least bit winded as she spoke. She'd likely be able to keep up with him and Sophie for a while. If she was barely more than a spirit, as she claimed, perhaps she'd keep up the pace much longer than either of them could.

Another tree came crashing down behind them, narrowly missing Sophie as she dove out of the way, gracefully rolling across the ground before hopping back to her feet to continue running.

"Can the creature swim?" he called out to her over the thundering of the beast's footfalls.

"Who knows!" she replied. "I summoned it from the earth. I did not create it."

If he'd had a spare moment, he would have sighed. "Lead us to the lake!" he demanded. "It seems our best option."

With a nod, Mara darted off ahead of him, impossibly fast.

With a competitive growl, Sophie picked up her pace and ran after her. Alaric dodged another tree, then followed them, praying that the creature would sink as quickly as it could run.

AFTER WE WERE ALL FED, we went back to the motel where Alejandro had gotten directions to the cemetery. Between us we had the cash and credit cards to rent a room for every single person, but we decided to just stick with two adjoining rooms. That way, if we were once again ambushed, we'd all be together. I could summon the banshees, and we'd be able to protect ourselves.

There was a second reason for the adjoining rooms, though no one said it out loud. Faas didn't trust anyone around me besides Frode, and we still needed to keep an eye on Maya and Marcos . . . just in case. Two rooms made that an easy task. We'd decided that one room would contain me, Faas, Marcos, and Tallie, while the other would contain Frode, Maya, and Alejandro. The adjoining door would remain open in case of emergencies, though in reality, it was just in case Maya and Alejandro decided to band together to eliminate Frode. I was to the point where I actually trusted Alejandro just as much as anyone else, but it was still wise to be cautious. Anyone who was previously one of Aislin's people needed to be watched, and that was that. I had a feeling Alejandro sensed our suspicions, but he didn't seem to mind. In fact, he seemed to find them amusing, quietly smiling at us as we debated the sleeping arrangements.

After receiving our flimsy, plastic key cards, we'd entered our rooms. They were done in typical cheap motel style, with ugly patterned quilts on the pairs of queen-sized beds, burgundy carpet that would hide most stains, and cheap particle board furniture to support the TV and bedside lamps.

Faas moved to shut the heavy drapes as I claimed the bed closer to the adjoining door. Marcos took the other bed, seeming quite content as he laid on his back on the bedspread and shut his eyes. He folded his arms across his chest, looking like a bad rendition of Dracula.

Tallie shifted nervously between the feet of the two beds, pawing at the ends of her loose, black hair.

I stared at her until I got her attention. "You can sleep with me," I offered. I cast a wary glance at Marcos, then added, "If you want."

She nodded quickly, then climbed into bed beside me.

With a sigh, Faas strode across the burgundy carpet and latched the additional security hinge on the room's main door and shut off the light, then returned to the window and made himself comfortable on the room's small couch. He was around my height, 5'9", so he fit better on the couch than Marcos would, but his legs still dangled off the end at an uncomfortable looking angle. A narrow sliver of light, not blocked by the heavy curtains, cut a vibrant line right across his face. With a groan, he put a pillow over his face and shifted until he was comfortable.

I sighed, then nestled my head against my pillow and closed my eyes. Frode had first watch, and would wake Faas when he was ready to take his turn to sleep.

The room was silent for several minutes, until Tallie whispered, "Madeline?"

I opened my eyes to see she'd turned her head toward me, barely illuminated by the sparse amount of sunlight creeping into the room.

"Yeah?" I whispered back.

"What's going to happen after we leave this hotel room?" she asked softly.

The question made her seem so childlike I was almost taken aback. While I'd sensed Tallie's fear many times, outwardly she preferred to project strength and capability.

"We're going to visit Estus' Salr and do our best to get Alaric and Sophie back," I explained quietly, though she already knew that portion of the plan. "This is just a rescue mission for now, unless we see an opportunity to do more."

She nodded. "Then what after that?" she whispered.

"Then we figure out a more organized plan of attack. We're going to do our best to flesh out our ranks. Then we're going to take Estus down."

She blinked at my explanation, then nodded again. "And after that? If we manage to survive, what will happen then?"

I sighed, wishing desperately for sleep. I had no idea how much information Tallie had gleaned during her time with us, but I saw no harm in telling her the truth, even if it was new information to her. She deserved to be prepared, and if she was going to have a problem with our plan, I wanted to know now.

"We're going to regrow Yggdrasil," I explained. "It's going to cause some chaos, but we're going to do our best to keep everyone safe."

She nodded again. I didn't sense any more fear from her than usual. "I'd heard that might be happening. I'd always thought Yggdrasil was just a myth." She smiled. "Of course, I always thought Norns and banshees were myths too."

I grinned. "Me too. If you would have told me a few

months ago about any of this, I would have called you crazy."

"Get some rest," Faas called from the nearby couch, interrupting our small bonding moment.

"Yes father," I said sarcastically.

"If Madeline doesn't have to sleep, neither do I!" Alejandro called from the other room.

"Smart asses," Faas mumbled before rolling over and putting his back to the room.

There were a few soft snickers from the other room, then silence as everyone drifted off to sleep. I appreciated the small moment of tension relief. I imagined that as soon as we woke, and the day unfolded before us, there would be little cause for further laughter, especially considering we might not even survive.

14

A laric didn't need Mara to lead him for long before he caught the scent of water. The lake had to be nearby. He wasn't looking forward to going for a swim, but it was the only plan he could conjure. They could swim to the center of the lake to lure the creature in, where it would hopefully drown. If, on the other hand, the creature refused to enter the water, they could perhaps swim to a region that would be difficult to access by staying on dry land. Of course, there was a third option. The creature could be a swift swimmer, and they would end up in a watery grave.

The lake came into view. There was no time to think things over. He quickly scanned the lay of the land as they approached.

The lake was massive. A gaping, sunny hole in the middle of the dense forest, with the trees pushed back away from the shore on all sides. At one end was a tall, rocky cliff face, jutting up against the water. Perhaps a suitable area to make an escape if they were able to find proper footholds.

His planning ended as they reached the bank. No one hesitated as their feet went splashing into the water. Moments later, once they were deep enough, they all dove in. Alaric briefly worried that Mara's velvet dress would impede her, but she quickly outpaced both he and Sophie as they swam. There was a splash behind them as the creature entered the water. Alaric spared a second to glance over his shoulder as he swam to see the creature swimming after them with large, exaggerated strokes, creating mini tidal waves as each of its arms cut down into the water. Fuck.

He turned forward and swam as fast as he could, knowing it would do little good. It wouldn't take the creature long to reach them. They were approaching the middle of the lake. Nice and deep for the creature to hold them under until they drowned, if it didn't break them in half first.

"Be still!" Mara shouted suddenly.

Alaric glanced forward at her in surprise. She stopped swimming, and bobbed ahead of them in the water, moving just enough to stay afloat. What the hell was she thinking?

"Trust me!" she shouted.

It went against every instinct he had, but he stopped swimming and did his best to float in place. Sophie stopped a mili-second later. The creature's violent splashing continued as it neared them. Though it was able to keep itself afloat, it wasn't a swift swimmer. Still, it would reach them in no time now that they'd stopped swimming.

He watched in horror as it approached, fighting every instinct to flee.

Suddenly, the creature's splashing increased. He thought at first it had lost its rhythm, and was flailing about trying to stay afloat, then a giant tentacle shot up out of the water near the creature's panicked face. Seconds later, another tentacle revealed itself, then two more. The deep purple skin of the tentacles pulsed with hidden muscles as they wrapped around the forest beast. The beast let out an ear-shattering scream like its lower body had been injured, then began to sink. It thrashed about, fighting for its life, but it was no use. Whatever monster dwelled beneath the lake's surface had to be enormous to take down such a large opponent. With a final, shrill scream, the creature disappeared beneath the water as the tentacles gave a final jerk. Everything was suddenly deafeningly silent, then massive bubbles sputtered on the surface of the lake above where the creature had disappeared.

"Float on your backs," Mara whispered. "Make as little movement as possible as we paddle to the other side of the lake."

Alaric and Sophie instantly obeyed. Alaric's heart thrummed in his head. He'd seen many terrible things in his long life. Epic battles, heinous crimes, unending violence, but nothing quite compared to the Morrigan's summoned creatures.

He kept his breathing steady and light while he floated on his back, making minute movements to slowly propel himself onward. His hair streamed beneath him. Hopefully the movement of the tendrils would not lure the creature, but if the theory he'd deduced was correct, it was drawn to larger movements in the water, like the thrashing paddles of the forest beast.

They seemed to float on for hours, surrounded only by the gentle sounds of their bodies treading water. They were headed in the direction of the rocky cliffside. He wanted to ask Mara a million questions, but didn't dare speak. Instead, he wondered what Madeline was doing in that very moment. Was she looking for him? Was Mikael keeping her safe? He smiled softly. Madeline was quite capable of keeping herself safe, but he was still glad she had the extra protection.

In the time they'd spent with the small Viking clan, he'd even come to trust Aila, Faas, and Tabitha to protect Madeline. Hell, he even sort of trusted Tallie and Alejandro, even though they'd been their enemies not long ago. It was an odd feeling, having more people to trust than just Sophie and himself.

He looked up at the sky as the clouds parted once more to reveal the sun. He would see them all again. He would get back to the future, and he would survive to meet his daughter. There was no other choice.

I ROLLED over and checked the bedside clock as I awoke. 12 pm. That meant I'd gotten less than four hours of sleep, but I couldn't afford any more rest.

I peered past Marcos' bed to see a vacant couch. Frode must have woken Faas at some point to take over watch duty, just as planned. I hoped they'd each at least gotten close to two hours of sleep, but knowing Faas and his tendency to worry, I doubted it.

I forced myself to sit up, then placed my feet on the floor. Tallie made soft grunts of protest, struggling into wakefulness. I stood, glancing once again at Marcos, who had opened his eyes to look at me. He didn't appear the slightest bit groggy, and instead watched me curiously. I turned away and headed for the small bathroom.

I sealed myself inside and let out a long breath, reveling in the small moment of solitude. It would have been nice to take a shower, but I didn't want to waste the time. Instead, I took a fresh white washcloth and wet it in the sink, then began scrubbing at the dirt on my face.

I straightened my crimson sweater and brushed it off until it was as clean as it was going to get, then used the cheap, plastic encased toothbrush provided by the hotel. There was only one visible on the countertop, so it was probably selfish of me to take it, but whatever. I didn't want to face my nemesis with stinky breath.

I used a flimsy plastic comb on my hair, pulling it into a braid to trail over my shoulder, then looked myself over in the mirror.

I looked pale and tired. My normally deep olive skin seemed sickly, and the giant bags under my eyes only added to the effect. Unfortunately, there was nothing to be done, and my appearance wasn't really a high priority at that moment. I finished preparing myself and left the bathroom to find Tallie waiting for her turn. Marcos had disappeared, but Faas was waiting calmly in his place, so I assumed the necromancer was simply primping in the other bathroom.

Faas remained seated on the edge of the nearest bed, pushing his long, blond topknot of hair out of his face. "I made a few calls," he explained, "but there are no rental cars in the area. We could have one delivered, but it would take several hours to arrive here from Spokane."

I frowned. Here I was, all ready to face off against Estus, and now we were delayed by something as mundane as not having a ride.

"I can use the banshees to travel, but I wouldn't be able to take everyone else," I explained tiredly. "Are there any bus or train stations nearby?" I added hopefully.

He shook his head. "We could attempt to hire someone . . ." he trailed off.

I sighed. "It's worth a shot. Either way, we need to get out of this town *today*. I can't risk Estus thinking that I'm no longer coming. He'd lose his reason to keep Alaric and Sophie alive."

Faas looked like he wanted to say something, but clenched his jaw to keep the words from coming out.

I took a seat beside him. "What is it?" I demanded.

He frowned, opened his mouth to speak, then closed it again, as if unable to decide upon the correct words.

I waited not so patiently.

Finally, he took a deep breath and let it out. "I just want to make sure you're prepared for all contingencies. If something ill befalls Alaric, you'll still have people depending on you. You'll still have the entire *world* depending on you."

I lifted a hand to rub at my tired eyes. "So you're worried that I'll break down and leave you all high and dry?"

He shook his head at my blunt statement. "Don't get me

wrong, you've done incredibly well given the circumstances, with first being separated from Alaric, then from
Mikael. You are doing just what a leader *should* do. You've
continued on in spite of everything. I am simply concerned
that certain outcomes may sway you from your course."

My palms began to sweat with nervousness, and I
wasn't sure why. I was pretty sure the worry over Alaric was
slowly killing me, but he wasn't dead. I *knew* it. Yet, the
assurance of my intuition probably wasn't going to be
enough for Faas.

"Alaric may be the person I care most about," I
explained evenly, "but he's not the only person I care about,
nor is Mikael. I will do my best to protect everyone here,
even those I would have once considered my enemies.
That's what a Doyen is supposed to do, right?"

Faas nodded with a now-confident smile.

Alejandro appeared in the doorway between the
adjoining rooms, leaning his shoulder casually against the
trim. "Well if I wasn't convinced about you being our leader
before, I sure am now. And I don't think transportation is
going to be a problem."

Faas and I both turned to him in surprise.

He grinned smugly. "The cute desk girl from last night
has a van. I had mentioned that we might need a ride to
Spokane, and she was more than happy to offer her
services, as long as we paid for the gas."

My jaw fell open in shock. "And you only decided to
mention this now?" I questioned in disbelief.

He lifted one shoulder in a half shrug. "We were about
to head to the cemetery to restore your phantom army.
Forgive me for being a little distracted."

I couldn't help but laugh. "Did you at least get her phone number?"

Alejandro waggled his eyebrows at me. "I *always* get the phone number."

"And for once, it's actually useful to us," Tallie muttered as she emerged from the bathroom.

She looked even more bedraggled than I felt. Deep purple marks rimmed the bottoms of her dark brown eyes, and her arms were covered with bruises, likely from her struggle to escape the initial ambush. The bruises had been hidden beneath her leather jacket the previous night, but now showed in stark contrast to her sleeveless, lilac silk blouse, now stained with dirt.

Alejandro held out his hand. "Cell phone please."

I stood and retrieved my phone from my purse, which rested on the bedside table. Before handing it to him, I turned it on and called Mikael's number. Straight to voicemail.

Alejandro had crossed his arms while he waited for the phone. "Trying Mikael again?"

I nodded as I approached and handed the phone to him. "You don't happen to know Aila's number, do you?"

He snorted, then pulled a piece of paper from his jean's pocket. "I didn't even know that Aila had a phone. There's no reason to have one for most of us. We can't get reception inside the Salr."

I sighed, and laid back on the bed as he dialed the number from the piece of paper and held the phone up to his ear. "Once this is all over, we are *all* getting phones and exchanging numbers," I grumbled.

Tallie laughed. "Good luck with enforcing that."

I chuckled. "You Vaettir and your disdain for technology."

Mikael, who liked to spend much of his time above ground, was a special case. Most Vaettir only participated in human society as much as necessary. For the most part, they remained hidden within the Salr. It was law to remain separated from the humans. Didn't want to get burned at the stake.

Alejandro started speaking, managing to be flirtatious even over the phone. I could just imagine the girl on the other end of the line grinning. She'd probably lose that grin when she saw just who she was giving a ride to, besides Alejandro. It could be unwise to pick up hitch-hikers at the best of times. Picking up passengers that looked like Marcos was just plain stupid.

Alejandro hung up, then handed my phone back to me. I resisted the urge to dial Mikael's number again. I wasn't sure I could take the disappointment of hearing his generic voicemail message once again. Him not answering his phone worried me. Logically I knew he could have just dropped his phone in the struggle, and was even now wandering the woods looking for me, but I couldn't help jumping to the worst conclusions. If Mikael was dead, our plan became twenty times more complicated, but I could admit, if only to myself, that the fluidity of our plan wasn't my main concern. Mikael was my friend. Probably my *best* friend besides Alaric. If he died because of me, I'd never be able to forgive myself. If Mikael was dead, I'd make Estus' death a painful one. I'd make him regret the day he had me stolen away into his Salr in an attempt to use me for his evil machinations.

I'm not really the vengeful type, and I may not be much of a killer, but I'd make exceptions to both rules, just for Estus.

TWENTY MINUTES LATER, we all waited at the curb of the motel for our driver to show up. Alejandro had assured us that she knew just how many people she was chauffeuring, and that she was okay with it. My first thought was that this woman was completely nuts to taxi around seven strangers, but I'd just spent the evening summoning banshees with said strangers, so who was I to judge?

Tallie tapped her foot impatiently as a large, beige van came rumbling down the road to stop in front of us.

Alejandro waved to the woman in the driver's seat. She seemed around thirty, with mousy brown hair styled into a shaggy bob. She lifted a dainty hand in greeting, her billowy, navy blouse draping around her upraised arm.

Alejandro stepped forward and slid open the side door of the van, then opened the passenger door and hopped in the front, chatting happily with our driver.

I glanced at Faas, who seemed to be questioning the road-worthiness of the van.

His eyes moved to me. "We don't really have a choice, do we?" he asked quietly.

"Nope," I replied, then turned away from him to hop into the van, feeling a bit like a teenager about to pile into a rickety vehicle with all of my friends. If only I'd been the type of teenager to pile into a rickety vehicle with all of my friends . . . if only I'd been the type of teenager to have friends at all.

I took a seat in the middle row, feeling a bit nostalgic, but not in a bad way. It was nice when you could compare the past to the future, and have the future win on so many levels . . . even though that future entailed the father of my child being in mortal peril.

Everyone piled in after me. Faas ended up in one seat beside me, and Tallie on my other side. Marcos, Frode, and Maya took the back row, all seeming uncomfortable to be so near to each other. Maya's injured leg seemed to be a little better this morning, though her attitude hadn't improved. She sat with her arms crossed, sullen, hiding half her face behind her dark curls.

After a quick introduction, our driver, Caroline, dutifully ignored us, her attention entirely on Alejandro. I had a feeling he was going to have a hard time parting ways with her once we reached Spokane. If only she knew what type of life she'd be trying to get herself into.

I checked my cell phone and tried Mikael's number one last time as the van pulled away from the curb. Voicemail once again, as expected.

Faas fidgeted beside me as the van made its way down the main stretch of town toward the highway. I didn't blame him for being nervous. I was nervous too. Just three hours and we'd reach Spokane, then we'd trek through the woods in search of an entrance. There were two that I knew of. One where I'd been taken the night I was kidnapped, and the other where James and I had escaped after Estus had him torture me. We'd try the prior first, as it wasn't far from the small house where I used to live, then the latter, which was deep in the woods, and would require an all day hike to reach.

At a sudden thought, I turned around to face Maya.

She looked back at me suspiciously.

"I just remembered that you were once part of Estus' clan," I explained. "Even if you were only there as a spy, you still probably knew where some of the Salr's entrances were."

She frowned. "Yes, I know of a few."

"Any that would be good for sneaking in?"

She raised an eyebrow at me. "You'll actually trust any information I give you?"

I deflated at that. I really shouldn't have even trusted Maya enough to leave her alive, but . . . "I trust that you want Estus dead as much as I do," I stated simply.

She nodded. "I know of several entrances, not that Estus was the one who let me know. Aislin tended to divulge more information than him. She was a cocky little bitch, not as paranoid and cautious as Estus."

"Would any of them be good for sneaking in?" I pressed. "I was unconscious when I arrived through one, so I don't even know where it leads, and the other was near the center of the Salr. The one *we* escaped through," I added poignantly, subtly reminding her that I was referring to the exit where she and Sophie had abandoned me to James' loving care.

She quirked the corner of her lip, but didn't comment. "*All* the entrances are going to be watched," she explained instead. "Do you remember how to find the one you went through when you were first taken? Maybe it's a lesser used portal. I imagine Estus will be keeping a special eye on any entrances Aislin knew about. He hasn't managed to recruit all of her people to his side, and likely fears retribution from some."

"But Estus didn't kill Aislin," I countered, confused.

Maya smirked. "Tell that to the rest of the clan. By all appearances, Estus and Aislin were in the middle of a war. When she disappeared, everyone just assumed it was Estus' doing."

"Hrmph," I replied, deep in thought. "It makes sense, I suppose," I said finally. "Estus is probably *still* telling his people they're in the middle of a war. I wonder how many know the truth."

Maya snorted. "Girlie, I don't even know the full truth. I knew Aislin was after a certain charm, then *you* found it, and she was gunning to get it back from you. Then we all heard word of banshees in Ireland, while at the same time Alaric allegedly swore fealty to Aislin and was going to bring you to her. Next we knew, Aislin was dead. She had a connection to all of her people that allowed her to track us, but it went both ways. When she died, we *felt* it."

I frowned, considering Maya's viewpoint. Caroline continued to chat happily with Alejandro, paying little mind to our hushed conversation.

"Alaric went to Aislin when he was trying to find me," I explained. "Tallie helped him track me." I glanced at the woman in question beside me, then back to Maya. "But Aislin found me too, along with Estus. They were working together all along."

"Then Aislin died, and Estus lived," Maya stated blandly, obviously desiring further explanation.

I turned my gaze to Marcos' impassive face. I just couldn't help it.

"No shit?" Maya muttered, catching on. "Killed by her own pet necromancer?"

If Marcos minded being referred to as a *pet*, it didn't show.

"It's complicated," I explained.

I wasn't about to tell her that Marcos had been possessed at the time. I felt uncomfortable talking about Mara with others. Almost like it was somehow a betrayal of her memory. I was willing to share certain things with Alaric, and some with Mikael, but the sharing stopped there.

Marcos turned his bored gaze to me. "I do not see why we are *sneaking* in at all. Let us take his Salr by force and be done with it."

I glared at him. "I won't risk Alaric and Sophie being killed."

"Killing Estus' people while our force is so small would do little good regardless," Faas interjected.

I turned around in my seat to give him my attention.

"We've been over this," he sighed. "We will instill doubt in his people, thin his ranks, then go in for an undeniable victory once the odds are all stacked in our favor."

I smiled at him.

His eyes widened. "Why on earth are you looking at me like that?"

I chuckled. "I've just never heard you sound so Viking-ey."

He rolled his eyes. "Focus, Madeline."

I snickered again, then turned my gaze back to Marcos.

"I agree with Faas. We are already taking a huge risk going in unprepared. I don't want to unnecessarily lose any lives."

He sighed. "Why not? I could simply reanimate them."

I blinked at him in surprise.

His face remained straight for several seconds, then he burst out laughing, while everyone stared at him in shock.

"Did he seriously just make a joke?" Maya asked in disbelief.

I stared at Marcos as he continued to laugh. The necromancer made a funny. If I hadn't been present to witness it, I never would have believed it.

15

The ride to Spokane was a *long* one. We'd exhausted all venues of conversation, and had planned our next course of action to death. None of us could seem to agree on *exactly* what we should do, so as de facto leader, I had to make the final choice.

I chose to check out the entrance I was originally kidnapped through, as per Maya's suggestion, and I chose to sneak in, rather than to attack with force. We couldn't bring the banshees into the Salr, but Marcos had gotten fully charged at the cemetery, and I found that I had too. Having the banshees around really had boosted my power more than anything else. I could feel it coursing through my veins. I could protect myself if need be, but would it be enough to help us escape with Alaric and Sophie in tow? I wasn't sure, but we had to try.

Tallie was going to stay above ground while we entered the Salr, a solitary messenger to spread word of our capture should we fail to return . . . if she could even find anyone to spread it to. At the very least, she'd be able to track us if we were moved. Our plan would put me underground with Faas, Frode, Marcos, Maya, and Alejandro. Frode and Alejandro were good back up to have with their elemental powers, but Maya unfortunately was a bit useless. She could fight, but she didn't have any extra powers to make her stronger than average.

The van came to a stop as we reached my old neighborhood. I'd had to direct Caroline down the residential streets I knew by heart. I'd lived in my tiny house alone for years, and now I was about to see it again, if only briefly. Our true goal was the Salr entrance a few miles into the woods behind the house.

I took a deep breath as Frode slid open the van door. One by one we stepped out onto the street to stand near my old driveway. It felt strange to be back where it all started. Back where I'd still thought I was human, even though I'd twice accidentally killed other humans with a single touch. It was also technically the place where Alaric and I had first met, though he'd been my kidnapper at the time. He'd been acting on Estus' orders, but I still gave him a hard time about it, even after we'd ironed out the kinks in our relationship. The flood of memories that passed through my mind as I exited the van made me miss him all the more.

There was a white car parked in the driveway of my old house. The world had moved on without me. My landlord had found a new renter, and likely hadn't divulged that the previous tenant was currently a missing person. To society, and the few friends I'd had, Madeline Ville was likely dead. No one knew that I was doing my best to save the world from a tyrant filled with the pure energy of chaos.

I found that I preferred it that way. My old life was behind me, and I could admit I'd left behind very little. I'd left behind the freelancing work that I didn't particularly enjoy, and eating alone every night. I'd left behind occasional calls from friends trying to get me to come out, all the while knowing I'd just give them some excuse to stay home. When I was kidnapped and told that I was Vaettir, I'd thought my life was over, when in reality, it was just beginning.

Faas cleared his throat, startling me out of my silent reverie. He glanced at my old house, then back to me. "We should get going."

I nodded, feeling almost close to tears for some reason as I looked at the white siding and gray roof of the little home. "Let's go," I agreed.

"We could at least get dinner," I heard Caroline argue.

I turned to see her pulling on Alejandro's arm while he desperately tried to disentangle himself from her.

I suddenly felt horribly guilty. We'd used the poor girl for a three hour car ride, six for her since she still had to travel back home. We'd given her cash to cover gas, but it was still an entire day wasted. It had been her choice, but still, I sympathized. She wasn't even going to get a date out of the deal.

Alejandro turned his gaze to me, his eyes pleading for help, as Caroline continued doing her best to persuade him.

I turned to Faas. "Aren't you going to defend your boyfriend's honor?" I asked loudly, figuring a fake boyfriend would invite fewer questions than a fake girlfriend.

Faas balked, but Alejandro instantly caught on.

"Come on sweetie," he pleaded, gazing at Faas with loving eyes. "I'd only hoped to make you a little jealous."

Faas glared at me, then marched right up to Alejandro, grabbed either side of his face, and planted a big kiss on his lips.

It was then Alejandro's turn to balk.

"Your little ploy worked," Faas stated apathetically, still holding onto Alejandro's face. "Now let us be off to consecrate our *love*."

Caroline looked back and forth between the two of them, utterly flummoxed.

I tried not to laugh. "Let's go lovebirds," I announced. "Times a tickin'."

I waved goodbye and said thanks to Caroline, though she still seemed to be in shock, before turning away to walk down the sidewalk, finally able to let loose my grin. I heard Maya whisper to Caroline that she was better off, before falling into step behind me. Everyone else followed.

A few seconds later, I heard the van's engine start, and turned to see Caroline speed away in the opposite direction. She really was better off. People that hung out with us tended to get killed, or at the very least maimed. She'd dodged a bullet.

The sun slowly began to set as we all marched down the street. I zipped up my black jacket and shoved my bare hands into my pockets, wishing for gloves and a scarf. My purse was across my shoulders, nestled against my side. It contained the pair of daggers Mikael had given me. I briefly considered wearing them at my hips, but dismissed the idea. I'd reconsider once we were in the woods, away from human eyes.

We all continued walking in silence, no one discussing the task ahead. I'd say I hoped we'd find the entrance quickly, but really I was just hoping we'd find it at all. Alaric had once told me it had been sealed, but I was pretty sure that had been to keep me from looking for it. The only problem was, I hadn't known where to look for the entrance from within the Salr, and I was fuzzy on where I should look for it within the forest. I'd been carried on my back toward the entrance, with my eyes facing the sky, and had been in quite a panic at the time. The only thing I had to go on was the faint memory of how far we'd traveled, and in what direction. Our saving grace was that we had two people that could sense energy with us. Between Faas and Tallie, if the entrance was there, we'd eventually find it.

Several houses from where we'd started, I turned left down a narrow path that led into the woods. Really, we could have just cut past my old house to exit through the backyard, but I didn't particularly want to risk getting the police called on us. We had enough problems.

Everyone filed into line behind me, and soon we left the rows of houses behind as we ventured deeper into the foliage. I could sense the banshees as we walked, though they remained out of sight. If I needed them, they could swoop in at a moment's notice. Unfortunately, magical wards kept them from swooping into the Salr with us.

I continued walking in the general direction of where I thought the entrance might be, keeping my worries to myself. When we were far enough away from the houses, I stopped to retrieve the daggers from my purse, sliding the sheathes onto my belt at either hip.

Faas raised an eyebrow at me, but didn't comment. He held no weapons, at least that I could see, but he was far more effective without them. A blade in his hand would only impede him.

I started walking again, silently praying that I was going in the right direction. My boots crunched over dry pine needles, accompanied by the sound of a nearby owl, just becoming active for the night. Just a normal evening walk in the wood, folks. Nothing to see here.

A few minutes later, Tallie was suddenly beside me, her hand on my arm. "Someone is near," she whispered.

Everyone fanned out around us. If Tallie claimed someone was near, she meant one of the Vaettir. She wouldn't have been worried about a human.

A small form tiptoed out from behind a tree further down the path. She was *tiny*, the size of a child, but I knew in reality she was ancient. Her translucent long hair mingled with her diaphanous white dress as she approached. Her skin seemed almost as colorless as her hair in the dim evening light. No shoes adorned her feet, which seemed to barely touch the ground as she walked. She smiled as I stared at her, revealing sharp little teeth.

"Sivi," I said. "What are you doing here?"

She took a few more steps, closing the remaining distance between us.

Frode moved to my side, opposite Tallie. "You know her?" he questioned.

I nodded. I knew her all right. Not only was she Kira's sister, but she'd made many attempts to sway me to her cause while I was in Estus' Salr. She wanted revenge on the humans too, and with a sudden start, I realized why she was so hell bent on her plan. It wasn't because of what the humans had done to the Vaettir as a whole, as I'd initially thought. She believed the humans had killed her sister.

Sivi's lilac eyes held amusement. "I knew you'd return as soon as I'd heard Estus had taken Alaric prisoner. You only knew of this entrance, and the one you escaped through. This one was easier. I've been waiting up here for you every day."

"So what do you want?" I questioned, doing my best to sound bored and not at all afraid. "If you're still part of Estus' clan, you know he now has the charm."

She nodded. "Yes, and it seems his plans fit with mine quite nicely."

I rolled my eyes. "Yep, so I must ask again, why are you here?"

"Curiosity, mostly," she admitted as she took in my entourage. Her gaze darted back to me. "I've heard you have banshees."

"What of it?" I asked instantly, not wanting to waste any more time.

She moved past me, and I turned to watch her approach Marcos. She circled around him, looking ridiculous with the huge height difference. His eyes remained on me the entire time, a subtle question in his eerie gaze.

"You've made some interesting friends, Madeline," she observed. Her attention next moved to Faas. "Three executioners in one clan. How strange."

"Is this impish woman important?" Faas questioned. "Or shall we move on?"

Sivi's playful gaze suddenly shifted to ire. "*Fine*," she snapped. "I'll leave you to fumble about as you search for the entrance." She raised her nose into the air as she aimed her cold gaze at me.

I shrugged like it didn't matter, though really we couldn't just let her leave to warn Estus of our arrival. "Do as you please," I bluffed.

She turned to walk away.

"By the way," I added, halting her progress. "Kira is looking for you."

Sivi whirled on me, her face contorting like a feral animal. "How dare you speak that name!" she shouted.

Tallie and Frode both closed in at my sides again, as if afraid Sivi might pounce on me with those sharp teeth of hers. Their fears were likely justified.

I forced a smile onto my face. "I only speak her name because she asked me to call her by it."

Sivi glowered. "Kira is dead," she stated.

"Little green haired girl, about yay tall." I held my hand around lower chest height on my body. "Has a penchant for making the plants grow?"

The shock on Sivi's face was worth the entire uncomfortable conversation. "Where is she?" she gasped.

I shrugged. "She came here with us, but we got separated during Estus' ambush. I don't know where she is now."

Sivi lifted her hands and cracked her bony knuckles, one by one. "He told me she was dead," she snapped. "He said he saw her burn!"

The *he* she was referring to had to be Estus. He'd probably lied about Kira's death to recruit Sivi to his clan.

"And you trusted what Estus told you, *why*?" I asked tiredly.

Sivi glared at me, then marched forward until she was within touching distance.

I resisted the urge to step back out of reach.

"I will take you to the entrance," she stated coldly, "and I will help you kill him."

"We have a plan for defeating him," I explained, "but our first priority is rescuing Alaric and Sophie."

"They do not matter!" she hissed.

I did step back then. She was teetering on a fine edge, and I really didn't want to experience those teeth first hand. She was also an ancient water elemental. I had no idea what she was truly capable of.

"You cannot simply kill Estus," I explained. "The charm will protect him. If you don't follow our plan. You will fail."

"I don't care," she spat.

"You should," I said instantly. "For Kira's sake. His people ambushed us shortly after our plane landed. We haven't heard from anyone. Estus may have your sister and the rest of our friends hidden away somewhere. If they have indeed been taken prisoner, I want them back too."

Sivi let out a small, frustrated scream as she tugged at her long hair, panting heavily. She clenched her eyes shut for several seconds, as if trying to calm herself.

When her eyes finally opened, she seemed like a different person. "Fine," she replied calmly. "We will rescue Alaric and Sophie, but so help me, if you do not return Kira to me, I will dance on your grave."

I nodded. "And if you betray us, you won't even get a

grave. I'll keep your soul trapped in your dead body forever."

Alejandro let out a low whistle. "You really do have the best threats," he mused.

Sivi glared at me, then stormed off into the woods.

We all followed.

Recruiting Sivi to our cause could either be very good, or very, *very* bad. She was a scary little loose cannon. What her final aim might be was anyone's guess.

Alaric offered his sister a hand up as she scaled the cliff-side above the lake. The climb fortunately had not been difficult, and there'd been no sign of tentacles since the forest beast had met its end.

Now that they were out of the water and could speak freely, Alaric found he had little to say. While they were still in danger, he'd wanted to curse Mara for summoning the dangerous creatures into the forest, but now he was wet, tired, and had lost most of his ire. Plus, Mara appeared incredibly dejected as she sat on top of the cliffside, her legs dangling over the edge, draped in the heavy wet velvet of her dress.

"Not happy to be alive?" he quipped, his eyes on Mara as Sophie wrung her clothing out behind him.

She lifted one shoulder in a half shrug. "Not happy to be so powerless," she explained, surprising him with her honesty. From what he'd learned thus far, the Morrigan was not one to easily admit defeat.

He sat on the cliff's edge beside her, wanting to

continue their journey as soon as possible, but also able to admit his body needed a small break after all the excitement.

"I'd say anyone who could summon such fearsome creatures is far from powerless," he consoled.

He wrung the water from his long hair, then flipped it behind his back. The sun had emerged fully now, and felt nice on his sore, cold limbs.

"I couldn't summon a bunny rabbit now," she replied with a bitter laugh. "I let my jealousy destroy who I truly was, back in this time. Now I am merely a shadow, nothing more."

He sighed. How had he ended up in the position of being the one to comfort the Morrigan? "Madeline would beg to differ," he argued. "She thinks quite highly of you."

Mara shook her head. Wet clumps of her red hair slithered forward over her shoulders. "I may have aided her with the banshees, but it was because of my actions that she ended up tied to a chair. The necromancer stole the key from her, and it was all my fault. Now the mission before her is more difficult than ever."

"You should stop feeling sorry for yourself," Sophie chided. She'd dried herself off as best she could without a towel, and now moved to sit on Mara's other side. "Madeline is a big girl, and it is no one's job to save her. In fact, I'd say she's quite a bit more capable than any of us."

Alaric glanced past Mara at his sister in surprise. "Are you actually complementing Madeline?"

Sophie rolled her eyes. "What I'm trying to say, is that we all have our *own* battles to fight. It is not our place to fight those belonging to others." She leaned forward to stare directly at Alaric. "This is a lesson we should *all* learn," she added.

He smiled ruefully. "Just because we *should* learn lessons, doesn't mean we will."

"I agree with Alaric," Mara stated, once again surprising him. "I'd much rather fight for others, than for myself. I spent an entire lifetime fighting for myself, making warriors bow before me in an attempt to soothe the rejections of my past. Striving for power to make myself feel safe. When I lost my mortal form, I wandered the other realms without purpose. I still had an identity, but it didn't matter. When Madeline accidentally summoned me, it was like I'd been awoken from some long, dark, dream. She might have feared me at first, but after we'd spent some time together . . . " she trailed off.

"She cared for you," Alaric finished for her.

Mara nodded, her face pinched as she held back the tears shining in her eyes. "She became my friend. She cared about how I felt, and cared when I died. No one cared when I died the first time." She turned to Sophie, giving Alaric her back. "If that isn't a reason to take part in someone else's fight, I don't know what is."

"You know," he began with a smile as Mara turned back to him, "I never thought you and I would actually have something in common."

She smirked. "Trust me, no one is as surprised as I."

Alaric stood and offered her a hand up. "We should get moving."

Mara nodded, then took his hand and stood. Pulling away from him, she offered a hand to Sophie, which she took after a moment's hesitation.

"We have much to discuss on our way to the castle," Mara explained as Sophie rose to her feet. "It will be difficult to convince the current Morrigan that you are telling the truth, and even more difficult still to convince her to help you."

"Then why don't you explain it all to her yourself?" Sophie questioned. "Surely seeing you would be all the proof she needs."

Mara shook her head. "She'd likely kill me on the spot. The first thing you need to know, my dear, is that the Morrigan hates no one more than she hates herself."

16

As we followed Sivi deeper into the woods, I began to realize my directional instincts were way off. We probably would have wandered through the woods for hours looking for the entrance.

"Can we trust her?" Frode whispered to me as we walked a few yards behind Sivi.

"No," I whispered back, "but having her on our side is useful enough to take the risk."

He raised a pale eyebrow at me, but didn't comment further.

The last few rays of sun slowly disappeared.

By the time Sivi stopped, it was full dark. We all approached where she stood near an expansive patch of vines. They were so thick you couldn't see any of the ground beneath. Suddenly my memories came rushing back to me. I'd been placed on the ground. Arms held me down while the vines encased me. I'd passed out from the shock of it all. Hopefully I wouldn't pass out this time.

"What part of the Salr does it lead to?" I asked, staring down at the vines, faintly illuminated by the moonlight.

"Is this not where you first entered the Salr?" she asked, confused.

"I lost consciousness that night," I explained. "When I woke up, I was already in my room."

Alejandro chuckled. "Couldn't handle your first trip underground?"

I glared at him. "You try living among humans for your entire life, only to be kidnapped and shoved through the ground."

He laughed. "Sorry, *that* experience is for executioners only. The rest of us never get the chance to live in ignorance."

Sivi sighed. "It leads into the dungeons."

Of course it did. "Not really the first place I was hoping to visit."

"Are you through stalling?" Maya asked.

Sivi was giving Maya a strange look, as if she'd only just noticed her.

I didn't bother asking what it was about. Instead I asked, "Who's going first?"

"I will," Frode volunteered instantly. "If Mikael is still alive, there's no way I'm risking him finding out that I let you dive into the enemy's Salr first."

"Then let's go," I replied, gesturing down at the vines. "And remember, our goal is to remain unseen for as long as possible. Conflict may be inevitable, but we need to find Alaric and Sophie first."

"They are not in the dungeon," Sivi explained, "but that is all that I know. I've seen neither of them since word spread of them being taken. Estus has been extremely guarded about their whereabouts. Most question whether or not they have truly been taken prisoner, but I heard it straight from Estus' lips."

"He told you?" I asked suspiciously.

She glared at me, the cool moonlight reflecting in her pale eyes. "It is easy to see and hear things, when most do not even notice you exist."

Ah, so she'd been spying. I would like to have said that I knew the feeling of being invisible, but my time among the Vaettir had been quite the opposite. I would have gladly given Sivi some of the extra attention placed on me.

Knowing that any other consolation I might give would probably just make her angrier, I moved on and asked, "Will anyone be guarding the dungeon?"

"Of course," she replied like I'd asked an incredibly stupid question.

I turned to Frode. "Take them out as silently as possible?"

He flipped his hand palm side up and emitted a little gust of ice, like a tiny snow flurry. "Not a problem."

I nodded. "Then let's go."

Sivi knelt down in the vines, and they slowly began to consume her.

"Hey, I wanted to go first!" Frode argued, then knelt down beside her.

Soon they both disappeared within the vines.

Maya and Alejandro went next, followed by Faas and Marcos.

Suddenly it was just Tallie and I above ground.

I turned to her. "Be careful, and don't do anything risky.

If it looks like we're in trouble, search for Mikael, or anyone else who might be sympathetic to our cause. Don't risk your life for no reason."

Her dark eyes widened in surprise. "You make it sound as if you truly care whether I live or die."

I smiled softly as I knelt down in the vines. "I do."

The vines slowly consumed me, and the next thing I knew, I was standing in a dark dungeon, way too close to Marcos' thin form for my comfort.

A small flame flared to life, illuminating Maya's face eerily as she held a lighter up between us. "I forgot how damn dark it was down here," she whispered.

Everyone froze at the sound of footsteps. The light of a torch could be seen as it moved down a nearby hall. We were in one of the cell-lined corridors that branched off from a central path on either side.

As soon as the torchlight passed, Frode crept away silently. A few seconds later, the crackling of ice could be heard, followed by a harsh gasp, then nothing. Maya lit her lighter again as Frode returned to us.

"I didn't see anyone else," he whispered, "but I wouldn't be surprised if there were more guards down here than one."

"Let's make for the main stairs," I whispered, low enough that my voice was barely audible. "We need to make this fast."

"Where are we going to check first?" Maya asked.

Sivi had claimed Alaric and Sophie weren't in the dungeon, which left only one logical place to try next. I swallowed the painful lump in my throat. "The torture rooms."

The thought of Alaric or Sophie strung up in one of those rooms made me sick, but it was a logical first place to check. Fortunately the rooms weren't far from the dungeons. We could check there, then move on.

Cupping a hand around the flame of her lighter, Maya led the way.

Within a few minutes, we passed the guard Frode had *encountered*. His head was frozen entirely in ice, and he was quite dead. I knelt quickly and released his soul, or life force, or whatever you wanted to call it. I felt the usual rush of energy. I could use that energy to harm or heal. Here was hoping I wouldn't need either.

We moved on, slowly approaching the massive steps that led out of the dungeon. Frode and Marcos had no trouble with the steps, while anyone under six foot had to reach their knees up higher than was comfortable, Maya and Sivi especially. Not for the first time, I was glad to be tall.

After the first few steps, the gentle illumination of the Salr encompassed us. Since it was nighttime, the lights were dim, but not dim enough. Anyone who spotted us would likely realize we were intruders, unless they were some of Estus' new recruits, who might not know anyone yet. Worse still, many others might recognize me on sight from my previous time spent in the Salr.

Alejandro and Frode reached the top of the stairs first, peeking out of the hall to look both ways. Alejandro gave the thumbs up. The coast was clear.

"I will leave you here," Sivi whispered. "I will try to find who you seek, and I will be ready to fight, but I will not be caught with you if I can avoid it."

I frowned, but she was right. She was only looking out for her own well being, but if she was captured, she'd do us much more good on the other side of the cell.

"This way," I whispered to the others as Sivi left us.

Stepping as lightly as possible, I led the way toward the torture rooms. My skin itched with the feeling that someone was going to jump out at us at any moment. I had the blades Mikael had given me on my hips, and a fresh helping of energy ready to blast someone away, but I still felt vulnerable. If someone alerted Estus to the intrusion, we wouldn't just be fighting a few opponents. We'd be fighting an entire clan. Our only hope would be to escape the Salr and use the banshees.

Sweat beaded at my brow as I forced myself forward. It wasn't particularly warm in the Salr. I was just that nervous. Risking my own life was one thing. Knowing the lives of Alaric, Sophie, and my unborn child were hanging in the balance was quite another. I couldn't just leave Alaric in Estus' care though. I couldn't wait around to find Mikael, even if he was still alive. I had to do this myself.

I froze as someone stepped out of a room further down the hall. I didn't recognize her. She had short, blonde hair, cut into a stylish bob, and large blue eyes. Noticing us instantly, she stared at us, her body only halfway out into the hall.

She opened her mouth to speak, scream, or *something*. I saw everything like it was happening in slow motion. Frode darted ahead of me and shot a stream of ice at her, but some sort of invisible shield went up, spewing the ice to either side seconds before it would have hit her. He tried again, and the shield went up again.

Faas pushed past me, raising both hands into the air, and the woman suddenly dropped to the stone floor, unconscious.

I looked at him in shock.

"Her shield was made of pure energy," he whispered.

I nodded, feeling shaky.

Frode dragged the woman across the floor, back into her room, and shut the door.

We moved on.

The torture rooms were now only a few yards away. Luckily, we continued on unseen, likely because all but the guards were sleeping. My thoughts darted off to what else might roam the halls at night.

James used to have a pet, a lindworm named Stella. The creature had a body shaped like a giant lizard, the face of a Rottweiler, and the fur and paws of a grizzly bear. I wasn't sure if the creature still lived, but I had no desire to encounter her. If she didn't slice us to bits on sight, she might sound an ear-splitting warning call.

We reached the first of the torture rooms. I placed my hand on the door and gently opened it, then gasped and reeled away at what I saw.

Faas put a calming hand on my shoulder, and I shook my head. It wasn't Alaric or Sophie. I just hadn't expected the room to be so . . . bloody.

I took a deep breath, then forced myself to walk into the room for a closer look. There were manacles on the wall, and a wheeled operating table, like you'd see in a hospital. Everything was blood soaked. The walls, the ceiling, *everything*. The room reeked of coppery blood and hints of other fluids, with an undertone of burnt flesh, like some sort of macabre perfume.

A severed foot lay on the operating table, still twitching with life. Apparently Estus hadn't found himself a new executioner to release the energy from his mangled corpses, else he just didn't care. I stepped forward and released the life from the foot with a gentle stroke of my fingers, accepting the extra portion of energy willingly. I was probably going to need it.

Without another word, I left the room. Everyone followed me further down the hall to the other torture chamber. I was even more nervous about this room. It was where Estus had kept the hearts of his victims, all in individual drawers in the wall. I'd released each and every one right before I escaped the Salr with James, but I was betting Estus had refilled quite a few.

Reaching the room, the others waited as I opened the door, not taking the time to prepare myself for what horrors might lurk on the other side. I peeked in and scanned the area, then let out a sigh of relief. The room was empty. No tortured corpse of Alaric or Sophie.

Of course, that led to a whole new problem. I had no idea where to look next.

I stepped back and gently shut the door. Deciding to follow my gut, I guided the others in the direction we'd been heading. Where else might Estus be keeping them?

During my previous time in the Salr, I'd done my share of exploring, but I knew there were many areas I hadn't seen. For the life of me, I couldn't think of where else Estus might keep prisoners.

I glanced at Maya, walking cautiously by my side. She'd

spent her fair share of time as Estus' prisoner. "Were you kept anywhere besides the dungeons or the torture rooms?" I whispered.

She shook her head.

I turned my gaze back down the hall, just as someone stepped into view.

He was just as I remembered him. Small, around Maya's size, with dark, loose-fitting clothing. His silver hair was twisted into an elaborate braid that trailed over his seemingly frail shoulders to reach his ankles. He smiled, crinkling the fine lines on his face.

"You're early, Madeline," he said pleasantly.

Faas and Alejandro were suddenly at my sides, while Frode and Marcos took up positions in front of us. Maya stepped behind me. I remained silent, waiting for him to speak. Why was he confronting us alone? It was a bold move, for a less than bold man.

"Is it Estus?" Faas whispered. "Or the key?"

I focused my attention on the man before us, and really couldn't tell. They had similar energy to begin with. If Mikael's theory was correct, the key would have fully possessed Estus, rather than sharing space like it had with me. But did it really have that kind of power?

"Where are Alaric and Sophie?" I demanded.

He smiled and took a step toward us. "You truly think I would hold them here, where you could so easily snatch them away?"

My heart sped. Was he lying? "Where are they?" I repeated.

He smiled wickedly. "Some place you will never reach them without my aid."

I shook my head. "I don't believe you."

He laughed, then lifted a hand to observe his nail beds, as if exceedingly bored. "Search the entire Salr if you like. You will not find them."

I gritted my teeth in frustration and balled my hands into fists, wanting nothing more than to rush forward and lash out at him. "And Mikael?" I asked through my clenched jaw.

His sudden anger hit me like a ton of bricks, matching my own. Mikael had done something that he hadn't liked, which likely meant he was still alive. It was a start. Now to stay alive long enough to find him.

"What do you want from us?" I asked. "Why take Alaric and Sophie at all?"

His anger was suddenly shut away, and I couldn't sense a single thing from him. Like he was afraid I'd learn his thoughts. Shielding was a skill the key had learned right along with me, but that still didn't tell me which energy inhabited the man before us. Estus could have learned to shield his emotions on his own.

"What are you hiding?" I pressed.

"Everything will be revealed at my inauguration ball," he replied. "For tonight, you and I have much to discuss. *Alone.*"

I frowned. I was leaning more and more toward the idea that we were speaking with the key, which was unnerving on so many levels. Estus was a clever man, who chose his words wisely, and he wasn't making any sense right now. I wasn't needed for his plans. He'd made that quite clear after he stole the key from me.

"He's afraid of us," Marcos stated coolly, referring to Estus. "Together we pose too great a threat."

Estus glared. "I am simply cautious. I did not enjoy being trapped, and lied to."

Well shit. He was the key after all. He was referring to his time spent inside my mind, when the Morrigan and I had kept our thoughts secret. Mikael had been right, which meant . . . I finished my thought out loud so the others could hear. "The key is afraid because I'm too much like it. My energy is what's needed to balance the chaos it embodies," I turned my gaze to Estus, but continued speaking to my companions, "He, the key, is planning something that involves my energy. Kidnapping Alaric and Sophie wasn't part of Estus' ploy for revenge, it was part of the key planning something entirely different. Estus didn't need me. The key does."

Estus/the key growled, then lifted a hand into the air. Suddenly my limbs seized, and I began to walk forward jerkingly against my will. Estus' powers were in telepathy, and mild telekinesis, and now the key had those skills too, only amplified.

"I fear nothing!" he/the key shouted, his curled hand looking like a claw as he used his mind to force me forward.

Alejandro turned and wrapped his arms around me, straining to hold me in place while Faas and Marcos stepped forward. I sensed Faas' power, so similar to mine, as it enveloped Estus. Faas was trying to drain the key's energy, but it wasn't working. It was like there was an impenetrable barrier around Estus. A barrier I knew quite well.

When the key had been a physical object, no one could

harm me unless it chose to allow it. When Alaric had tried to rip the key from my throat, he'd been thrown backward by an invisible force. Now that force was protecting Estus from having his energy drained. It wasn't like when Faas had kept me drained. I'd had control over my own body, even with the key, and I had *allowed* Faas to take my energy. Neither the key, nor Estus, if he had any control, were allowing Faas to drain them now.

A sudden force tugged at my chest, as if I were a marionette, and Estus held my strings.

Maya joined in the fight to keep me away from him, but her small body didn't add much weight. Frode rushed forward and tried to freeze Estus, but his ice stopped and dissipated in midair, not even getting close to touching him.

I felt it the moment Marcos added his energy to Faas', and the force tugging on my body began to subside.

With a snarl, Estus shifted his focus to them. He swept his arm outward, and both men were flung back like they weighed nothing, narrowly missing Alejandro where he held me.

Estus turned his attention back to me, and I was jolted forward. Alejandro, his arms still wrapped around me, pushed me back, but I was moving on waves of the key's power, not just with my own force. Alejandro was no match for that pull.

Tears rimmed my eyes as I struggled to simply not move forward. It took so much concentration I almost didn't notice the small form behind Estus. A few feet behind him, Sivi held her arms out in front of her. An impossibly large wave of water erupted from her palms. It parted and flowed around Estus, then grew in volume as it collided with us, knocking us all off our feet.

Alejandro lost his grip on me, and I struggled to paddle upward as suddenly the entire hall was filled with a heavy current of water. Knowing I stood no chance of swimming against it, I swam with it, just trying to keep my body afloat.

Maya's head crested the surface of the water beside me. She gasped and sputtered for breath. We picked up speed down the hall, and I almost didn't believe my eyes as the unnatural water took a sharp left turn. It flowed down the stairs of the dungeon like an invisible barrier had diverted it, leaving the hall further down perfectly dry.

Suddenly I realized that Sivi hadn't been trying to attack Estus, nor had she tried to attack us. She saw that we were about to lose, and was helping us escape.

I tried to turn with the current as I reached the hall that led to the dungeon, but there was no need. The water contained itself like there was an invisible barrier adjacent to the dungeon's entrance. I bobbed in the water for a few seconds as I bumped into that barrier, then shot along with the water down into the dungeon. The water splashing in my face obscured my sight. Were my companions still around me? I hoped so, but I couldn't worry about them at that moment. I just had to worry about staying on top of the current.

I had picked up so much speed that the long, cell-lined corridors whooshed right by. Once I reached the corridor we'd entered through, another invisible barrier diverted the water. Yet this time, the water didn't flow forward into the corridor. I was thrown out of it, like I was reaching the end of a long amusement park water slide. I hit the stone ground *hard*, then barely managed to roll out of the way as Alejandro came flying out of the water right after me.

His reflexes quicker than mine, he leapt to his feet and grabbed my hand, dragging me back as the rest of our party shot out of the water to land in a groaning heap.

We helped everyone to their feet wordlessly, then Alejandro tugged me toward the vines that would take us back above ground.

I tugged back. "Alaric could still be here!" I shouted.

The others could leave, but there was no way I could depart without searching for him. Estus had claimed he wasn't there, but Estus was also a liar. So was the key. They both lied to themselves even more than they lied to everyone else.

"You can't help him if you're dead!" Alejandro shouted, taking both my arms in his.

His wild emotions stopped me, and I nodded numbly. He was right. I was being stupid. We all rushed forward into the vines that would carry us back into the cold moonlight, no closer to saving those I cared about most.

17

Two by two, we emerged from the ground into the chilly night air. Our clothes were sopping wet, adding to the cold, though only some of us seemed to be affected by it.

"Where's Tallie?" Alejandro questioned.

I glanced around in the darkness, but didn't see her.

"We need to get away from here," Faas cautioned. "Once we're safe, we'll regroup and come up with a new plan."

I felt like I might vomit, but nodded, then took off at a run, back toward civilization. I was worried about where Tallie might have gone, but it wouldn't do anyone any good for us to wait around for Estus to surface, even with the banshees aiding us. I just wasn't sure who would win.

My brief thought of the banshees brought them to close in around us. I thought of Tallie, urging them to find her. Their dark shapes whirled around me for a moment, then veered to the left, leading us in a different direction. Desperately wanting to return to civilization, but not wanting to leave Tallie behind, I followed. Nobody questioned me as I darted away into the woods. They just fell into step around me.

I ran on, occasionally stumbling. My sopping wet clothes tugged at my skin uncomfortably as my over the shoulder purse thunked irritatingly at my side with every step, catching on the blade at my right hip. I frowned as I thought of the blades, which had been utterly useless. If Faas' powers couldn't touch Estus, there was no way mundane steel would.

We ran for around a mile, and I felt just about ready to collapse when we heard voices. Several figures were standing roughly thirty feet away, softly illuminated by moonlight. At our approach, the nearest one turned to face us. It was Tallie. My knees felt weak with sudden relief as I realized who was with her.

Tallie trotted in our direction, spewing apologies as soon as she reached us. They fell on deaf ears. I rushed past her toward the six-foot-five figure she had been speaking with.

Mikael wrapped me up in his arms as I reached him, lifting me off my feet and spinning me in a small circle. "When Tallie told me she let you go into Estus's Salr without me, I could have killed her," he explained, letting me down to my feet. "How could you be so stupid?"

I smiled despite his harsh words. "I didn't know if you were alive or dead, and I couldn't just leave Alaric and Sophie down there to rot."

"But you didn't find them?" he asked, quickly taking in those gathered behind me.

Aila moved to stand at Mikael's back, along with several other people I didn't recognize.

I shook my head, then lifted my eyebrows at Mikael in question. "Care to explain what *you* have been up to?"

"We will discuss everything," he explained. "But first I must know, did you encounter Estus?"

I nodded, then glanced over my shoulder reflexively, even though we hadn't seen nor heard any signs of pursuit since leaving the Salr. "I think you're right about everything," I explained, turning back to meet his gaze. "I believe the key has fully possessed Estus, and is carrying out its own plans. It seems to want me for some reason, while in contrast, I served no further purpose for Estus. Without Sivi's help, we probably wouldn't have escaped."

"Sivi?" he questioned.

I looked around us and realized she'd remained back with Estus, unless she'd jumped into the water that had carried us, but we'd seen no signs of her as we left the Salr.

"Nevermind," I muttered, feeling too overwhelmed to explain everything in detail.

He wrapped his arm around my shoulders, then guided me forward. Everyone fell into step around us.

"After we were attacked," he explained, "most of us remained to fight Estus' people. Many were killed, but those who lived eventually surrendered. Once they heard what we had to offer, most were willing to switch sides. Those who would not have been . . . taken care of."

I grimaced, but didn't comment. I supposed we weren't really in the position to take hostages.

He removed his arm from my shoulders, then offered me a

hand over a fallen log. "At that point, we searched the woods for you, but you had done quite the job of escaping. Without Faas and Tallie, we were unable to track you. Our few new recruits let us know of the various Salr entrances. It was sheer luck I was with the group that came to check this one, and that we were near enough at the correct time for Tallie to sense us."

"You could have called," I replied, remembering my frustration at trying to get a hold of him on his cell.

"My phone was destroyed, which wouldn't have been worrisome since I have your number memorized and could get to another phone. I tried to call as soon as we reached civilization and a pay phone, but *someone* had their phone turned off, and your voice mailbox was full."

I abruptly stopped walking, suddenly feeling like the biggest idiot on the planet. I had kept my phone off to preserve the charge, assuming if anyone managed to call me they would leave a voicemail that would appear as soon as I turned the phone on. I'd always been terrible about deleting old voicemails, but I'd never thought it would come back to bite me in such an awful way.

"Well *I* feel like an idiot," I muttered.

Mikael laughed. "It all worked out. I bought a new phone, and one for Silver as well. I sent you a text as soon as I did, but it was recent. I'm guessing your phone is dead by now?"

I nodded. "And probably a bit . . . *wet*."

"It's okay," he continued. "We can move on with our plans, and we now know that Estus has been possessed by the key, and that it is the key trying to lure you in, not him."

"He also claimed Alaric and Sophie aren't in the Salr, though we have no reason to believe him," I explained.

Suddenly Mikael grabbed me and shoved me behind him. I was about to curse at him and ask why, when I noticed someone running toward us. Moments later, Sivi came to a skidding halt in the dead leaves. She looked up, *way* up, at Mikael.

She panted for a moment, out of breath, then peered past Mikael to me. "You could have waited for me, Madeline," she snapped.

"You know her?" Mikael asked, his eyebrows raised high as he glanced back at me.

I stepped up beside him. "This is Sivi. She saved us from Estus."

She snorted. "You left me little choice. You were clearly all about to die."

I opened my mouth to argue, then shut it. It didn't matter. What mattered now is that we were safe, for the time being.

"I take it you had no time to search for Alaric and Sophie?" I questioned.

She shook her head. "And I heard what Estus claimed, that they are not within the Salr at all. I am inclined to believe him."

"But there's no way to know for sure," I grumbled.

Mikael motioned for us to continue walking. "Our new recruits do not believe they are being kept in the Salr," he explained as we all moved on. "Or else they are extremely well hidden. No one has seen them."

Sivi trotted to catch up with us, then grabbed my arm. Her small, bony hand clenched my bicep tight enough to pinch through my damp jacket.

"Where is Kira," she demanded.

Mikael stopped and looked at her, then glanced at me. "I thought I saw some resemblance there."

"They're sisters," I explained.

"You've seen her too?" Sivi gasped, gazing up at Mikael.

"She's safe," he assured. "If we can manage to get out of these woods any time soon, you'll see her shortly."

That shut Sivi up. She hurried past us to the forefront of those who walked ahead. I imagined they knew where we were going, because I sure didn't. Hopefully somewhere warm, where my luggage and phone charger awaited.

I wrapped my arms around myself as we began to walk once more, debating whether I'd be colder with or without the damp jacket

"Here," Mikael offered, shedding his brown leather coat.

I shucked my damp jacket off without a word, then handed it to him in exchange for his. I donned it quickly, reveling in the dry warmth.

"You really need to learn to just ask for things when you're uncomfortable," he chided, slinging my damp jacket across his arm, not seeming the least bit uncomfortable baring his arms to the cold

"Honestly, I didn't think about it," I replied.

"That's my point," he explained. "If you don't think about your well being often enough, eventually you will no longer be well."

I smirked, though in the darkness, he probably didn't see it. "Vaettir don't get ill," I countered.

"But they can still suffer from exhaustion," he countered right back. "Exhaustion slows your reflexes, and can mean the difference between life and death."

"Point taken," I sighed. "Just don't forget that you have well being to look after too."

He laughed. "Oh no, I'm invincible, hadn't you heard?"

I smiled, glad to have my friend back by my side. The task of rescuing Alaric and Sophie, and of beating the key, seemed far less daunting with Mikael's help.

Never underestimate the value of friendship at any time, but especially when you're ass deep in alligators. Mortal peril is never a good place to be alone.

SOPHIE'S CLOTHING had mostly dried by the time the castle came back into view through the trees, a small blessing since night had fallen, and it was cold as Hades in ancient Ireland. They'd spent the past hour listening to Mara as she briefed her on what to say. She hoped she could remember it all, as her life quite literally depended on it.

She would enter the castle on her own. She didn't like leaving her brother in the dangerous forest, but really, she probably faced just as much danger going into the castle as Mara and Alaric would waiting outside.

The more immediate problem though, was the massive portcullis guarding the castle against intruders. She observed the heavy barrier warily from their hiding place within the dense trees. Past the portcullis, the dark inner courtyard of the castle could be seen. The courtyard was eerily still. Such a large castle brought to her mind scenes of its inhabitants, tending the grounds, having grand feasts, and otherwise occupying the space, but there was no one there. Mara claimed the Morrigan lived in the massive castle entirely alone.

"So I should just walk up and wait to be spotted?" she whispered, then bit her lip.

Mara leaned her hand against a tree, her gaze intent on the castle. "Yes, she will at least take the time to speak with you. Few venture into her forest and live to tell the tale. Your presence will pique her curiosity."

"Then I just blatantly state that I've been sent from the future, and that I have the knowledge to prove it?" she pressed, wanting to make sure she had the plan just right in her mind.

Mara nodded. "Your modern clothing will support your point, and the things you know are things only the Morrigan could have told you herself. I took many secrets to my grave."

Sophie took a deep breath, smoothing her hands over her still-damp black jeans, then took a step forward.

Alaric grabbed her arm, bringing her gaze to him. "Be careful," he ordered. "And if it seems like she may be overly hostile, scream and we will do our best to rescue you."

Mara snorted. "There will be no rescuing her. If the Morrigan does not believe her tale, we're all as good as dead."

Sophie sighed, now more nervous than ever. She'd faced death many times, but facing the Morrigan was another story entirely. "On that reassuring note, let's get this over with."

Pulling away from Alaric, she stepped forward, out of the cover of the dense trees. She approached the stone walkway leading to the portcullis. Her boots seemed loud as they hit the stones, one step after another. She felt like the Morrigan might jump out of the darkness and attack her any moment, or maybe a banshee. Soon she reached the heavy iron bars of the portcullis, and suddenly wasn't sure what to do. Should she knock? Or perhaps call out?

Her decision was made for her as a loud, clinking sound nearly deafened her, then the portcullis began to raise. She took a step back, resisting the urge to glance over her shoulder into the forest. If anyone was watching, she didn't want to give Alaric and Mara away.

Once the portcullis had raised fully, she took a deep breath and darted through the entryway, almost laughing at the thought of the portcullis crashing down on top of her to end things right then and there. Yet, it remained raised as she entered the well manicured courtyard.

She suspected the perfectly level green grass and ornately trimmed shrubberies were maintained by magic, as she couldn't really picture the Morrigan out there trimming them herself.

Straight ahead was an ornate, heavy wooden door that would lead into the center of the castle. She approached it, but before she could reach out to open it, the door unlatched and swung slowly inward. She stepped inside, feeling like she was entering a haunted house in a movie. The type of movie where the audience screams at the heroine to stay out of the creepy building. That's where the monster is.

The door swung shut behind her, leaving her in a candlelit entry room. The castle's stone walls reminded her of the Salr, though this structure was above ground, and set firmly in the human realm. As far as she could tell, she was alone.

She stepped onto a finely woven burgundy runner rug as she ventured further into the castle. The entry room branched off into long hallways in either direction. At the end of one hall, she could see a stone staircase rising upward. Deciding the Morrigan was likely the type to reside at the top of the highest tower, she made her way toward the stairs, wondering why the Morrigan was forcing her to seek her out in the first place. The opening of the portcullis, then the door meant the Morrigan knew of Sophie's presence and had magically opened them. Else the castle had a mind of its own. She shivered at that thought as she reached the stairs, then journeyed upward. And upward. The stairs seemed to go on forever.

She reached the top to find an open, expansive room, ornately decorated with shiny wooden furniture and copious candles. Beautifully carved friezes of elements of nature had been installed as part of the walls, replacing the heavy stones in certain areas. Tapestries draped the walls further into the room, all leading up to a raised dais. In the center of the dais, rested a wooden throne. In the throne, sat the Morrigan.

She had the same appearance as Mara currently possessed, not like the corpse she'd inhabited in the future, but still with long red hair, and a lovely, angular face. She wore a red silk dress, trailing past her feet to pool on the floor. The bodice was a tight corset with long sleeves to cover her arms, draped elegantly on the armrests of the throne.

"Have you come to kill me?" the Morrigan asked with a

small smile. Before Sophie could answer, she continued, "Few make it through the forest, but those who try always wish to kill me."

Sophie took a step forward. "Actually, I've come to ask a favor."

The Morrigan's laugh was rich and throaty, echoing through the space to reach Sophie's ears from all directions. She stood, pushing her red hair over her shoulder to mingle with the deeper red of her dress.

"I don't believe I've heard that one before," she replied. She gestured to Sophie with a theatrical wave. "Please, proceed."

Sophie took a steadying breath, then launched into her explanation. She detailed everything that had happened with the Morrigan in the future, including the new information Mara had given her on their walk. She detailed just how the Morrigan had come to be, and just why she was the way she was now, including the betrayal of the one she loved. She then went on to explain just how she'd come to the past, and the implications therein.

She finished, then took a shaky breath, realizing she'd spat everything out at an almost unintelligible rate.

The Morrigan puckered her lips and wrinkled her nose like she'd just eaten something foul. "Who sent you here?" she demanded. "Who told you these things?"

Sophie straightened her spine and took on an almost aggressive stance, belying her fear. "*You* told me. You are the only one who knows these things."

The Morrigan shook her head, then marched up to Sophie like she might hit her.

Sophie stood her ground, not bothering to defend

herself. She'd never win in a fight against the Morrigan. Her only hope was to convince her.

Instead of lashing out, the Morrigan lifted her hand and placed it around Sophie's jaw, holding her face immobile. She peered into Sophie's eyes for several heartbeats, then released her.

"Where is this future me?" she demanded. "Bring her here, and perhaps I will aid you."

Sophie slumped in relief. "She's in the forest," she explained, "with my . . . brother."

The Morrigan eyed her sharply at the mention of a man, but did not comment.

"Fetch them," she demanded.

Sophie nodded quickly, then turned and hurried out of the room. There was the possibility that the Morrigan simply wanted to gather them together before killing them, but it was a risk she had to take. Without the Morrigan's help, they were as good as dead, and Sophie would rather end it all now, than waste her life away in a world that could never be home.

18

We escaped the woods and took two SUVs to regroup at an expensive hotel with everyone else. It had to be twenty stories high, but we ended up on the eighth. I had just started walking into the room Mikael had led us to, when Kira came running out, flinging herself at me. Her small arms wrapped me in a hug.

"I was so worried!" she exclaimed. "Where have you been?"

I gently pried her off me. She backed away, smoothing her green hair in sudden embarrassment. Her motions halted as she glanced past me. Her jaw dropped.

I moved out of the way to give her a clear view of Sivi, who stood silently in the hall. Judging by her blank stare, one would never guess she was seeing her long lost sister for the first time.

"Sivi?" Kira questioned in shock.

I backed away, putting myself closer to Mikael. "We'll

give you two some space," I said softly.

Sivi shuddered as life seemed to return to her. "There is no need for that," she snapped, then strode past Kira into the hotel room.

Tears rimmed Kira's eyes. She looked up at me, completely at a loss.

I shooed her into the room. *Talk to her*, I mouthed.

Kira nodded, but still seemed unsure. I didn't blame her. Sivi was downright scary. I was trusting that she wouldn't harm her long lost sister, especially with how demanding she'd been about seeing her. I had a feeling Sivi simply hadn't shown true emotion in so long, she just didn't know how to handle what she was feeling.

Mikael took hold of my arm. "Let us see if Silver has returned yet."

I nodded, gave Kira one last encouraging look, then allowed Mikael to pull me away down the polka dotted rug of the hotel hall. Apparently my fresh clothing and phone charger would have to wait. Everyone else had either gone to their rooms, or were down in the hotel bar/restaurant, waiting for those still out investigating the Salr's entrances to arrive.

"Let's get a drink," Mikael suggested as we walked, "and you can tell me exactly what happened while we were apart."

I frowned. "Why didn't you just ask me on the drive over here?"

He raised an eyebrow at me. "Have you shared every aspect of what's happening with Alejandro and Tallie?" he questioned. "I assumed you would not want everyone to know what we'd discussed before the ambush."

I blushed. "I didn't explain everything directly, but they have probably pieced together most of it."

He laughed. "Well then my caution was for naught. I just assumed you wouldn't want everyone to know you're . . . not like everyone else."

We reached the elevator and Mikael pushed the button to summon it.

"*I* don't even want to know it," I quipped.

The elevator dinged, and the doors slid open, revealing a man. We entered the elevator along with him, doing that awkward thing you do in elevators, where you all pretend you don't see each other, but at the same time, you don't speak, and you all know that you're not speaking expressly because of the extra person's presence.

The doors shut, and down we went, not stopping until the ground floor. We exited, eyeing the man as he walked out of hearing range.

"So let's begin with when we got separated," Mikael suggested.

We walked into the nearby hotel bar, which was mostly empty, given it near eleven, and most travelers had early morning work conferences, or family vacation plans. Mundane life at its best. I couldn't say I missed it, except for the not being in danger part.

A table in the back of the dimly lit establishment held familiar faces. Silver sat having a conversation with Aila and Faas. Marcos was nowhere to be seen, but I knew neither Mikael nor Aila would have allowed him to run off. He was likely in one of the hotel rooms, under heavy guard.

Mikael motioned for me to walk ahead of him past the gleaming, freshly wiped, empty tables. The lone bartender perked up as he noticed us from behind the bar, amidst towers of expensive looking bottles and sparkling clean glasses.

I reached the table first, taking the empty seat next to Faas, leaving Mikael to sit on my other side, near Silver. It wasn't that I didn't like Silver. Well, that's a lie. I really didn't like him, and I wasn't sure why, other than the fact that he unnerved me. Bad first impression, I suppose.

He ran a hand over his perfectly styled, black hair as he nodded to both Mikael and I in greeting, then lifted a glass of amber liquid to his lips. Faas took a long swill of something similar in color. In front of Aila sat a white mug of coffee. Even at the late hour, the aroma wafting from the steaming cup made my mouth water.

The bartender approached our table and asked for our drink orders. Apparently in a hotel bar at midnight, you didn't get cocktail waiters, just the lone bartender. I ordered a cup of decaf, and Mikael ordered, surprise, whiskey.

Once we had our drinks, we all leaned forward conspiratorily.

Silver's eyes flicked up to meet mine. "I'm told you have restored your banshees," he whispered. He maintained an uncomfortable amount of eye contact as he sipped his drink.

I nodded, glanced at Mikael for reassurance, then began to tell everyone all that had happened once we separated. From reaching the small town and visiting the cemetery, to Marcos sharing his power with me to strengthen the banshees, to finding and invading Estus' Salr. Faas took in my story silently, not bothering to add any tidbits from his perspective.

I glanced at Mikael hesitantly before stating the next part, even though Faas already knew, and Silver and Aila had been present in the vehicle when we'd first discussed it. "I think the key has taken control of Estus," I admitted, "and it's planning something that involves me. That's why Sophie and Alaric are being held hostage. It wants me to cooperate with it."

"We've been working on discerning where Alaric and Sophie are being held," Mikael replied. "If we can find them before the time stated on Estus' invitation to his *ball*, then we can ignore his requests. Instead, we'll continue to grow our forces in preparation for trapping Estus long enough to meet his end."

I nodded. "The key protected him from all the attacks we threw his way. He will not be easy to subdue."

Mikael lifted his glass to his lips and drained it in a single swallow. "I believe our best chance is to lure Estus out into the open where he'll have to face the banshees and the executioners at once."

By executioners, he meant Marcos, Faas, and *me*. It was going to be an epic battle of death vs. chaos.

"I'd like to speak with Marcos more about all of this," I said. "We haven't even had a chance to discuss what happened with the banshees. I'd like to make our plans very clear to him."

"I still don't like that he's involved at all," Faas replied. "We can't trust him."

I bit my lip, debating on whether or not to tell Faas about Hecate sharing our goals, or about both Marcos and I being descended from similar deities. Faas was different from us. He manipulated energy, granting him the skills of an executioner, but he wasn't aligned with death. I briefly debated asking which god he was aligned with, but wasn't sure if it would be rude. Those aligned with lesser gods seemed to be a bit touchy about it.

I wasn't sure if learning about Hecate would make Faas value Marcos' participation more, or less. Though, I supposed it really didn't matter. We were all going to do what we needed, regardless of how we felt about each other. I just didn't like the constant unease coming from Faas. As an empath, it only added to my nerves.

"There are plenty of people we can't trust," I decided. "It doesn't mean they aren't useful."

Mikael chuckled. "Spoken like a true queen."

I took a sip of my decaf, then pursed my lips in distaste. It just wasn't the same as the real deal. I glanced at Aila's cooling coffee longingly.

Raising a pale eyebrow, she slowly slid the cup across the table toward me, tempting me with its soothing goodness.

Screw it. I took the mug gratefully and took a sip. She'd added way too much cream and sugar, but it was still better than the decaffeinated abomination I'd ordered.

Movement caught my eye, just as Mikael's eyes slid toward a red-haired woman I recognized as one of his people. She entered the bar along with Tabitha and Rose. I was proud I'd managed to remember Rose's name after only interacting with her the one time, the day she'd arrived at the Salr in Dublin with Maya.

Spotting us, Tabitha rushed forward, followed by the others. She wrapped me in a brief hug as she reached our table, then moved on to start chiding her brother in Old

Norsk. I couldn't understand much of what she was saying, but the tone was quite clear. *How dare you make me worry about you.*

Their argument made my heart ache as I thought of Alaric and Sophie. We needed to figure out where they were, and fast.

Unable to watch the scene any longer, I turned to Mikael. "Do we have *any* ideas on where to look for Alaric and Sophie?"

"I have a few," he admitted, swirling the ice cubes around in his glass. "It's likely they're not in Estus' Salr, but it's also a possibility they'll be moved there sometime before the ball." He furrowed his brow in thought. "Or perhaps not. It might all be a ruse. He, or the key, might just be using them as a ploy to get their hands on you. Once you are lured into the Salr, that will be that."

I shook my head. "I don't think that's it. I have a feeling the key needs my cooperation with something. The key wanted to speak with me alone. I think Alaric and Sophie are the leverage to force me into doing something I don't want to do."

"The only thing the key might need you for is to regrow —" Faas interjected, then cut himself off as he glanced at Rose, standing awkwardly beside the red-haired woman near the edge of the table. They seemed reluctant to pull up seats, as if waiting for an invitation.

Not wanting to be the one to give it to them, I turned back to Faas and nodded. The only thing the key might need me for was to regrow Yggdrasil, which was *our* plan, not the key's.

I took another sip of Aila's coffee as I thought about the

key's possible intentions. "Maybe there's something else we don't know about. In all this time, I haven't been able to discern the key's true intent. To cause chaos, yes, but maybe there's more to it. It was going along with *my* plan before, so there was obviously some end in that direction it desired. It was probably just waiting to act until the perfect moment."

Mikael stroked his chin in thought. "Perhaps we should discuss things further with the Norn. She is the other part of this puzzle. I would not be surprised if she and her sisters have kept a great many things hidden."

"Like why Estus killed those who held Sophie and Alaric hostage?" I suggested. "Maybe she knows the *real* reason for her sisters' deaths."

Mikael nodded. "The only problem, is that she has yet to rejoin us. Hopefully she will appear to us soon."

I let out a frustrated breath. It felt like we were just going around in circles. We needed to *act*. I had a sudden thought.

"The Norn said we could bring back a portion of the Morrigan's energy, but we'd need Marcos to do it," I explained. "Maybe we can go ahead with that plan. Having the Morrigan's input, even in a small way, could help us determine what the key is planning."

Everyone, except Mikael, was looking at me like I'd just sprouted a second head.

"Summoning her didn't work out very well the last time," Aila grumbled.

We'd actually attempted to summon Freyja, Aila's patron goddess, but the Morrigan had come forth instead. I had a feeling Aila was still a little bitter about what she perceived as a rejection, though really, the Morrigan had only been able to come forth because she wasn't truly a goddess.

"Not true," I argued. "She's the only reason we have the banshees and other phantoms, and she came up with the plan to regrow Yggdrasil, our only way to truly defeat the key."

Mikael sighed. "Madeline is right." He turned his gaze to me. "I do not relish the thought of once again seeing the Morrigan peeking out through your eyes, but at the very least, your survival is important to her. I believe adding her energy to yours is a worthwhile cause."

I nodded. "The Norn said she wouldn't be as strong this time. Her energy is too far depleted. I'm not worried about losing myself."

Silver, who had sat back silently through most of the conversation, leaned forward with a frown. "You truly intend to summon a goddess?"

I eyed him cautiously. "She's not a true goddess, you know."

He steepled his fingers together in front of his face, leaning his elbows on the table to look somewhat menacing. "Close enough."

I glanced nervously to Mikael, who nodded in reassurance.

Mara was as close to a true goddess as I wanted to get. Though part of me missed her, the other part was still fearful. She'd awakened things in me I hadn't been ready to face. I still wasn't. I'd faced violence, war, and a force of pure chaos. It had all been scary, but I could admit, if only to myself, that my own true nature scared me most of all.

19

Tabitha had informed us that Marcos was in one of the hotel rooms with Frode and Alejandro. After a long, silent elevator ride, Mikael and I made our way down the hall toward the aforementioned room. Aila and Tabitha had decided to abstain from the meeting, while Silver and Faas each wanted another drink. I didn't mind. The fewer people I had to discuss things with, the better.

We passed the room where we'd left Sivi and Kira as we walked. It was difficult to resist checking on Kira. She seemed so sweet and defenseless in comparison to Sivi, but it wasn't my place to meddle. They had a lot to catch up on, no matter how painful it might be for both of them.

Soon we reached the room Tabitha had detailed. Mikael knocked, and moments later, Frode answered. He had light bags under his blue eyes, standing out vibrantly against his pale skin. He gestured for us to come inside without a word.

Marcos sat against the headboard of one bed, while Alejandro sat on the foot of the other, flipping channels on the TV with the remote in his hand.

Marcos met my eyes as Mikael shut the door behind us.

"I need to talk to you," I stated. I glanced at Alejandro, then at Frode. "Anyone who doesn't want to be involved in talks of summoning goddesses may leave the room now."

Alejandro stood. "Sorry, summoning banshees was more than enough for me." He walked past, winking at me on his way out of the room.

"I could use a drink," Frode added tiredly, then followed after him.

Marcos remained on the bed, staring up at us. His long, white hair was now slightly wavy, having dried without a good brushing after we'd all gotten soaked by Sivi's wave. He didn't seem to care. Nor did he care about his still damp, black clothing. Of course, my clothing was still slightly damp too, so who was I to judge?

I sat on the bed Alejandro had formerly occupied, facing Marcos. Skipping any pretenses, I explained, "The Norn seemed to think you would be capable of returning some of the Morrigan's energy to me. Know anything about that?"

He smiled, then cocked his head as if listening to a voice whispering in his ear. Maybe he was.

"My powers are associated with the old dead," he explained, "so I may be able to connect with the Morrigan's energy. Whether or not she can return to you in a larger way, is more up to how much power she has left in this world, and how much you are able to give her."

I nodded in acceptance. "Let's try."

He smirked and raised a white eyebrow at me. "Right now?"

I shrugged. "Why not?"

"You are quite the strange individual," he mused.

"Are you sure you want to try right this moment?" Mikael asked, taking a seat beside me. He turned his gaze to Marcos before I could answer. "Is it even possible to try right this moment? Last time there was blood and fire involved."

"It would work better to at least be outside," Marcos explained, his eyes on me instead of Mikael. "Your goddess is connected to the earth. You should be as close to her as possible."

I stood. "Then let's go."

"Madeline," Mikael cautioned, standing to tower over me. "Are you sure you're up for this? You've had very little sleep."

Come to think of it, I wasn't even sure how I was still standing. I was exhausted, and now that the adrenaline of escaping Estus' Salr had long since worn off, I felt jittery and dizzy.

"You know I'm not going to be able to sleep with everything up in the air," I sighed. "Let's at least try to contact the Morrigan, then I'll rest for a few hours . . . maybe."

Mikael sighed. "Let's go," he conceded.

I smiled, though a small part of me almost hoped he'd try to stop me. I seriously needed some sleep.

I waited while Mikael retrieved his new phone from his pocket, then sent a quick text. "Silver and Faas will finish their drinks and meet us in the lobby," he explained, returning the phone to his jeans.

I frowned. "Faas I understand, but why Silver?"

Mikael glanced at Marcos, then back to me. "I want an extra pair of empath eyes to make sure death incarnate over here doesn't pull any funny business."

Marcos chuckled, apparently enjoying being referred to as *death incarnate*. To each his own, I guess.

Mikael gestured for Marcos to stand, then waited as Marcos led the way out of the room. I followed behind, feeling an odd mixture of excitement and dread. It would be interesting to see Mara again, and I was pretty sure she'd be proud of how far I'd come, but I also feared the effect she had on me when we shared the same body. It was simply too much power, similar to what happened with the banshees. It was addictive, and made me a little *too* bold.

My only hope was that Mara's spirit had been weakened enough that she'd be little more than a small voice in my head. I felt guilty for thinking in such a way about my friend, but there it was. If I had to share my headspace with someone, it was better for them to be as non-influential as possible.

The door closed behind us, locking automatically, and we made our way to the elevator. Mikael pressed the button on the wall as we reached it. We all waited in silence for the little *ding* to signal that the door was about to open.

The doors parted to reveal a pair of inebriated woman, dressed to the nines. They both appeared to be in their mid-thirties, probably having a nice girls' weekend together. Was it really the weekend? I'd lost track.

We entered the elevator and stood with our backs against one wall, while the women stood against the other. The doors slid shut, leaving us in silence. One of the women looked Mikael up and down, being horribly obvious about it. She seemed to like what she saw.

Her friend gawked at Marcos. Her sudden anxiety washed over me. She had good instincts, or maybe a bit of natural empathy, to be fearful of Marcos. He was creepy looking, but not enough to instill instant fear in random women.

Mikael leaned slightly forward, his eyes on the frightened woman. "He's single if you're interested," he whispered.

The woman jumped, turning her horrified eyes to Mikael.

I tried to hide my smile. "You're mean," I chided quietly as we reached the bottom floor and the doors slid open.

Marcos smiled and gave the scared woman a slight bow of his head.

Her eyes widened, then she grabbed her friend's hand and tugged her out of the elevator. Her friend looked longingly at Mikael as she was pulled out of sight.

"You're both mean," I corrected as we exited the elevator. "It's not nice to pick on humans."

Marcos raised an eyebrow at me. "You want to release wild magics into their world, completely altering existence as they know it, and you're mad at us for teasing them?"

I blushed, because he was right. What I was going to do to them was far, *far* worse.

I scanned the lobby to find Silver and Faas, leaning side-by-side against the wall near the vacant help desk. There was little noise coming from the nearby bar. From my current angle I couldn't see into the establishment, but I was betting our elevator friends weren't in for much excitement.

Silver pushed away from the wall and approached, followed by Faas. Even after the long day and night, Silver's white suit looked unwrinkled, and his hair was perfect. Or maybe it was a different suit, and he'd had the honor of a shower and sleep, unlike the rest of us.

"Are we sure this is a good idea?" he asked, coming to stand before us.

"It's our *only* idea," I replied.

He nodded, but didn't seem to fully believed me. "Fair enough." He gestured for me to lead the way out of the hotel.

I frowned at him, then made my way toward the exit, though every step was a battle as I imagined how good it would feel for my head to hit a pillow. Marcos had said being outside would be better, but he hadn't specified *where* outside. Hopefully a nice, grassy nook somewhere near the hotel would be good enough. Given the late hour, we'd likely go unnoticed hanging out and chanting in the grass, and if we were, I didn't really care. I just wanted to get this over with as quickly as possible.

I wasn't sure where Mara's spirit had gone when she *died*. Hopefully she wouldn't mind being pulled back into our world. Did spirits have *lives* in the afterlife? Did they mingle with the gods?

We were about to find out.

ALARIC LEANED against a tree with Mara a few feet away

from him. Both watched the night-shrouded castle. Sophie hadn't been gone long, but it felt like ages. He'd heard no sounds of commotion, but it was a large castle. For all they knew, Sophie might be screaming her lungs out in an underground dungeon.

He'd just made up his mind to go in after her when she appeared in what could be seen of the central courtyard from his vantage point. She ran through the still-open portcullis toward their hiding spot.

She reached them in less than a minute, then grabbed onto Alaric's hand and began tugging him forward. "The Morrigan has demanded everyone's presence. She claims if we bring her Mara, she'll help us."

Alaric turned to look at Mara, who took a step forward, then clutched her stomach as if in pain.

"Something is wrong," she groaned doubling over. She fell to her knees, then looked up at them. "Oh shit," she said, seeming to realize something. "I'm being summoned."

"What?" he asked frantically, rushing toward her. He crouched in front of her hunched over form. "By whom?"

Mara's eyes pinched shut. "I think it's Madeline," she panted, "but not just her. Someone very powerful is helping. I won't be able to resist for long."

"Someone powerful?" he questioned desperately.

"You can't go!" Sophie interrupted. "The only reason the Morrigan is willing to help is because she thinks I'm bringing along the future version of her!"

"I can't help it," Mara rasped. "I'll try to return as soon as I can."

"Who is helping her!" Alaric demanded, fearing she was about to disappear.

Mara licked her dry lips. "I think it's the necromancer. It's an energy I've felt before."

She faded out of existence as if she'd simply been an illusion all along, leaving both Alaric and Sophie to stare at the ground where she'd been, just seconds before.

"This is not good," Sophie groaned.

"For more reasons than one," Alaric replied.

Not only had Mara left them, but she'd mentioned a necromancer. Had Madeline allowed Marcos to regain much of his power? What was Mikael thinking allowing such a thing to happen? It was as good as going to sleep beside a poisonous viper.

I RESISTED the urge to pull away as I held Marcos' bony hands in mine. We'd walked roughly a mile away from the hotel to a small park. I'd always taken the plentiful parks of Washington for granted, but now I couldn't be more grateful for the state's focus on trees and greenery. I was not up for a late night drive to the woods.

Mikael, Silver, and Faas stood off in the grass to one side, observing, though there wasn't much to see. This new ritual wasn't anywhere near as flashy as pouring blood over my hands into a roaring fire. Of course, we weren't trying to summon one of the gods in full. We were only trying to summon Mara's remaining energy in a less substantial capacity. All it took, apparently, was power and concentration. Oh, and a necromancer. Mustn't forget that part.

Marcos had his eyes closed in concentration. I was supposed to have my eyes closed too, but I couldn't help stealing a few peeks. The park was large enough that we were able to distance ourselves from most of the street-lights, but the moon still cast an eerie glow upon Marcos' face.

"Concentrate," he demanded, his eyes still closed.

I snapped my eyes shut, and did as he asked, though I felt spacey from exhaustion. I was supposed to focus on Mara's energy, the *feel* of her, while Marcos supplied the actual power needed to bring her energy back into the world.

As I thought of Mara I felt a sudden tug, then cool energy spread up through my body from Marcos' hands. Suddenly I could sense every tree, every bug, even the three men standing roughly ten feet away, their energies shining like captive suns in the darkness.

I pulled my thoughts away from them and concentrated on Mara's fierce energy while I became engulfed in a feeling of oneness. At that moment, I was connected to all living things. In reality, that connection always existed, but I never took the time to *feel* it. All my fears washed away, replaced by a feeling of certainty in my gut. I was in control, and I could do this.

The power built between Marcos and I to the point where it felt like molten metal was running through my veins. The metaphysical heat slowly increased to an unbearable temperature. I stifled a scream. It was too much. Marcos clamped his fingers tightly around my hands to keep me from pulling away.

Just when I thought I couldn't take it anymore, the power released, forming a glowing sphere between us. My body suddenly cooled. The sphere stretched upward and elongated into a tall oval, then slowly began to take on the form of a woman.

This wasn't right. I was supposed to have summoned Mara into my mind. She couldn't sustain herself in our world on her own.

Confused, I stared at the glowing figure as its details morphed. Soon I could see a face, and a distinctly feminine body draped in a tight, long dress. Something was wrong though. She was transparent, and looked almost like . . .

"A banshee?" Marcos questioned. His hands were still gripped in mine, forming a circle around the glowing woman.

We both craned our necks to look up at her, then let our hands drop. We backed away as the figure's feet floated downward until they hovered just above the grass. The glow faded, leaving a white, ghostly figure behind.

I didn't recognize the phantom's face staring down at me. It was different than the corpse Mara had inhabited while I'd known her, but somehow I knew we'd gotten the right woman. Maybe it was how she'd looked originally.

"Mara?" I questioned.

"Oh Madeline," she groaned, shaking her incorporeal head. "What have you done?"

What *had* I done? It was a good question. From the looks of it, I'd turned the Morrigan into a banshee.

"WHAT DO WE DO?" Sophie gasped, holding her hand up to her mouth.

Alaric glanced at the space were Mara had been. "The Morrigan will only help us if we bring Mara to her?"

Sophie nodded, her eyes pinched in worry.

"Then we're screwed."

"What is the meaning of this?" a voice called out from the direction of the castle.

Alaric peered past Sophie as she turned to see a woman in a tight, red dress striding toward them. The dress trailed behind her across the stone walkway, then into the dirt as she approached. Her long red hair blew away from a face matching the one Mara had been using in this time, looking eerie in the darkness.

Sophie stood in an almost submissive stance, not a stance Alaric saw on his sister often, but he supposed he couldn't blame her. The Morrigan walked forward in a cloud of her own anger.

"Where did she go?" she demanded, halting before them. "I only caught a glimpse of her before she disappeared. Is this some sort of trick?"

"Um," Sophie began in reply. "Remember how I told you there's a woman named Madeline in the future, made in your image?"

The Morrigan nodded sharply.

"She summoned her, *you*, um," she paused. "She summoned Mara back to our time."

"Why?" the Morrigan snapped.

Alaric moved to stand near Sophie's side. He was worried his presence might make things worse, but he couldn't stand to see his sister acting so unsure and afraid.

"They're friends," Alaric answered. "Madeline probably needed her help."

233

The Morrigan sneered at him. "I take it you are this one's brother?" she nodded in Sophie's direction.

"Yes," he replied simply.

"And the father of this *Madeline's* child?" she pressed.

He shifted nervously. How much had Sophie told her? "Yes," he answered again.

The Morrigan seemed to think for a moment, then turned on her heel and started walking back to the castle.

He was just about to call out to her when the Morrigan shouted, "Come with me!" in a tone that left little room for argument.

Alaric and Sophie both obeyed. When a woman like the Morrigan told you to do something, you didn't make her say it twice.

20

"How did this happen?" I gasped, still stuck in a state of disbelief.

Shortly after Mara had stopped glowing, the banshees had shown up. I hadn't summoned them, but they'd been drawn to the power Marcos and I had manifested all the same. They now gathered around Mara. She blended right in with the crowd.

Ignoring the banshees around her, she eyed me tiredly, though coming from her ghostly face, it was more unnerving than guilt inducing. "Madeline, I was in the process of returning Alaric and Sophie to you," she explained. "You couldn't have summoned me at a more inopportune time."

"What!" I shouted, then clamped my hands over my mouth. I glanced around the shadowy park, but it didn't seem any strangers had heard me. "What?" I asked again more softly, lowering my hands.

Her shoulders slumped in defeat. "You don't even realize where they are, do you?"

I shook my head. "At first we thought they'd be in Estus' Salr, but we couldn't find them."

"They're in the past," she explained patiently. "In the year 1707, in Ireland."

I shook my head rapidly, feeling like I might faint. Mikael was suddenly beside me with an arm around my waist, keeping me from falling to my knees.

"How?" I croaked. Tears began to fall down my face.

"The key," she replied like I was being stupid. "It's holding them hostage in a place you cannot reach. It's quite clever, really."

A whole myriad of emotions hit me at once. Alaric and Sophie were trapped in the past. It was confusing and horrible, but also wonderful, because at least they were alive. At least we might stand some chance of rescuing them. We'd gone back in the past before. There had to be a way to do it again. Even if it took regrowing Yggdrasil, then using the tree's power to go back myself.

Mara sighed. "Well it's too late for me to go back now. Hopefully *she* will find it in her black little heart to help them."

"She?" Mikael and I questioned in unison.

Marcos had moved to stand at my other side, but I didn't see Silver anywhere. Faas was still in the same place, only now he was alone. I'd been so distracted I wasn't sure at what point Silver had left.

"The Morrigan," Mara explained, drawing my attention back to her. "We were on our way to ask for her help. She still had the key in that time. In fact, it was only months before she destroyed herself. I can't help but think there was some meaning to the key sending them back to that exact point in time, but I haven't been able to figure it out."

I held up my hands to stop her from speaking. It was all too much. "Rewind a little. You were somehow in the same time as your previous self?"

She tapped her incorporeal foot impatiently. "I'm just energy, Madeline, or at least I was. I was able to exist more strongly in that time because my physical form was still anchored to the earth. Of course, now you've gone and anchored me to the earth in a whole new way. Or really, you've anchored me to *you*."

I frowned, wiping at the drying tears on my face. "What do you mean? I was just trying to summon you back into my mind."

She huffed in irritation. "You've turned me into a banshee. You've anchored my soul in this time to yours. I'm just like the others now."

"I didn't mean to do that!" I argued, unable to help the shrill tone in my voice. Had I really taken her away from Alaric just moments before she would have helped him return to me?

Now that I was steady on my feet again, Mikael removed his arm from me and stepped forward. "What do you mean, she anchored your soul to hers?"

Mara sighed. "I mean exactly what I said. My soul is now permanently connected to hers."

I shook my head. Fresh tears dripped down my face. What had I done? "I don't understand," I muttered.

Mara hovered closer to me as she explained, "The banshees exist because they were unable to let go of their old lives. They were all women who were wronged in some way. Murdered, tortured, or worse. Unlike normal ghosts, which are just residual energy of souls that have moved on, the banshees' souls have remained in this realm. They cling to their graves, unable to let go of what happened to their bodies. Before I was more like a ghost. My energy was here, but I did not exist entirely in this realm. You brought me fully over, including my soul, my *anchor*, into this world. I have resided, at least in part, in the spirit world since my mortal body perished. Now I cannot go back."

Marcos, who had remained silent through the entire exchange, finally cleared his throat to speak. "That's not quite true. If you are anchored to Madeline, then you will go back to the spirit world if she dies."

Mara glared at him, and with her spectral face, the look was twenty times more terrifying than it normally would have been. "Drawing my attention to *you* is not a wise choice." She turned back to me. "Why is he even still alive?"

"Um," I began nervously. "We need him to return the key to me," I bit my lip. "And he helped me restore the banshees," I added quickly.

She turned her glare back to Marcos. "I should have killed you when I had the chance."

He smirked. "You never had the chance. You possessed my body to kill Aislin, but you only accomplished that task because I also wanted her dead."

Mara's sudden rage was palpable.

"Now, now children," Mikael interrupted. "There's no sense arguing, as these are the cards we've been dealt, and we have more pressing concerns. It will be morning soon, and Madeline needs to rest before we can face Estus."

"But what about Alaric?" I argued. "We have to figure out how to bring him and Sophie back to the current time."

"There's no way for you to do that now," Mara explained. "Perhaps the Morrigan of that time will aid them. If not, they need only stay alive long enough for you to regrow Yggdrasil. Once that is done, you can use the tree's power to retrieve them."

My shoulders slumped in defeat. I finally knew where Alaric and Sophie were being kept, and I was powerless to save them. At least in the past, the key wouldn't kill them on a whim, but the Morrigan might.

Mikael laid his hand gently on my shoulder. "Time for rest."

I nodded, then turned back to Mara. "I—" I hesitated, unsure of what to say.

"I know," she said with a soft smile. "I'll be fine. We'll figure everything out after you've had some rest."

I smiled back and nodded. "I'm sorry for what I've done, and I'll do my best to fix it, but even so, it's nice to see you again."

She nodded her agreement. She was taking the whole being made into a banshee thing like a real champ. Of course, she'd just been fluid energy before, so maybe it wasn't a huge change, except for being stuck in this world.

She glanced back at the other banshees, who watched on silently. "I guess I'll wait with them until you wake up." She turned her gaze back to me. "It serves me right for how I used them in the past. A taste of my own medicine, I suppose."

I cringed. "Sorry."

She rolled her eyes at me, then turned away to join the banshees. Once she'd reached them, they faded from sight.

Mikael put an arm around my shoulders, urging me back in the direction of the hotel. Marcos walked ahead of us. Faas fell into step on my other side, but didn't speak. He was being unusually silent about this whole ordeal.

I was too tired to think about it. Instead I turned my gaze toward Mikael as we walked. "Where did Silver go?"

He chuckled. "He once encountered the banshees in his distant past. It was a rather . . . unpleasant experience. He probably ran all the way back to the hotel when they arrived."

I smiled, feeling somewhat satisfied. Even thousand year old empaths had fears. I glanced forward at Marcos' thin frame, wondering if he had any fears. What did someone with power over the dead fear? Sunshine? Flowers? Who knew. Maybe he was afraid of bunny rabbits. I sure hoped so.

ALARIC HAD LIVED LONG ENOUGH to visit many castles in his time. In fact, he'd been alive in the current year, so he didn't find the imposing stone structure terribly awe-inspiring. That was, until they reached what could only be called a throne room. *Of course* the Morrigan would have a throne, but that wasn't what held his interest. The candlelit friezes and tapestries adorning the room were marvelous. If he weren't in such a dire situation, he would have loved taking the time to observe them more extensively. As it was, his full attention was demanded by the red-haired woman glaring at him from a few feet away.

"Tell me again," she snapped.

They'd already told her *everything*. She was particularly interested in Madeline, which unnerved him. What was her true motive? Both he and Sophie had assured her that she'd meet Madeline in the future, although they failed to mention what form she would be in when that meeting occurred. How do you tell someone that they will soon destroy their human form after growing no longer able to cope with their human emotions? The answer, you didn't. They couldn't tell her she would soon die, else they might alter the course of history. They might have already altered it, but hopefully not. Mara had assured them it would be nearly impossible to sway the Morrigan from her path.

"There is no more to tell," he stated once again. "We need to return to the future to aid Madeline, and since she has summoned *you*, we'll be helping you as well."

She pursed her lips in thought. "Okay," she agreed slyly, causing Alaric's heart to race. "But I want a favor in *this* time first."

His heart sank. He didn't have time to go around doing favors. He needed to get back to Madeline.

"What favor?" Sophie asked suspiciously.

The Morrigan smiled sadly, surprising Alaric. "I will not remain on this earth much longer," she explained.

Alaric and Sophie both gasped. She knew?

She eyed each of them in turn. "I have committed many crimes since my creation, but there is one I simply cannot bear. Though he wronged me, what I did was unnatural."

Alaric had no idea what she was talking about. He knew

the Morrigan wasn't fond of men because of some past betrayal. Was all her ire truly due to one individual?

"Cúchulainn," she muttered. "I trapped his soul in his remains, and sealed them within a barrow. If I leave this earth without releasing him, he will be trapped forever. I cannot expect him to atone for his crimes for eternity, when I can face my own no longer."

"You trapped his soul?" Sophie balked. "Talk about a woman scorned."

The Morrigan eyed her sharply, wiping away all traces of previous emotion as if the sadness and admission of guilt had all been a brief dream.

Alaric stepped forward. They needed to get this over with so they could get the hell out of the past. "Where is the barrow?"

"I will send you there," she stated simply, not answering his question.

"Why can't you go yourself?" Sophie asked.

Alaric groaned. Did she really have to choose *now* to regain her bad attitude?

Worry crossed the Morrigan's face, then was gone in the blink of an eye. She sighed. "I trapped him on sacred ground. Land protected by the old gods. I have toyed too much with death, and can no longer travel there."

He knew he shouldn't ask. He knew he should just go to this sacred ground and get the task over with, but . . . "What's stopping you?"

The Morrigan was suddenly angry again. "Will you truly require me to lay all of my indignities bare? Can you not simply accept that I have been rejected by the land from whence I came?" Before he could answer, she snapped, "*Fine.* The place you are to go was where Yggdrasil once took root. That land *created me,* but I have tainted my energy to the point where I cannot set foot there."

Everyone was silent for a moment.

Alaric heard his sister audibly gulp before she asked, "And we can? We are mere mortals. Can we truly step foot in such a place."

The Morrigan seemed to deflate. She walked wearily to her throne, then slumped down upon it. She held a hand to her eyes as if warding off a headache. "You are Vaettir, the children of the gods. Even though you destroyed Yggdrasil, the fates and the gods still love you. You are welcome in what remains of their pathetic earthen kingdom."

The bitterness was clear in her tone. She'd been rejected by the gods for her crimes, but the Vaettir were still accepted, even after all they had done.

"We'll find his remains for you," he said softly.

He was surprised at the compassion he felt for her, but there it was. She'd never had a family or a true home, and the one she'd loved had betrayed her. It might change history if they helped her, but it was a risk he was suddenly willing to take.

She sighed in relief, then stood. "I am prepared to send you now, but I'll leave you with a warning. I do not know what sort of creatures may roam the lands near the barrow. Though the pathway to the gods has been destroyed, their energy still lingers. It attracts many things. Be careful."

Alaric nodded as his sister moved to stand at his side.

The Morrigan lifted her hands toward them.

"Wait," Sophie implored. "Once we have Cúchulaiin's remains, how will we return here?"

The Morrigan's hands dropped an inch. "Return to where you will first arrive. I will place you near the border of the sacred land. Once you cross back over that border, I will be able to retrieve you."

Alaric took Sophie's hand in his. "We're ready."

The Morrigan raised her arms again.

"Like hell we—" Sophie began, but her words were cut off as the castle's interior blurred around them.

He gripped his sister's hand tightly, overcome by an odd floating sensation. He felt stationary, but with a dizzying feeling of momentum. Like the world was zooming past him while he remained in place. The movement was too fast to make out much with his eyes. Everything was a blur.

Suddenly the world seemed to stop, and they both went tumbling forward, as if they'd been in a moving vehicle only to have it completely halt, flinging them both onto the ground.

Alaric lifted himself off the rocky earth to a sitting position, nearly falling back over with dizziness.

Sophie slowly sat up beside him. "Why do I have the feeling she made that ride more . . . exciting than necessary?"

Alaric groaned, then forced himself to stand. A salty smell pervaded his nostrils. They were near the sea. "Because you've spent enough time around both Mara and the current Morrigan to understand their irksome natures."

"I wouldn't say that too loud," Sophie grumbled, rising to her feet. "*One* of them can probably hear us right now."

Alaric wouldn't have been surprised if the Morrigan was somehow magically looking in on them, but at the moment he didn't care. He was more focused on not throwing up.

Feeling unsteady on his feet, he glanced around, attempting to get his bearings. The Morrigan had claimed that she would place them near a border, but it apparently wasn't a visible one, at least as far as he could tell in the first hints of morning. The trees in the area were sparse, unlike the dense enchanted forest they'd travelled through to reach the castle. Looking around, there seemed to be nothing out of the ordinary. He spun in a slow circle until his ears pinpointed which direction the ocean was. Judging by sound alone, they were maybe a mile or two off.

"This way," he stated as he began to walk, his boots crunching on the rocky soil.

Sophie jogged to catch up to his side. "How do you know which way it is? Everything looks the same."

"Madeline told me about her encounter with Yggdrasil," he explained. "She claimed it was within sight of the sea. Therefore, we follow the sound of the surf."

"Then what will we do once we get there?" she pressed.

He shrugged and continued walking. "Beats me."

"We should probably have a plan," she stated dryly.

His eyes scanned the scenery around them, searching for signs of life. "We have no idea what sorts of men or beasts might dwell on this *sacred* land. Any sort of plan we might formulate will be worthless without knowing what we're up against."

Sophie stopped walking.

He halted and looked back at her, taking in her desperate expression, framed by her long black hair fluttering around her face in the breeze.

"Alaric," she whispered, her voice cracking with emotion. "The Morrigan claimed the energy of the gods still resides here. How on earth are we supposed to face that?"

"I don't know," he answered honestly. "All I know, is that we must."

She looked like she might cry. "But aren't you scared?"

"Of course I am," he replied. "But I will find my way back to Madeline no matter what. Even if I have to face gods to do it."

She looked down at her feet for several seconds, then back up to him. "If Madeline has supplied you with bravery, then you will have to do the same for me. I can face the gods if it means saving my brother. I can face anything."

Now it was Alaric's turn to fight tears. Sophie had changed over the past few months, or perhaps she'd always been the person standing before him, only she'd been too scared to show it.

Either way, they would face the gods together. If they fell, they would both fall. Neither would die alone.

It was a lot more than most people could say.

21

I gasped and sat up in bed, my mind slowly pulling itself out of my nightmare. I'd dreamed I was locked in Estus' dungeon, and all of my teeth were falling out. Wouldn't have to be a therapist to read much into that one. Lack of control, feeling trapped, you name it.

I checked the bedside clock to find it was nearly noon. The heavy curtains blocked out most of the sun, but left me enough light to see Tabitha and Tallie asleep in the bed next to mine.

I struggled out of the covers, throwing my legs over the side of the bed to place my feet on the carpet, thinking of what I'd done to the Morrigan, and of Alaric and Sophie being stuck back in time.

There was nothing I could do about any of it. Tonight was the night we would go after Estus. The Norn was yet to be found, but we would have to move on without her. Maybe even regrow Yggdrasil without her. All of her sisters had been killed, but that energy had to go somewhere, didn't it? Maybe it would be called back to the tree. It was our only hope.

I stood and padded quietly across the carpet toward the bathroom. I knew someone was likely standing guard outside our room, but I didn't bother to check. I was relatively safe, and my toiletries awaited me in the bathroom. It was finally time for a much needed shower.

I took a quick left into the bathroom, then nearly jumped out of my skin. The light was already on, and Frode was standing over the sink, shaving the stubble from his face. His hair was twisted up in a towel. Next I noticed the steaminess in the bathroom, and the small circle he'd cleared on the mirror with his palm.

"What the hell are you doing in here!" I exclaimed.

He was clothed in black leather pants and a black tee-shirt, making his pale skin and hair stand out in sharp contrast. I was glad he was at least clothed, but my face still felt suddenly flushed. We weren't at a point in our friendship where sharing innocent bathroom time was comfortable.

He eyed me calmly, his razor poised inches from his face. "Shaving."

I narrowed my eyes at him. "Yes, I can see that. I meant what are you doing in *our* bathroom. Claiming this as a girls' room was intentional."

He shrugged and turned back to his shaving. "Aila took over the bathroom in our room. I didn't want to wait around."

I crossed my arms and glared at him. He'd roomed with Mikael and Aila by choice. "You chose which room you would stay in. Now return and suffer the consequences of your actions."

He sighed and lowered his razor, then walked past me with shaving cream still on his face. "As you wish, *Phantom Queen*," he replied snarkily. A moment later, the main door opened and shut behind him.

I swear, sometimes being part of a clan was like being at teenage summer camp, except in this case, half of the campers were six foot tall Vikings with a penchant for violence.

Finally alone, I shut and locked the bathroom door, looking down at the dirty sink in distaste. With a sudden feeling of dread, I turned toward the towel rack, then exhaled in relief as I saw one single clean towel left over for me. Normally I preferred two towels, one for my body and one for my hair, but it would have to do. I guess it's understandable we'd go through a lot of towels when most everyone around had long hair, including the men.

I heard the room door open and shut, then a knock on the bathroom door. With a heavy sigh, I opened it and peeked my head out.

Faas looked back at my grumpy expression warily. "I was just checking to see if you wanted to come to the lobby for lunch."

I continued to glare. "How did you get a key to our room?"

"I saw Frode in the hall and he gave it to me."

Of course he did. I sighed. "I'm going to take a shower now, and anyone else who interrupts me is going to face the banshees come nightfall."

Faas smirked, then held the key card out to me. "Yes ma'm."

I took the card from him, then resealed the bathroom door as he turned away. If anyone else knocked, I was ignoring them.

I kneeled down beside my suitcase, which had been pushed into the corner next to the sink. I pulled out my toiletries and set everything up for my shower, wondering how I was still able to go about things so normally after all that had happened. Perhaps I was becoming a stronger person, or maybe I was just becoming numb. You can only experience so much terror and turmoil before it stops affecting you like it once did. Once you'd been through enough, nothing could truly touch you. Or maybe I was just being melodramatic. Yeah, that was it.

I turned on the water in the shower, adjusted the temperature, then disrobed, glad to finally shed my dirty crimson sweater. I'd been so exhausted after summoning the Morrigan that I'd simply collapsed on my bed in a heap, falling asleep in my dirty clothes with unbrushed teeth.

I stepped into the shower and closed the curtain behind me. The hot water instantly relaxed my tense muscles and soothed my nerves. I hadn't even realized the tension was there until that moment. Of course, I hadn't had a quiet moment to think about it until then.

I had shampooed my hair and was just starting to relax, when a strange feeling overcame me, and a voice echoed in my head. *Time is running out. Please help.*

I lost my footing, then barely managed to catch myself on the metal bar built into the wall for disabled or elderly guests, banging my ankle on the wall of the tub. My ankle throbbing, I leaned against the bar for a moment, then shifted all my weight to my unharmed foot.

I recognized the mental voice as the Norn. I closed my eyes and shifted out of the water, lowering my shields in hopes of hearing more. As soon as I did, images flashed through my mind. The woods, in a place I recognized.

She was in danger. I didn't need words to explain her fear. I had to go to her.

I did my best to mentally convey that I'd soon be on my way. The mental communication was muddled at best, probably because of the distance between us. The Norn's telepathy was stronger with nearness, and was most clear with touch.

There was no reply.

I turned the water off and stepped out of the shower, muttering a deluge of curses. This was just what we needed. Just when our plan had been settled.

I quickly dried myself off, then wrapped my long hair up in the towel. I grabbed the first clothes I came in contact with from my suitcase. A long-sleeved, green cotton shirt and black jeans. I dressed quickly, then feeling like my heart was about to pop from anxiety, I discarded the towel from my hair, grabbed a clean pair of socks, and rushed out of the bathroom to find my boots.

Tallie and Tabitha were both awake, and sat on their bed chatting with cups of coffee in hand from the small, hotel-supplied coffee pot. They both looked at me like I'd rushed out of the bathroom spewing fire from my lungs, a mix of shock and fear at my flustered, yet determined, expression.

"The Norn is in trouble," I explained as I tugged my boots on one foot, then the other. "Tell everyone. I'm going to find Mikael."

I didn't wait for them to answer before I turned around, grabbed my purse and black jacket, then hurried out of the room.

Alejandro was outside the door on guard. His reaction was similar to Tallie and Tabitha's. I didn't blame him. I was sure I looked crazed with my unbrushed wet hair, flushed face, and turmoil-filled expression.

"Where's Mikael?" I demanded before he could speak.

"I don't kno—" he began, but I had already turned away.

Faas had said he was going to the lobby for lunch. Maybe Mikael was with him.

I hurried down the hall toward the elevator. Alejandro followed behind me, calling out for me to stop, but there was no time.

I reached the elevator and waited impatiently for the doors to open as Alejandro caught up with me. Rather then asking questions, he simply darted into the elevator alongside me, then waited as I pushed the button for the lobby.

"Mind telling me what the hell is going on now?" he asked, just as the elevator began to descend.

"The Norn . . . *contacted* me," I explained. "She made it to Washington, but she's in trouble. We need to go save her."

The elevator reached its destination and the doors slid open. I walked out into the lobby, not waiting for Alejandro's reply, then turned toward the bar/restaurant.

I scanned the tables all filled by the lunch rush, then

exhaled a sigh of relief as I spotted Mikael, Faas, and Aila seated together with mostly empty plates of food before them.

Mikael spotted me first, and watched as I approached with Alejandro at my back. Likely just judging my frazzled appearance, he seemed to deduce it was time to go. He stood and threw a wad of cash on the table, then gestured for Faas and Aila to follow him.

He met me halfway across the room, near the bar. "What happened?" he asked, his eyes lingering on my messy wet hair.

"The Norn is in trouble," I explained in a low voice.

"Let's go," he stated simply as Faas and Aila reached his back.

He pulled out his phone and started typing while he walked. Likely sending a text to Silver, since he was the only other one who seemed to have a phone, besides Aila.

He returned his phone to his pocket and we left the restaurant, then the five of us walked across the lobby and exited the hotel.

"We don't want to take any backup?" I questioned.

We walked across the parking lot toward one of the SUVs. The sun was shining brightly, an odd occurrence in Washington State in the middle of winter.

"Silver will gather reinforcements," he explained, his eyes scanning the parking lot for possible threats. "I'll tell him where to go as soon as you tell me."

Alejandro, Aila, and Faas fanned out around us like proper bodyguards as we reached the vehicle.

I thought back to the images that had briefly flashed through my mind when the Norn had contacted me. I recognized the area portrayed in the images as Woodborough Park. It was a recreation area right past a small suburb on the outskirts of Spokane. There was a hiking trail I had frequented back in my normal days that led to a secluded picnic area. I'd recognized the memorial plaque at the base of one of the trees. I'd sat by myself under that tree many times. It was either fortuitous that I knew the area, or it was a trap.

"Woodborough Park," I explained. We all piled into the SUV. I took the front passenger seat while Mikael drove. "It's about twenty minutes east of here."

"Was the Norn able to communicate the location's name?" he asked quizzically as he backed the vehicle out of its parking spot, then aimed us toward the exit.

I shook my head. "I recognized the area. This may be a trap."

Mikael seemed deep in thought as he steered the vehicle out onto the street, then picked up speed and changed lanes to merge onto the nearby highway. "Would Estus be aware that you'd recognize this location?" he asked finally.

"I'm not sure," I replied. "He had people watching me most of my life. Sophie was one of them, actually. But I'm not sure if anyone would have reported such an insignificant detail."

"There is another option," Faas interjected, peeking his head forward between the seats. "The key had access to your mind before you learned to shield. It could have gleaned many memories."

I frowned. "I went to Woodborough Park *a lot*, so it was a more prominent memory than most. It's entirely possible the key saw the information and stored it away for later use, though how it could have planned that far ahead is beyond me."

Alejandro cleared his throat from one of the back seats, drawing my gaze back to him. "Or else the location is entirely coincidental," he suggested. "You lived in this area for most of your life, right? The odds that you would recognize any given location are high."

I pursed my lips in thought. "True. I guess there's only one way to find out."

I turned my gaze back to Mikael in time to see him grin. "Show up and kick some ass?"

I nodded. "Pretty much."

It was as good a plan as any. We couldn't just let the Norn die. Estus and the key would both know that, so it was the perfect trap, if it really was a trap. I only wished it was nighttime so the banshees would be at full power, though they could be pretty scary during the daytime too.

Not to mention that Mara was now part of my phantom army. She could kill a man with her bad attitude alone.

"I can't believe her," Sophie growled, going on her second half hour straight of griping. "She probably placed us in this desolate, ugly place on purpose, knowing there was nothing here."

Alaric kept quiet. He wouldn't exactly call the expansive coastline ugly, but he also saw no sign of a sacred barrow. It would have helped to have someone like Tallie with them, who could sense energy. As it was, they were searching based on sight and smell alone, but they didn't know what the barrow looked like, nor if there were any distinguishing scents nearby. All they could do was keep walking and hope they weren't going in the wrong direction.

"We're going to die out here," Sophie muttered.

His boots sank in the sand as they continued to walk. "I don't think she tricked us," he stated finally. "Though she's a bit crazed, she's still the woman Mara once was. There's humanity lurking behind her bitterness. I believe she truly wants us to accomplish this task."

Sophie snorted. "When did you become so trusting?"

He lifted a hand to shade his eyes as he peered down the coast. "When I realized that there's usually more to everyone than what meets the eye," he muttered.

Sophie stopped beside him and shaded her eyes, gazing in the same direction. "What is that?" she questioned softly.

"I'm not sure."

It was a small stone structure. *Very* small. It didn't seem grand enough for a tomb on the land of the gods, but perhaps a building's looks could deceive as much as a person's.

He lowered his hand and continued walking, an extra spring in his step now that they had finally spotted something out of the ordinary. "There's only one way to find out."

Sophie caught up to his side and they both hurried toward the distant structure.

"Be on your guard," he advised as they jogged. "We've no idea what sort of creatures might be lurking about. After the Morrigan's forest, I wouldn't even be surprised if we ended up facing a dragon."

Sophie groaned. "That's not at all comforting."

"It wasn't meant to be," he replied. "We must be prepared for anything."

"We have no weapons, and I can't even remember the last time I ate," she whined. "I don't even feel prepared to battle a mouse."

"You bring shame on Bastet," a deep voice rumbled from behind them.

Alaric and Sophie both skidded to a halt and quickly turned around.

The baritone rumble of the voice had made Alaric suspect some sort of giant, but the man who stood a few feet away was of normal size. What was not normal, was that he appeared to be made of stone. His features were expertly carved, his face animated like a living being, but there was no mistaking the texture and tone of his skin and unmoving clothes. The robes draping his masculine frame seemed rigid, as did his body for that matter. All that moved at the moment were his eyes. He stood in a statuesque pose, staring at them.

"And who might you be?" Alaric asked, wondering if this was some sort of odd trick, and the statue was not actually animate.

"I am Terminus, the guardian of boundaries," the statue man explained.

"As in the Terminus out of Roman Myth?" Sophie inquired.

Alaric turned to raise an eyebrow at her. He was well versed in many of the myths, but had not been aware of that one.

"Indeed," the statue answered simply.

A few silent seconds ticked by.

Alaric found it troublesome that the statue had appeared just as they were about to reach the small stone structure. That he'd called himself the guardian of boundaries was more troublesome still. Was he here to enforce the boundary the Morrigan had referenced?

"The children of the gods are no longer welcome here," the statue stated finally.

"And how is it that you are here?" Alaric countered. "The gods have left these lands."

The statue made a *hmph* sound. "I am merely one of many guardians. I am no god."

"Terminus was a god," Sophie argued.

The statue tilted its head. The movement was fluid, with no signs of crumbling stone. It led Alaric to believe the statue could move the rest of its body just as easily, which meant it was a threat.

Though the statue was several feet away, he spread his arm in front of Sophie to push her back with him. "We simply need to retrieve some human remains and we'll be on our way," he explained.

The statue tilted its head to the other side. "You must leave now."

So it was capable of movement, but obviously not very bright. He glanced over his shoulder at the stone structure. It was still maybe thirty feet away. They could probably reach it well before the statue could catch them, but that was assuming the stone man had no other powers, and no accomplices.

"What are you meant to do to any who refuse to leave?" Sophie questioned. She had glanced back at the structure several times, likely considering the same thoughts as Alaric.

The statue took a graceful step forward. "Any who refuse to leave must die."

Alaric glanced at his sister. "You go," he whispered. "I'll hold him off."

"No," she answered instantly. "We have no idea what he might be capable of."

"We have no choice," he muttered. "Find the remains and get back to where we started. I will meet you there." Not for the first time, he desperately wished for a weapon. He had a feeling teeth and claws would be as useless against Terminus as they would have been against the forest beast.

Sophie cursed under her breath, glanced at the waiting statue, then nodded. She darted away in the direction of the stone structure, while Alaric waited for the statue to charge. It did not disappoint.

With a shrill battlecry, the statue unsheathed a massive stone sword from somewhere within his robes, lifted the blade high in the air, then sped toward Alaric.

Alaric took on a fighting stance, ready to dodge the oncoming attack. This would not be the first time he took on an unnatural foe. Here was hoping it wouldn't be the last.

22

We sped down the highway toward Woodborough Park. Silver had called Mikael shortly after we'd gotten on the highway to let him know reinforcements were on the way. I found it funny that two of the oldest Vaettir around were the ones most comfortable with cell phones, but I wasn't in the mood to laugh about it. I wasn't in the mood to laugh about anything.

There had been no more mind messages from the Norn, which had me worried. Her contact with me should have only increased as we closed the distance between us. As it was, we'd be flying blind as soon as we reached the park.

With that thought, I realized we wouldn't need to be *entirely* blind. I thought of Mara and the other banshees. There was an echoing reply in my head, faint, because their powers were dimmed when the sun was out. I thought of the park, imploring them to scout ahead.

Mara's sarcastic voice shot through my mind. *Yes mistress*, she quipped.

I couldn't help my small smile. She was pissed about becoming a banshee, but it definitely hadn't killed her spirit.

"What are you grinning about?" Mikael asked, darting his eyes between my face and the road.

I shook my head. "I sent the banshees ahead to scout out the park. They're less powerful during the day, but can at least tell us what we might be up against."

"Good call," Alejandro chimed in from the back seat. "It's far too nice a day to go waltzing into a trap."

"Will the banshees be able to fight?" Faas asked seriously.

"They can fight," I replied, keeping my eyes ahead of us, looking for the road sign that would signal our turn off, "just not as effectively. They're still dangerous, but at night their power is amplified."

I pointed as the green and white sign for Woodborough park appeared ahead of us.

Mikael slowed the vehicle and exited onto the off-ramp. Soon we took a left toward the underpass, then continued on as the road narrowed and became shadowed by massive redwoods. I instructed him to take the first right leading toward the campgrounds as the road changed from asphalt to gravel. We pulled into a large, circular loop, bordered by heavy picnic tables, and parked. There were no other cars in sight.

Still seated in the vehicle, I mentally reached out to the banshees. As soon as I opened myself up to them, voices flooded my head. *There is no trap. Hurry. Time is short.*

I unbuckled my seatbelt and opened the door. "Let's go," I ordered as I hopped out of the vehicle.

I rushed into the trees, directed by the banshee's thoughts in my head. Mikael and the others shouted behind me to wait. I realized as I ran that I'd failed to tell them there was no trap, but I couldn't take the time to explain things now. There was a sense of urgency pounding in my head. *Hurry*, the banshees urged me again.

The others soon caught up to me, but no one tried to swoop me up to run more swiftly, given I was the only one who knew where we were going. Fortunately, we didn't need to run faster. We were almost there.

I slowed my pace, reaching a clearing in the trees. A large shape lay in the yellow grass. The tips of deer antlers glinted in the sunlight.

I raced to the Norn's side, along with Faas. The others hung back, scanning the woods for danger.

"There's no trap!" I called out to them. I reached the Norn, then gasped.

Her robes were covered in blood. Blood speckled her narrow face, and a thin line trickled from her mouth. Her eyes turned up to me. *I tried to find you,* she whispered into my mind. *I found the entrance of a Salr where you had been, but they found me there.*

I could sense the pain of her wounds, plucking my nerves like guitar strings. I didn't have to ask who *they* were. It had been Estus' people. Perhaps even Estus himself, or really, the key.

I placed a hand on her bloody chest and her pain hit me full force. Though I couldn't see her wounds beneath the blood and fabric, I suddenly knew every injury she'd suffered. They'd tortured her. I retracted my hand, feeling sick.

"I don't have much energy stored up," I explained gently, gazing down into her eyes, "but I'm going to try healing you."

No, her voice whispered in my mind. *It is too late.*

I shook my head, fighting the first of my tears. Faas crouched across from me, his eyes on the Norn, while Mikael came to stand behind me. Alejandro and Aila stayed back.

Ignoring what the Norn had said, I gathered my energy. I'd managed to pull Sophie back from the brink of death before, but I'd just released multiple lives. I didn't have much juice at the moment. Still, I wasn't willing to give up. I placed my hands on her bloody chest, taking all the pain and unpleasant emotions that rushed forward with my touch.

No, she said more firmly. *I want to join my sisters.*

"But we still have to regrow Yggdrasil," I argued, my voice quavering. "I can't do that without you!"

She smiled softly. *Then take my energy into you. Take it entirely. Use it when the time is right. I cannot bear this life any longer. I cannot bear what our children have done to us.*

My tears fell harder. Mikael knelt beside me and placed a hand gently on my back, offering comfort. It didn't help.

"I don't know how to do that," I whispered. "I don't know how to take all of your energy, nor do I want to."

You must.

I shook my head over and over. It was just *wrong*. She'd come all this way to help us. She'd been looking for us, and we'd carelessly led her right to Estus. She'd been tortured because of us.

As if reading my thoughts, she chuckled, then coughed up blood. She took a few shallow, rasping breaths, then spoke into my mind, *Do not feel sorrow. You have shown me love. That is all any of us ever wanted.*

"It's not right," I said, shaking my head back and forth.

I couldn't just steal her life away.

Mikael and Faas were both watching me, obviously not hearing the other side of the conversation, but I couldn't bear explaining it to them.

Please, she said calmly into my mind. *Take my life and regrow Yggdrasil. It is the only way my sisters and I will know peace.*

My body was wracked with sobs as I pushed my hands more firmly against her chest. I could feel her heart beating underneath the fabric and blood. She wanted me to stop its gentle rhythm.

"I can't," I argued, even though I knew I had to. If it was truly what she wanted, I couldn't force her to live.

Her eyes turned up to the sky. There was so much peace in that single look, I could no longer deny her.

I took a steadying breath and quieted my tears.

As if sensing my resolve, her voice whispered in my mind, *Thank you, and do not fear. We will see the old gods together, you and I.*

With that, I drained away her life. It wasn't difficult. She was badly injured, and willing to give up. Her life flowed into me. Normally I focused just on the release, and I would let most of the energy return to the universe where it belonged, but I couldn't do that this time. I pulled on her life force, refusing to let any of it slip away.

"Madeline," Faas said softly, his eyes wide.

I stared at him across the Norn's body while the last of her life force poured into me. It wasn't like when Mara or the key shared space in my mind, I was just suddenly *more*. It was a small shred of fate's collective energy.

"Madeline," he began again, "what have you done?"

"Just what she asked," I replied bitterly.

I stumbled to my feet away from the Norn's body. Mikael caught my arm before I fell. I felt strange. The world looked somehow different.

Faas walked around the Norn to approach me. His eyes looked me up and down, though I knew he wasn't looking at my body. He was reading my energy. For some reason, I felt like I should stop him.

Before he could say anything, the banshees approached. They were barely visible in the daylight. Kind of like looking at a shimmering outline that could easily be passed off as the wind rustling the trees and the yellow blades of grass.

I felt Mara's energy as she came to stand on my side, opposite Mikael. It appeared as if her insubstantial face was looking down at the Norn, but I wasn't sure.

"What does it feel like?" she asked softly.

I didn't have to question what she meant. She'd been partnered with the key before. Its energy had melded with hers because they were supposed to be one. The Norn's energy was the other missing piece, but Mara had never rejoined with that energy. Not since Yggdrasil had been destroyed.

"Not like it was with the key," I explained. "I feel odd, like I'm a slightly different person now, but there's no extra presence in my head."

She nodded. "This step was necessary."

I didn't agree with her. I would much rather the Norn had lived.

We all turned to see several figures appear, walking toward us from where we'd parked the SUV. Silver and the reinforcements. With him were Frode, Dominic, Tallie, and to my surprise, Marcos and Sivi.

As they neared us, their focus drifted down to the Norn's body.

Across her corpse, Marcos' eyes met mine. He smiled. He could sense if a soul remained in a body just like I could. He knew I'd released her. "It feels amazing, doesn't it? The Norns' energy is like nothing else."

I felt like I was going to vomit. Marcos had participated in the murder of several Norns so he could drain their energy. I stared straight into his eyes and spat, "You're an evil bastard." Then I moved around the Norn's body and walked past him. I walked past them all.

His words had gotten to me because they were true. The extra energy *did* feel amazing, but that didn't mean I wanted it. Plenty of things in life felt great, but if they came at a great cost to others, they just weren't worth it. The fact that most of the Vaettir took so callously, *killed* so callously, was really starting to piss me off. Being descended from the gods shouldn't be a *get out of jail free card* for immoral deeds. It wasn't religion, or law. It was the blaring difference between right and wrong, good and evil.

The Norns deserved justice for their deaths. Marcos

would have to wait, but Estus was just begging for cosmic retribution. If I had to be the one to give it to him, then so be it.

ALARIC ROLLED across the sand of the coast, gracefully returning to his feet as the stone sword narrowly missed him. Terminus was deceivingly quick. Each time Alaric recovered from one attack, another was already on its way.

He saw no method of truly fighting the creature. He had no weapons, and the man was made of oddly fluid stone. All he could do was distract him while Sophie searched for Cúchulainn's bones. Even if she managed to complete her part of the task, his chances of escape were slim. Now that he was within attack range of Terminus, it would be difficult to escape without getting a sword in the back.

He briefly considered the nearby ocean. Perhaps Terminus would meet a similar end to the forest beast . . . but he quickly dismissed the idea, then rolled and dodged another attack. The water would likely slow down his movement far more than it would the stone man.

Soft footsteps raced up behind him in the sand, interrupting his thoughts. He rolled away from another attack, placing himself so he could see whomever had approached while keeping Terminus in his sights.

Sophie threw a square canvas bundle, roughly two feet wide, into the sand, then turned to fend off her own attackers.

Alaric rolled away from Terminus once more. Two women shot spouts of glowing energy at Sophie. One woman had golden skin and hair to match, while the other had ebony skin and pure black hair. Their diaphanous clothing sparkled like the fabric was made from stardust. White gems glittered in their long, streaming hair. Sophie narrowly dodged another burst of energy. The women wailed at her like banshees.

Terminus took another swing at Alaric.

"What are they!" he shouted to Sophie. He dove out of the way, landing near her discarded parcel.

"The Zorja!" Sophie screamed. A burst of energy spewed sand in all directions, right where she'd been standing only seconds before. "They are the Morning and Evening Stars," she panted. "Guardians of the constellations."

Alaric dodged another attack, putting himself back to back with Sophie. "When the hell did you learn so much about mythology?" he asked breathily as their attackers circled them.

"I can read a book!" she shouted. Each of the Zorja attacked her once more. "Now take the bones and get out of here!"

Alaric glanced at the canvas parcel, then back to Terminus. Their attackers now seemed to be considering their opponents, wondering how best to catch them.

"I told you to get to the border with the remains," he growled. "I'll find a way to meet you."

"We're not both getting out of this alive," she snapped, slowly spinning along with Alaric to keep their respective opponents in view. "You have more to return to than I, and I will not be responsible for my niece growing up without a father."

"I will not leave you," he argued. It killed him to say it, to sacrifice his chances to be with Madeline. To be there for the birth of his child. Yet he could not allow Sophie to sacrifice herself. He'd protected her for over five hundred years. He wasn't about to stop now.

Suddenly their attackers closed in all at once. Sophie and Alaric both managed to dodge the initial attacks, but it was clear they would soon be overcome. Now that they'd been herded together, they each needed to watch for attacks from all three opponents, though the Zorja only seemed to attack in unison.

Alaric narrowly missed a swing of Terminus' sword, then Sophie screamed. Alaric back-pedaled to see her lying in the sand, clutching at her chest. One of the Zorja must have hit her with their strange energy.

He tried to rush toward Sophie, but Terminus spun and attacked with a backward thrust of his blade. Alaric wasn't fast enough. He was about to die.

"Enough!" a voice shouted, opposite the direction of the sea.

Terminus halted his attack, his blade inches from Alaric's chest. Sophie groaned on the ground in pain, but the Zorja did not attack her again.

He stepped out of harm's way, then moved to Sophie's side.

All turned toward the source of the voice.

The Morrigan approached them, moving with halted motions like every step caused her great pain. Her red hair and red dress billowed around her with the coastal breeze, illuminated by the sunlight to make her look like some sort of fire goddess. Her face, though scrunched in pain, showed determination.

"You are not welcome here," Terminus stated.

He took a step toward the Morrigan as the Zorja moved forward to stand at his side.

Now that their attackers had a new target, Alaric quickly snatched up the bone-filled parcel, then crouched beside his sister. Her eyes were shut and she groaned in pain, but at least she was alive.

"The earth will not tolerate your presence here," one of the Zorja stated in a breathy, melodious voice. "Soon it will swallow you whole."

"I know," the Morrigan said through gritted teeth, forcing herself forward step by step. "I have come to atone for my sins."

Alaric wrapped an arm around Sophie's back, under her armpits, then lifted her up to stand beside him. She hung limply, kept aloft only by his hold on her. He began walking a wide circle around Terminus and the Zorja with the parcel under his free arm. Sophie tried to move her feet along with his, but mostly they dragged in the sand.

Ever so slowly, Alaric and Sophie reached the Morrigan's side, while Terminus and the Zorja watched on.

Terminus turned his stony gaze to Alaric. "You have fought well, but we have other matters to attend to. Leave now, and I will allow you to live."

Alaric handed the parcel to the Morrigan, then hoisted Sophie up to get a more secure grip on her. She seemed to have lost consciousness. "We all leave together, or not at all," he replied.

The Morrigan looked at him in surprise.

"No offense," he whispered, "but you're kind of our ride out of here."

She chuckled, then coughed. Globs of mucous and blood spewed out of her mouth to land in the sand. It was like something was attacking her from the inside.

His eyes widened as she coughed up more blood.

"The earth is reclaiming her," the darker of the two Zorja explained. "Soon she will be no more."

The Morrigan nodded in agreement. "Yes, I will soon perish. I will not fight my fate, but I will not leave this earth before I have righted my most grievous wrong."

She tried to kneel in the sand, but as her knees landed she fell forward, bowed over the parcel. Slowly, she forced herself upright, knees digging into the sand, and undid the bindings on the parcel, revealing a full set of old, yellow bones.

She placed her hands over the bones, and Alaric suddenly realized what she was doing. He'd seen Madeline do it many times before. She was releasing the soul trapped in the remains.

"Stop her!" the lighter of the two Zorja shouted.

All three charged them, but they were too late. The Morrigan suddenly stood, no longer appearing to be in pain. She'd gained energy from the release, just like Madeline could. She motioned with her arm and shot a wave of energy at their attackers, casting them aside effortlessly.

Alaric looked from their downed attackers to the Morrigan. "We need to get out of here."

She smiled. "*You* do. This is where my story ends. Tell Madeline I am sorry she must bear the same curse as I. My only hope is that she bears it more gracefully."

He nodded. "She is purely good, despite the darkness she is capable of."

The Morrigan's expression took on a dreamy quality. She turned her gaze out to the sea. "Thank you for giving me peace," she muttered, then waved a hand in front of Alaric and Sophie.

He was overcome once again by that odd feeling of still momentum. Everything began to go gray.

The last thing he saw was the Morrigan collapsing over the bones of her one-time love, then everything went black.

23

We all walked in silence back toward the vehicles. Mikael remained by my side the entire way. No one had attempted to speak to me since I'd called Marcos an evil bastard, and I was glad for it. I wasn't in the mood to talk.

Madeline, Mara whispered in my head.

I shook my head. *Whatever it is, we can discuss it later,* I mentally replied.

No, she pleaded, *something strange has happened. I feel odd.*

I stopped walking.

Mikael glanced at me in question.

"Something's wrong with Mara," I explained distantly, focusing my energy on her. Pain riveted me. I was suddenly crushed to the ground.

"What the hell!" someone yelled from behind us, while Mikael shouted "Madeline!"

I'd managed to brace myself with my forearms as I fell forward into the dirt, but now something heavy pinned my back. Someone groaned on top of me. There were *people* on top of me, like they had just fallen from the sky.

"Madeline?" a voice questioned near my ear.

My heart stopped. I knew that voice. Tears instantly began streaming from my eyes. "Alaric?" I croaked, barely able to coerce my voice into functioning.

The weight rolled off me, and I turned over and sat up to find Alaric and Sophie seated less than a foot away. My breath left me as Alaric dove for me and wrapped me up in his embrace. "Please tell me we didn't hurt you with that landing!" he said frantically.

Though I'd landed on my stomach, my arms had taken most of the impact. That was as far as my thoughts went. I couldn't seem to stop crying. "I'm fine," I sobbed, "but how did you get here?" I pulled away from him enough to see his tear stained face. His perfect dark eyes. And the smile I had missed so much.

The Morrigan sent them, Mara's voice echoed in my head. Her voice was filled with joy. *She released Cúchulainn from his eternal imprisonment. She atoned for our sins before her body perished.* I could sense her shock and awe. She'd destroyed herself because of her guilt, which encompassed many things, but most of all it had been centered around what she'd done to Cúchulainn, the man who'd betrayed her love.

I wrapped my arms tightly around Alaric as he pulled me into his lap. The numbness of shock still had possession of my body. Alaric felt so real against me, but part of me expected him to disappear. I turned my face up to him, and he buried my lips in a kiss. After a moment he moved from my mouth then showered my face with kisses where my tears had fallen. His tears started anew as he pulled back a few inches to show me the sheer joy in his eyes.

"Would someone mind explaining to me what the hell just happened?" Alejandro asked.

I turned my gaze up to him and everyone else gathered around us. I couldn't help my grin as I replied, "Fate decided to stop being such a bitch, for once."

My brief glance at those surrounding us brought my gaze to Sophie, who still sat in the dirt, looking bleary eyed and rejected. The visible skin on her chest was bright red and welted, like it had been severely burned.

With a grin still plastered on my face, I rolled my eyes at her, and held out an arm. "Get over here, you idiot."

She glared at me. "You know I'm not the cuddle puddle type."

I continued to hold out my arm and she continued to glare, then she finally moved close enough for me to wrap her in a half hug. Alaric removed one arm from my waist and wrapped it around his sister, trapping her against us.

Sophie only tolerated the hug for a few seconds, but her responding emotions let me know she'd appreciated the inclusion, even if she'd never admit it.

Letting go of her as she struggled away, Alaric wrapped his arms back around me. "Mind telling me why we're sitting in the middle of the woods . . . " he trailed off as his eyes took in everyone standing around us, lingering on Sivi. " . . . with such an interesting entourage?" he finished.

I supposed it *would* seem interesting to him, since he'd

never even met Silver, and the last time he'd seen Sivi was back when we'd all lived in Estus' Salr.

"I'll explain everything," I assured with a smile, "as long as you tell me all about being back in time with the original Morrigan."

"Since you know that," he began, "I'm assuming Mara is here? She thought it was you summoning her, but then she disappeared before we could ask her more."

I bit my lip, trying to figure out how to best explain things. She hadn't spoken into my mind again since Alaric had arrived, and remained out of sight, but I knew she was probably watching.

"Madeline," he said cautiously, knowing my nervous look all too well, "what happened?"

I glanced away from him. "Well, um . . . "

"She turned her into a banshee," Mikael answered for me.

I turned back in time to see Alaric's eyes widen. "How? *Why*?"

I shrugged. "It was kind of an accident."

He sighed. "Where is she now?"

At his question, Mara appeared before us, though she was still barely visible in the midday light. She stood silently, but those near her backed away.

I tensed as Alaric's uneasy energy hit me, then I remembered something Mara had said right before Alaric had appeared. He'd somehow freed Cúchulainn, her one-time love turned enemy.

I watched Alaric as he stared at her.

"Do you feel any different?" he asked her hesitantly.

"Quite," she replied with her eyes on me before turning

her gaze toward Alaric. "You know you shouldn't go around changing history," she chided, then softened her tone to add, "but yes, I feel quite different. I feel . . . free."

"So it worked then?" he pressed. "I mean, I saw her release his soul, but we weren't able to hang around and ask questions."

Mara's transparent lips smiled. "It worked. I have the memory of the entire experience now in my mind. She was me, after all." She turned her hollow gaze back to me. "I was quite impressed, really. They fought Terminus and the Zorja."

"Terminus and the Zor-what?" I asked her, confused.

"Ancient guardians left over by the gods," she answered simply.

"Not to interrupt," Mikael interrupted as he stepped forward, "but we really should get back to the hotel to plan our attack."

I'd been so wrapped up in getting Alaric back I only then realized that everyone else probably didn't share my excitement, and wanted to get on with the mission. I reluctantly rose from Alaric's lap. He followed me up, standing close, his shoulder touching mine.

Mikael stepped in front of Alaric. "It's good to have you back."

"You don't have to lie," Alaric replied instantly.

"I'm not," was Mikael's simple reply before turning to walk the rest of the way toward the vehicles.

We all followed. I didn't dwell on the odd moment. I had Alaric and Sophie back, and Mara was practically singing with joy in my mind. I had the energy of the Fates within me, and even though the Norn's death caused me sadness, the idea of fulfilling her wishes lifted me back up. Between Mara and the Fates, I had two pieces of the puzzle. Now I only needed the third. The key. Together we could create a whole new world for my daughter to grow up in. One filled with magic and excitement. Or at least that was my hope. In reality, releasing magic into the world might be a very bad thing, but I had to have faith the Fates wouldn't steer me wrong.

Okay, so they had steered me wrong before, but forgive and forget, right? Ri-ight.

OUR VEHICLES WERE a little crowded with the extra passengers, but everyone managed to fit, sort of. Luckily we didn't have far to go. Mikael took the driver's seat again in the SUV we'd arrived in. Aila climbed into the passenger's seat. Alaric, Sophie, and I took the middle row, while Faas, Tabitha, Alejandro, and Tallie all crammed into the back row, sharing the three seats uncomfortably. It was lucky Tallie and Faas were small, else they never would have fit. Silver took everyone else in the other vehicle they'd arrived in.

On the drive back I'd filled Alaric and Sophie in on everything they'd missed, including our failed attempt to infiltrate Estus' Salr.

"So Sivi is on our side now?" Alaric asked suspiciously as we neared the hotel.

I nodded. "More out of spite against Estus, than out of a need to help us. He lied to her about Kira being dead. They spent hundreds of years apart because of him."

"Can we trust her?" he pressed, still sounding unsure.

I shrugged. "She saved us that night, so she's at least useful, and I trust Kira. If Sivi is plotting something, I believe Kira would try to stop her."

"So how did their little reunion go?" Alejandro interrupted from behind us.

I turned around to look at him. "I haven't had the chance to ask yet. In fact, I haven't seen Kira at all. It's been one thing after another since we got back."

Faas rolled his eyes. "Yes, you've kept us *all* very busy," he quipped.

I smirked. "Hey, no one made you come along for any of it."

"Well I couldn't very well leave you to your own devices," he replied sarcastically.

We pulled into the parking lot of the hotel, distracting me from my forthcoming clever retort. We parked, and with Alaric's hand firmly linked with mine, we all filtered out of the vehicle and into the parking lot. The clouds had moved in to obscure the sun during our drive, making me feel more at home. As a life-long Pacific Northwesterner, I wasn't used to much sun.

Alaric and I fell behind while everyone else walked toward the hotel ahead of us.

"You all seem quite comfortable with each other," he said softly, leaning his head near my shoulder. "I'm surprised."

I shrugged. "I've had to rely on everyone a lot since we got here. You can't help but make a few friends when death lurks behind every doorway."

"Hmph," he replied.

I tilted my head and raised an eyebrow at him as we neared the front entrance. "Correct me if I'm wrong, but are you jealous?"

He smiled softly as we entered through the sliding doors. "I didn't like missing out on that time with you. I'm grateful to everyone for keeping you safe, but at the same time, I wish I could be the only one with that job."

I grinned at him. "Don't worry, you can keep me the *safest*."

He laughed, then we were interrupted by Sophie. She'd reached the end of the lobby near the restaurant entrance, and was now shouting at the hostess. Aila stood at Sophie's side trying to calm her down.

Mikael turned away from the scene as we reached him. "It seems Sophie wants food, and she wants it now."

I laughed, then rubbed my small baby bump. "I could stand to eat too."

Alaric placed his hand over mine on my tummy. "I was hoping for some alone time," he admitted, "but what baby wants, baby gets."

Mikaels took a breath through his teeth. "You two are disgusting," he muttered, feigning horror at our cuteness.

Or who knew? Maybe he wasn't feigning and we really were that disgusting. Either way, he led us toward Sophie and Aila.

The hostess sighed, then gave in and agreed to seat them in the overly full restaurant.

We ended up sitting at two little round cafe tables pushed together in the corner of the room. It was somewhere around 4 pm, but we all ordered coffee. I even went for the real stuff. Screw my leftover human instincts. I was

Vaettir, and everyone had assured me a little caffeine wouldn't harm my baby, so I was just going to go for it. Of course, maybe I was more than Vaettir, something else entirely, and that made me question my ability to even have children. I shook my head and focused on the menu in front of me. I wasn't about to let my mind go there until we were all safe. I had too much to think about as it was.

Once we all had our coffee, we ordered food. Pancakes for me, and a burger for Alaric. While we waited for our food, Alaric and Sophie regaled us with the story of their adventure. By the time our food arrived I was suffering from a mixture of surprise, and a bit of jealousy. Forest beasts, the original Morrigan, and ancient guardians? It all sounded exciting . . . and terrifying. It also made me feel a bit ill that Alaric had come so close to not making it back to me.

We all waited in silence as the waitress doled out our plates from her large tray. Once she was gone, I forced myself to take a bite of my pancakes. Everyone at the table silently dug into their food. The pancakes were fluffy and delicious, and sat like cardboard in my stomach.

"As for tonight," Mikael announced, drawing everyone's attention to him. He had an untouched bowl of french onion soup sitting before him. "Most of us will enter the Salr together to attend Estus' *ball*. We have deduced that he wants to convince Madeline to help him in some way, but he's lost his leverage." He glanced at Alaric and Sophie. "Still, he will likely try to force her into aiding him. Our job is to not give him the chance."

Everyone around the table nodded in agreement,

including me. I was just fine with passing up a personal meeting with Estus/the key.

"Faas, Madeline, and Marcos will remain together," he continued, "as they can feed each other's powers. This extra display will be needed, as the banshees cannot enter the Salr. Most of our numbers will enter the Salr along with them, though a small force will remain outside with the phantoms."

I narrowed my eyes at him in confusion. "You speak as if we have hundreds at our disposal," I commented, interrupting his speech. We'd gathered quite a few people to our small group, but it was still just that. *Small.*

He chuckled. "You did not truly believe we were all just sitting here twiddling our thumbs while you did all of the work, did you?"

I kept my eyes narrowed, waiting for him to explain.

"Many of Aislin's people have joined our cause," he stated smugly, "and the smaller clans are coming over from Ireland and Norway. They all understand what is at stake, and are willing to fight."

My jaw dropped. "So you're saying we have an army?"

"A small army, but yes. They will be little help against the key, but will be invaluable against those still loyal to Estus."

Faas nodded along with what Mikael was saying. "Many will still have to die."

"More power for Madeline," Mikael stated, his voice void of emotion.

Many would die, I thought to myself. It had been the plan all along, but it still didn't sit well. Many had died already.

Alaric watched me like he knew just what I was thinking. He probably did.

"We'll rest until nightfall," Mikael continued. "Then we shall depart together." He looked at each individual around the table. "Prepare yourselves well. Tonight we fight for our lives."

"And to restore balance," I added.

"And for vengeance for those we've lost," Aila chimed in.

"And for love," Sophie added, surprising everyone.

We all raised our coffee mugs into the air, clinking them together, then drank heartily of the most noble of beverages.

As we lowered our mugs we laughed, relieving some of the tension after the dark discussion. The conversation was light as we finished our meals, paid, and left the restaurant, well-fueled and prepared for the night ahead.

AFTER OUR MEAL, we'd all made our way to our rooms to rest. Now that Alaric and Sophie were back, we'd had to switch up the room arrangements just a bit. Tallie and Tabitha bunked up with Faas, Alejandro, and Maya, while Sophie was added to Mikael's room along with Frode and Aila. She hadn't been happy with the arrangement, but preferred it to rooming with Maya.

It had been blatantly obvious that everyone was trying to give Alaric and I a room by ourselves, and I wasn't about to argue with them. It was actually quite a sweet gesture, and horribly out of character for most of the Vaettir.

Still, Alaric and I did end up with a room to ourselves, and suddenly everything felt well and right in the world, even though we would soon have an epic standoff with our long time enemy.

Now we stood in that dark room, all by ourselves. Alejandro had given Alaric some fresh clothing, since they were roughly the same size, but he'd wait to change until after a shower and some rest.

Speaking of a shower . . .

We both glanced at the open bathroom door, providing the only light in the room, other than what crept in through the shut curtains. We only had a few hours to rest before it was time to go, but it seemed neither of us was overly concerned with going to sleep.

Alaric glanced at the bathroom again. "Shall we?"

"You should probably get some rest," I sighed.

He hadn't slept the entire time he was in the past. I knew he was much better at going without sleep than most, but he still had to sleep sometime.

He gently laid his hands upon my shoulders. "I haven't seen you in days. We're about to go up against Estus and the key. I'm not going to waste these few hours with you on sleep."

"But—" I began to argue, only to be cut off by his lips on mine.

All arguments ceased. He took my hand and led me toward the small bathroom. I'd just taken a shower in there earlier that morning, but I didn't mind another one. Especially since I had company this time.

Once in the bathroom, he dropped my hand to slip his into the shower to turn on and adjust the water, then repositioned himself in front of me. He put his hands on my waist, then slowly tugged my shirt up to my ribs.

With a smile I lifted my arms, and he drew it the rest of the way up over my head, sliding the sleeves off my arms one by one. He let my shirt drop to the floor, his eyes intent on me, even as he began to undo the button of my jeans, snug under my belly. He paused, eyes cast downward as his hands encircled my waist.

"Did it get bigger?" he asked, excitement in his tone.

I smiled. "It's only been a couple days, I don't think it's really changed much."

He shook his head, still staring down at my belly. "Nope. I'm pretty sure it's grown."

I laughed, then glanced at the running water. "Are we going to shower or not?"

He nodded, then quickly removed his shirt as I slid off my jeans.

He frowned at me as I wiggled them down to the floor. "Hey, I wanted to do that."

I smirked. "Your going to *have* to do that when my belly is too big for me to bend over, and I'm wearing those fun maternity jeans with the big elastic waistband."

He pulled me close and kissed me, then pulled away enough to whisper, "I can't wait."

The rest of our clothes fell away quickly, then we both stepped into the shower. He focused the stream of water on me, making no move to wash himself.

I squinted my eyes against the water running down my face as I looked up at him. "You should probably get yourself clean if you hope to get any rest before we leave."

He shook his head. "No way. We are staying in this shower for the next hour. No arguments."

I laughed. "I knew there had to be some hidden benefit to the endless supply of hot water in large hotels."

He nodded and kissed me again. If he could go without sleep, so could I.

24

———

Alaric and I watched out the window of our hotel room as darkness slowly encased the world like a foreboding cloud. Time was up. The banshees would now be at full power, including Mara. It was finally time to storm the castle. This was our chance to regrow Yggdrasil and take down the key forever. Failure wasn't an option. Only death for one side or the other.

"We should go," Alaric said softly in my ear as his arm encircled my lower back.

I smiled. "We said that ten minutes ago."

A knock on the door drew both our gazes.

"Damn," Alaric muttered, then took my hand. We both padded barefoot across the carpet toward the door.

Alaric had gotten dressed in Alejandro's clothes. The black jeans fit him perfectly, but the black tee-shirt was a little snug in the shoulders. I'd begrudgingly pulled on leather pants for the umpteenth time since joining the Vaet-tir. I hated wearing them, but Alaric had made a very good point. We were going somewhere people might try to beat me up. My injuries would be less if the leather took some of the damage instead of my skin. I didn't mind, however, slipping on a crimson silk blouse. We were going to a ball, after all. I wanted to look nice. Else I just liked the way Alaric looked at me when I wore the blouse. Silly, but true.

We opened the door to reveal Aila, Mikael, and Sophie. Aila and Mikael were in their normal Viking gear. Mikael carried a long, canvas bundle under one arm. Sophie wore all black, like her brother. I didn't know where she'd gotten fresh clothes, but I was pretty sure I recognized the top as one of Tabitha's.

"Time to go kids, get your shoes," Mikael teased, glancing down at our bare feet.

We both sighed, then led the way into our room. The others followed, shutting the door behind them. I searched around for my boots. I found them near the window, retrieved some socks from my nearby suitcase, then sat on the bed beside Alaric to tug them on.

"Now you remember the plan, correct?" Mikael asked, standing by the foot of the bed looking down at me, the mysterious bundle still under his left arm.

I nodded. "Waltz in like we own the place and don't give Estus the chance to make the first move."

Mikael smiled. "And what else?"

I sighed. "Let everyone else protect us from Estus' people. Our main goal is luring Estus outside."

He nodded, then offered me a hand up as I finished putting on my black, low-heeled boots. "It will not be an easy task. He knows about the banshees, and thus will try to remain within the Salr. We must give him no choice but to follow us."

"Knowing he's lost his leverage will help," Alaric said as he finished lacing up his boots. He stood up beside me and took my hand. "The goal is to make him desperate enough to make a mistake."

I nodded. "The key's energy combined with Estus' power is terrifying—" I halted what I was about to say as what should have been a blaringly obvious thought struck me. "What if he tries to send us or our people back in time? He'd instantly regain his leverage."

Mikael shrugged. "It's a possibility, but I'd say it's not a likely one. Time travel takes a great deal of power, power the key will not want to waste when confronted with the banshees, along with the energies of the Morrigan and the Norns."

"It's still a risk though."

He shrugged. "Everything is a risk. It doesn't excuse us from doing what we must."

I sighed. "You're right. I'm just stalling."

"But that still leaves us needing to lure him outside," Alaric added.

I nodded, then turned back to Mikael.

He shrugged. "We have the numbers we need, so we're as prepared as we're going to get. I was just planning on winging it."

"*Winging* it?" Alaric asked skeptically.

Mikael nodded, then turned to me with a smile. "From what I've observed, that's how you function best. Though you may not agree, Lady Luck has been on your side. Statistically speaking, your best chance of success is to simply act on your gut instincts."

I had to swallow the sudden lump in my throat before I could speak. "You're placing an awful lot of faith in me."

He continued to smile. "Madeline, if there's one thing you've taught me in our time together, it's that you must always have faith in your friends."

I let out a long breath, then answered, "If you say so."

"Don't look so glum," he chided. "I bought everyone new weapons."

Aila's face lit up at the news.

Mikael placed the bundle he'd been holding on the foot of the bed and unrolled it. Inside were two big-ass swords in leather sheaths, a one-sided axe, too big to be a hatchet, but still shorter than the swords, and a whole bunch of sheathed knives of varying sizes.

I stroked my finger down the handle of the ax. It seemed to be made of smooth bone or ivory. The blade was a dark metal, ancient, but finely honed. "I recognize this," I muttered, then the lightbulb came on in my head. I turned my gaze to Mikael. "This is the axe you brought back from the past."

When we'd gone back to Viking times to meet Mikael's long-dead wife, Erykah, he'd brought the ax back with him. I'd never gotten a true explanation, and this was the first time I'd seen the weapon since then.

"It was my father's," he explained distantly.

Sophie let out an abrupt laugh.

We all looked at her.

She blushed. "Sorry, it's just odd thinking about the ancient Viking's father." She turned her dark gaze to him.

"No offense, but I can't really imagine you as a child with parents."

Aila rolled her eyes. "Everyone has parents."

I looked down at the floor, hoping no one would realize Aila's faux pas.

"Except Madeline," she added awkwardly, pointing out her own mistake before anyone else could.

I blushed. I hadn't fully discussed our theories with Alaric since his return.

He and Sophie both stared at me.

"Yeah," I muttered, then forced my gaze up to them. "We're not sure if I was really born, or somehow created, like the Morrigan and the Norns."

They both gasped.

A million silly thoughts rushed through my mind. Would Alaric view me differently now, knowing I wasn't like him? Would he worry that our daughter wouldn't quite be Vaettir either? I should have trusted him to accept me for exactly what I was, or what I might be, but I was finding it difficult, which explained why I'd neglected to tell him.

Taking in my unsure expression, Alaric stepped forward and reached his hand out, gently lifting my chin so I'd meet his gaze. "Madeline," he said patiently, "I've always known you were special, and we've been questioning your lineage for some time. This changes nothing. Do you think of Mara as less of a person because of how she was created?"

I frowned, then answered honestly, "Not in the slightest."

He smiled. "Then give me a little bit of credit here. I

don't care where you came from. I'm just grateful you exist."

Sophie started making exaggerated retching noises.

I briefly considered stabbing her with one of the knives.

With a laugh, Alaric pulled me into a half hug and we all turned our attention back to the weapons.

"As I was saying," Mikael continued, making it clear in his tone that he was dealing with a bunch of children, "I've purchased everyone new weapons. We'll keep the larger ones wrapped up until we leave the hotel, but the knives can be donned now."

"I still have the two blades you gave me when we first landed," I commented, "so I'm good."

Mikael rolled his eyes at me, then picked up two of the smaller knives. They were in sheaths of thick, black nylon, with adjustable loops at either end. "Hold out your arms," he commanded.

With a sigh, I did as I was asked, and he slipped a sheath on each of my wrists, securing them so they wouldn't slip around.

Meanwhile everyone put on their own knives. Some went on ankles, or around the waist underneath shirts.

With my wrist sheaths secured, I turned to watch Alaric as he donned his own wrist blades. "I feel like if we're to the point of needing all of these blades, we're as good as dead."

"They may try taking our weapons when we enter the Salr," Alaric explained. "The more we hide, the more likely they will be overlooked. Plus, a blade an enemy doesn't know about is always better than one they can see."

My mouth formed an *oh* of understanding. When it came to matters of war and weaponry, I really needed to learn to stop asking questions and just let the professionals work.

Once everyone was done securing their blades, Mikael wrapped up the few larger weapons. We all donned coats. My short black jacket barely covered the wrist sheaths, but since they were black too, they blended fairly well.

We were officially ready. All we needed to do was drive to the Salr's entrance, and pray we made it out alive.

We all stared at each other for a moment.

I felt like my heart was about to pop. We were really doing this. We were going to face the key and attempt to regrow Yggdrasil. We were going to reopen a highway straight to the old gods and other realms.

I took a deep breath. "Let's go."

Alaric took my hand and gave it a squeeze, then Sophie, Mikael, and Aila turned to exit the room. I paused, my hand still in Alaric's, to retrieve my purse from the floor. It contained the larger blades to be worn at my hips, my fake ID and passport, some chapstick, and that was it. To say I felt underprepared was a monumental understatement. I couldn't do this. I couldn't face down an entire clan led by the key in Estus form. There was no way I could do this.

I sucked in a breath and held it, waiting a few seconds to let it out. I *had* to do this.

I'd been through a lot of terrifying experiences over the past few months, but I'd never been as scared as I was in that moment. This was the end. No more running. No more plotting.

Alaric, seeming to sense my unease, pulled me into a tight hug. "I love you," he whispered against my loose hair.

"And I believe in you. I've never believed in anything more in my entire life."

I pulled away from him with a soft smile. "You always seem to know what I'm thinking."

He chuckled. "You're an empath. I have to at least be a bit perceptive to stand any chance of leveling the playing field."

He took my hand once more and led me out of the open door and into the hall where the others waited patiently. As the door shut, I heard the click that confirmed it had locked behind us. Faas, Marcos, and Silver had joined our group. Faas was dressed like Aila and Mikael in Viking garb, while Marcos wore his usual black, and Silver what I'd come to think of as his usual white.

The eight of us would be riding together, and would protect each other throughout the night. Everyone was divided into units like that, ensuring someone always had someone else to watch their back. Those who would wait above-ground with the banshees were divided in a similar way, groups of six to eight.

With just a brief nod of acknowledgement to me, Silver led the way down the hall toward the elevator. We all followed his slender back silently.

The ride down in the elevator was spent in silence. Was everyone as nervous as I, or were they just conceiving battle strategies in their minds? I was betting on the latter. Many of them had gone to war before.

My only source of comfort was Alaric at my side, though part of me almost wished he'd remained in the past until after the battle. It would have been nice if he could have remained relatively safe until it was all over, then I could have used Yggdrasil to retrieve him. As it was, I was terrified something would happen to him and I wouldn't be able to stop it.

My thinking wasn't fair though. I knew he held the same fears for me, and he was pushing forward. He deserved a chance to fight for a better world for his daughter just as much as I did. We were in this together, to the bitter end.

More of our people were already waiting in the lobby as we arrived. The other hotel guests and staff cast us odd looks. No one's weapons were visible, and most looked like fairly normal humans, but a large silent group, most dressed in leather, would stand out anywhere.

Alaric and I led our group in continued silence toward the front exit. We entered a surprisingly crowded parking lot.

A whole fleet of black SUVs were lined up to transport us to our destination. No wonder the hotel staff had been eyeing us. They probably thought we were a celebrity entourage, or members of the secret service. Else maybe they had all decided that the *Men in Black* were real, and we were all going out to hunt aliens. It was a more likely scenario than the truth. A truth they would eventually find out if we were successful.

We approached the nearest SUV. This time Aila took the driver's seat, with Sophie in the front passenger's seat. I ended up sandwiched between Mikael and Alaric in the middle row, with Faas, Marcos, and Silver sitting behind us.

Aila started the engine and found her place in the line of SUVs as they exited the parking lot. Soon we were on the highway, and all was silent in the vehicle's dark interior. I watched as the frequently passing headlights lit up Alaric's face one after another. The people within the vehicles were all on their way to have nice normal nights. Family dinners. First dates. You name it. Or who knew? Maybe some of them were serial killers searching for prey, or men and women on their way to the airport to fly off to a human war zone.

I closed my eyes and took a deep breath, forcing away my dark thoughts. Alaric leaned over and kissed me on my cheek, but remained silent. We all did. Our planning was done. All we could do now was act.

Our drive didn't take long. We were going to an entrance I'd never been to. Aila slowed the SUV as we exited off the highway. We took a right, then continued on down the dark, one lane street. No lights of homes or businesses lit our way, which was for the best. Didn't want the humans getting in the way of the phantom army.

We pulled off onto another dark street that soon turned into a bumpy, dark road. We were in the middle of bumfuck nowhere, where no one would hear us scream.

The SUV bounced for several more minutes. It was almost bright outside with so many pairs of headlights, but farther off the land was encased in inky blackness, save the now distant lights of the highway. Another turnoff into a more wooded area, a few more minutes of driving, then one by one the SUVs came to a halt.

We all spilled out into the darkness, accompanied by the sound of the doors opening and shutting on roughly fifteen other vehicles. As soon as my feet hit the ground, a cool wind blew the hair back from my face. The banshees. They were ready for war.

Mara's presence sent a minute shiver through my brain. She was pissed off. She wanted to go into the Salr with me, but would have to remain outside with the others. I didn't blame her for being upset. I wanted her to come too.

I took a moment to retrieve the blades from my purse, fastening the sheaths at either side of my belt before throwing the purse back into the SUV. My ID's and chapstick wouldn't be needed.

Once everyone was out in the open, I shut the SUV door and thought of the banshees again, focusing my energy on them. Marcos came to stand by my side, then took my hand. I flinched, still as uncomfortable with his touch as ever, then slowly relaxed.

His energy joined mine, and fed into the banshees, which in turn fed their own brand of power back into us. It was like a perfect symbiosis. We all fed off each other, but gained just as much, if not more, in return.

Many among our large group gasped as the banshees began to take shape before us, followed by the other phantoms. I could feel the fear of our people like a cloying perfume on the back of my tongue. All we'd needed to make them join us was our shared hatred for Estus, but it was fear of my phantoms that would keep them in line after the fact.

I turned my focus away from the banshees as more headlights illuminated the small backroad. I glanced at Mikael in question, who nodded, letting me know those headed our way were more of our new recruits. Including those around us, there had to be over one hundred.

I shivered, and it had nothing to do with the banshees,

or Marcos still holding my hand. There were so many new Vaettir. Who knew if we could trust them?

Mara's voice echoed through my mind. *They will not move against you. Their need for freedom from Estus is too great.* Her voice paused in thought for a moment, then she added, *Once he is dead, you will need to reconsider their allegiance.*

Well that was comforting. I'd have to think about it later though, after we all survived. As long as they would fight for us tonight, then I didn't need to worry about them, and beyond everything else, I trusted Mikael's judgement. He would not have brought them here if he thought mutiny likely.

I turned my attention back to the banshees. They were now at full power, and knew their orders. They would slay any who moved against our people outside of the Salr, but their primary focus was Estus. The moment that little rat emerged, they would spring the trap.

I dropped Marcos' hand without a word as Alaric and Sophie came to stand on either side of me.

"Are you ready?" Alaric asked.

I wanted to say *no, not at all*, but what came out was, "Ready as I'll ever be."

With that, around fifty of us moved forward, guided toward the Salr's entrance by Mikael, leaving our extra people behind with the banshees. Out of the kitchen, and into the fire, as it were.

25

I t was a ten minute walk to the Salr's entrance, and we saw no sign of Estus' people along the way. The night was quiet and still around us. Alaric and Sophie didn't smell nor hear anything unusual, nor did Faas sense anything. There was no trap waiting outside. Imagine that.

The entrance was similar to Mikael's Salr in Norway, disguised as a massive tree. At a touch from Faas, the doorway shimmered into existence, revealing a stairway down into the earth. Down into a Salr I'd already visited far too many times for my liking. Hopefully the third time would be a charm, because the first and second had ended in torture and near death, respectively.

Frode and Alejandro had joined us to lead the way into the Salr. Followed by Mikael and Aila, then Sophie and Alaric. Next came Faas, Marcos and I, with me in the middle. Then everyone else slowly filtered in.

Soon I realized why this particular entrance had been chosen by our people for our arrival. It opened up into a room connected to the large throne room. We could come in as an organized group, not risking the first to enter being picked off while they waited for everyone else.

I stopped dead as we entered the throne room. Previously barren stone walls were decked out with massive tapestries, their gold and silver thread glinting in the light of hundreds of candles. Banquet tables lined the room, their surfaces entirely covered with fancy food and casks of what I assumed was wine.

The crazy bastard really was throwing an inauguration ball, and here we were dressed for battle.

I glanced around as everyone gathered near us, but saw no sign of Estus. I saw no sign of anyone, for that matter. Maybe we were early.

Just as I was about to open my mouth and ask what we should do, movement caught my eye. The far side of the room to our left opened into a main hall. Though moments before it had been empty, the hall now slowly filled with people. A few I vaguely recognized, but most were strangers to me.

Their outfits matched the setting, with the men in antiquated tuxes, and the women in shimmering ballgowns. They didn't seem prepared for a fight, but with the Vaettir, looks can be deceiving. They formed a long procession, filtering into the room to stand opposite our large group.

At the end of the procession was Estus. He stepped into the room, his head held high, not looking at anyone. He wore his usual dark loose clothing, with his long silver braid trailing on the stone floor behind him. He walked forward, cutting a perfect line between his people, and mine.

My palms began to sweat as I waited to see what he would do, but he still wasn't looking at any of us. Instead, he approached an ornate wooden throne on the dais in the back of the room. There had never been a throne there before. I wondered if it was Estus' idea, or the key's.

He turned and sat delicately upon the throne, then looked past everyone else to smile pleasantly at me. "Welcome home, Madeline," he purred.

His polite words filled me with sudden rage. I stepped forward, flanked by Marcos and Faas. I looked directly into Estus' eyes and knew for a fact that one of us would die that night. If it was in my power to kill him, I would. If I was given a choice to either be used by him, or die, then I would do my best to take him down with me, but I would be used no more.

"Let's end this," I stated simply, raising my voice loud enough for everyone in the room to hear.

Estus/the key cocked his head. "Now Madeline, what about my leverage? Surely you haven't given up on your love so easily."

I held in my nervous laughter. He didn't know that we'd gotten Alaric and Sophie back. He wasn't all-seeing after all. The pair in question stepped forward out of the crowd.

A slight twitch of Estus' eye was the only hint of his surprise. His mouth formed a tight, angry line. He returned his cold gaze to me. "I see I have underestimated you. How irritating. What of the Morrigan?"

"What of the key?" I asked in reply. "Or is that who's speaking right now?"

His sudden grin was one of the most frightening things I'd ever seen. "I truly have underestimated you. It was never fair that the Norns and the Morrigan were given living forms and not I. I have simply remedied that injustice."

My entire body felt abuzz with nervous energy. Was I really speaking to the key? I'd had it in my mind before, so I knew it was sentient. I knew it was capable of anger and surprise. Yet the abomination before us seemed almost . . . human. Just like Mara.

I spared a second to glance at his waiting followers. They all stared forward at us with dead fish eyes. I hadn't noticed their lifeless gazes before, but something was very wrong.

"He's done something to them," Faas whispered in my ear. "I cannot see anyone's energy."

Estus/the key chuckled, drawing my attention back to him. "I could not have you stealing any more of my people away. I'll need them before the night is through. Now come to me, Madeline," he demanded.

He lifted a hand and I was overcome with a tugging sensation. I took a staggering step forward. Both Marcos and Faas were quick to grab hold of me, having stood witness the last time this particular form of magic was used.

I felt a wave of scalding anger behind me, then Alaric and Mikael stepped past us to face Estus, weapons in hand.

"Get them," Mikael commanded, pointing his axe in the direction of Estus' people.

"*Wait*," Estus snapped, suddenly releasing his hold over me. "Madeline must hear my proposal before any action is taken. This is a celebration, not a standoff."

"He's completely out of his mind," Faas muttered, gazing at Estus. His grip tightened on my arm.

Between that and Marcos' firm grip on my other arm, I felt utterly useless.

I pulled away from them both and stepped forward of my own volition. I glared at Estus sitting primly upon his throne. "Speak your words quickly," I demanded. "We haven't got all night."

He stood, and all the energy in the room shifted. It wasn't something that could be seen, but even those who couldn't sense energy probably felt it. It was like the pressure before a storm broke, when the earth was dry and cracked, the sun beating down, but you knew any moment the clouds would move in and a torrential downfall would be released.

"I'd rather not speak in front of an audience," Estus said dryly. "But I can assure you, you'll want to hear what I have to say if you hope to survive after Yggdrasil is regrown."

Several of our people gasped around us. For them, rumors about regrowing the World Tree just became reality.

"What do you mean?" I asked.

He smirked, then moved to close some of the distance between us. I noticed with a start that his feet were no longer touching the ground. He was moving on waves of the key's power.

"You truly believe the old gods will let you live?" he laughed. "You are an abomination Madeline, just like me. They will kill us both."

My first thought was that if we regrew Yggdrasil, the key would already be as good as dead, but I didn't say it out loud.

"You're lying," Faas accused from beside me.

Estus chuckled, keeping his gaze on me. "Ask the necromancer if you don't believe me."

Everyone shifted nervously around us.

I turned my gaze to Marcos.

He did his odd little bit of tilting his head to the side, like he was directly listening to Hecate. "It is a possibility that some will want you dead. Others will not see you as a threat."

"I have a way to ensure the old gods cannot touch us," Estus said, drawing my eyes back to him.

Mikael let out a growl of annoyance. "We tire of your games. Spit out what you have to say and let us get on with this."

"I want to grow a new kind of tree," he explained, his eyes never leaving my face. "Instead of reaching into the heavens, we'll reach into the underworld. Instead of connecting with the old gods, we'll embrace the dead. I sense the power of death within you, growing every day. Together we will be more powerful than ever before."

"Yeah, no thanks," I answered. "I think I'm going to go with my plan." I resisted the urge to place my hand on my belly. What would happen to my child if such a fate came to pass?

He sighed. "This would have been so much easier if I didn't have to force you." He glanced at his waiting people. "But alas, everyone has come for a ball." His eyes flicked back to me. "We wouldn't want to spoil it for them with bloodshed."

If we weren't going to fight, then what the hell were we doing here? I needed to get him outside so we could end this.

He grinned as he met my eyes, almost as if he'd read my thoughts. I half-expected him to comment, but he didn't. If I ran now, would he follow me? I desperately wanted to go back outside where the banshees could protect us all.

I took a shaky breath and mustered my courage. "Are we going to duke it out or what?"

He tsked at me. "You really are a troublesome girl. If you don't want to play nice, I'll give you some motivation. My people are stationed all over the country, ready to march on the humans. All it will take is a single thought from me, and they will begin the attack. Play nice, and perhaps you and I can eliminate the need for unnecessary bloodshed. With our powers combined, we will have full control over all."

"You're lying," I countered. "You haven't had enough time to set that up."

"Am I?" he asked with a wry grin. "Would you care to test that theory?"

I would have liked to say yes, but I wasn't sure. I glanced at Mikael. He'd had more dealings with the key than I.

"Many of Aislin's smaller clans have gone missing," he explained softly. "If they are not dead, it's possible they have been recruited to this scheme. There would not be enough to take over the country, not by a long shot, but they could cause a great deal of death and chaos."

I frowned. "Or they might just be dead."

"Are we celebrating, or not!" Estus called out, interrupting us.

"*Sure*," I replied.

I wasn't willing to risk the slim chance that Estus might attack humanity, and playing along might benefit us in the long run. We needed to figure out a way to lure Estus outside. This would buy us time.

"Excellent," he replied, then began to chant.

I didn't recognize anything he was saying, but I recognized the building power in the room. Suddenly Alaric had a hold of my arm and was dragging me toward the exit.

"He's going to transport us!" he shouted. "This is what happened when he sent us back before!"

The sudden panic of those around us made me weak in the knees.

Sophie, who'd obviously jumped to conclusions as quickly as Alaric, came barreling back out of the room we'd entered through. "The way is sealed!" she shouted. "Attack!"

The bodies around us erupted into motion. They all charged toward Estus, just as Estus' people moved to cut them off.

Alaric pulled me against him as a tugging sensation overcame my body. We were too late. We hadn't expected him to use the energy to transport us, and we'd been wrong. I held on tightly to Alaric as everything went black. No matter where we went, I wasn't losing him again.

I clenched my eyes shut and we both suddenly became weightless. We were floating in empty space. I almost thought Estus was going to leave us there, then my boots touched down on soft sand. A cool ocean breeze gently pulled my hair away from my face. I huddled in the circle of Alaric's arms, with my face turned to the side against his chest.

"This cannot be." I recognized Faas' voice. We weren't the only ones who'd been transported.

I opened my eyes, but maintained a tight grip on Alaric.

We were on a desolate beach. A beach I recognized. I pulled away slightly to glance over my shoulder to where Yggdrasil once stood. I remembered touching the tree and stealing its energy like it was yesterday.

Large bonfires dotted the beach, illuminating everything.

Around us stood Mikael, Faas, Marcos, and Aila. Faas and Aila both held on tightly to Mikael's arms. I had a feeling they'd deduced that he'd be transported, and had clung on for the ride. I wasn't sure why Marcos was brought along, as he stood on his own. Everyone else had either been left behind, or transported somewhere else.

A scream cut through the night air, and we all turned to find Estus, holding on to Sophie with one arm wrapped around her waist. The hilt of a blade stuck out from her ribs. The light of a nearby fire showed her black clothing growing even darker with blood.

"Sophie," Alaric gasped, then began to pull away from me.

"I wouldn't do that, if I were you," Estus chided, his pale eyes on Alaric. "Madeline's power is death. The only chance she stands of defeating me is to gather more energy."

Sophie slumped to the ground as Estus released her. I could feel her life slowly draining away. It called out to me.

Before any of us could react, Estus lifted a hand and Aila collapsed to the ground, screaming in agony. Her hands lifted to the side of her head as she doubled over. He flicked his wrist, and her body jerked to the side, ending with a horrible cracking sound. She went still, then slumped forward into the sand.

Mikael screamed in rage beside her. Drawing his axe from his belt with a feral growl, he rushed toward Estus. Alaric hesitated beside me, as if unsure whether to remain by my side, or to check on Sophie.

Estus held up a hand and Mikael suddenly halted. Mikael's rage and pain over losing Aila were almost over-whelming. She had been by his side for hundreds of years. He took an agonizing step forward, pushing through the key's magic.

The power coming from Estus' body was staggering, but Mikael managed yet another step.

"I will kill him," Estus said, his focus all on me. "Then I will kill Alaric and the rest. Feed from the lives of the women. Use your friends' sacrifices to defeat me. It is the only way to save the rest of them."

Faas stood near me with tears running down his face. "He's trying to align your powers," he breathed. "He's wants to make you the death that he needs, so that he can grow the tree of his choosing."

I looked to Alaric, who appeared completely at a loss. Fresh tears clung to the rims of his eyes.

I turned back to Estus. He'd left me with no choices. If I stole the remaining energy from Sophie and Aila, I might be able to defeat him. To regrow Yggdrasil as it was meant to be. We were at war, and there were casualties in war. Death to the few to benefit the many.

"No," I growled.

Estus raised an eyebrow at me. Mikael was still strug-gling toward him. He flicked his wrist and blood blossomed at Mikael's throat, almost like Estus had thrown a knife at him, though no blade could be seen. Still, Mikael struggled forward as blood dripped down, soaking his shirt. His face held fury while his red hair blew wildly in the breeze, making him appear like some sort of vengeful god.

"Soon he will be weakened," Estus explained, seeming slightly annoyed that Mikael was still standing. "Surely with his energy you could defeat me. Use your necromancer to aid you, if you wish."

Marcos stood off to the side like a dark shadow. Offering neither help, nor resistance.

I turned back to Estus. "No," I growled again.

"*No*?" he questioned with a cruel smile. "Then you shall have me kill them all? Alaric is next."

Alaric suddenly collapsed like Aila had. His pain-filled face looked up toward mine. "Don't do it," he said through gritted teeth. "Don't give him what he wants."

"If you defeat him with death, then you will grow what he wants to grow," Faas said calmly from behind me. I felt his pain as Estus attacked him next.

"No!" I shouted, rage and agony taking over my mind. I would not be what he wanted me to be. I would not plunge the world into darkness. We were all better off dead.

I began marching toward Estus.

"You are too weak to harm me," he said, watching my approach. He turned his attention back to Alaric and Faas.

They both screamed out in pain.

I continued to approach, with only my power, and the power of the fates within me.

"I've seen great evils in this world," I muttered, bringing Estus' attention back to me. "I've seen death, pain, and injustice. I've seen plenty of things that could turn a woman toward darkness."

He released his invisible hold on Faas and Alaric as I continued toward him. I prayed they were alright. This had to end. Right here. The death of a few to save the many.

"But I've also seen love," I continued. "I've seen love persuade a man to turn his back on vengeance. I've seen love creating families for those who long ago gave up on the idea."

Estus/the key watched me, confused.

I smiled. "Love has given me more strength and bravery than fear and pain ever did. Love is what makes us face our fears. Love shines light into the darkness. Love is the glue that holds fate and life together."

"What are you babbling about?" Estus asked snarkily, though his voice quavered. Good.

"Love is more powerful than chaos," I continued. "It's more powerful than death. I may be death itself. I may be capable of darkness. But my love will always shine more brightly."

I took a few more steps forward, putting us face to face.

I hugged him, and he was too stunned to react. Yggdrasil required the energies of fate, chaos, and all that the Morrigan had embodied to be reborn. She might not have been with me, but I had that energy too.

"If you regrow Yggdrasil this way, we'll both die!" Estus shouted into my ear.

I continued to hug him as I opened up my connection to the earth. I could feel the energy of the ocean pounding in my skull. I could feel the lives slowly leaking out of my loved ones around me.

This was the right thing to do. My child and I would become part of Yggdrasil, along with the key. The lives of the few to save the many.

Power swept over us as Estus/the key began to cry in my arms. *Chaos is love too*, I thought. *It's love and hate, life and death. We're the same*, I realized.

That was something I had to accept long ago, a voice echoed in my mind. Mara's voice.

As I thought of Mara, she was suddenly there. She pushed her phantom form between Estus and I, forcing me away as she embraced him.

Suddenly knowing what to do, I pressed my hands against her back, pushing all of my energy forth. I released the energy of the Norn into them both. As the last bits of power left me, I was thrown back into the sand like I'd been hit with a turbulent gust of wind. The forms of Mara and Estus lit up in a golden ray of light. It shot up into the sky, and down into the sand.

I tried to sit up, but the power of it forced me flat onto my back. All I could do was watch as the golden branches of a tree formed. They stretched up endlessly while the light at the center of the tree increased. Mara and Estus could no longer be seen.

I laid in the sand and sobbed like a baby. Mara had sacrificed her soul to save me. She'd been hated in life. Feared. Now she'd sacrificed everything to save the race she'd once despised. To save us all.

I stared up at the golden light as it wove its way through the sky like tiny veins in a giant leaf. The sand beneath my back grew warm, and suddenly I realized why. It was lit up with that same golden light. The roots of the World Tree were taking hold.

Suddenly there was a presence above my head, then hands gripped beneath my armpits to pull me backwards. Soon I was nestled in someone's lap, with my head against a muscular chest. Alaric turned my face enough to kiss me, encasing us in his dark hair.

I felt another presence at our side, and pulled away to see Sophie. Her wound was gone. She sat in the sand beside us, staring up at the glowing tree.

Next came Mikael, then Faas and Aila, all uninjured.

I stared back up at the tree, surrounded by my family, and smiled despite my sadness. This is what Mara and the Norns had wanted. How things were supposed to be.

The air grew chilly. I sensed the banshees at our backs. Though Mara was gone, they were still here. Still ready to serve me.

It's pretty, one of their voices sounded in my mind, speaking of the tree.

I had to agree with her. It was a miraculous sight. The golden branches reaching up into the sky would bring the old gods down upon us. Wild magics would be released into the world, and we had no idea what that might mean for any of us.

There would be many consequences to come, but for now, we had won.

"You're free now," I said out loud, speaking to the banshees. "Your task is done, I release you."

Alaric watched me, his face close to mine, but didn't comment.

You must return us to the earth, one of the banshees replied.

No, I thought back. *It's time for you to let go. Your true Phantom Queen is now free. So too are you.*

A flurry of confusion raced through my mind, then excitement. The banshees had waited a *very* long time to be free. It was probably a bad move to give up my best weapon, but I knew what it felt to be used for the goals of others. I wouldn't be anything like Estus or the key.

I relaxed against Alaric. We'd still have to deal with the old gods, but we'd do it just like we'd done everything else.

Together.

26

Three Months Later

"You need to eat more," Faas chided, shoving another piece of buttered toast near my face from his seat next to me at the table.

I snatched the toast from him with a glare and placed it on my plate, just as Alaric added another heaping scoop of scrambled eggs from my other side.

I sat back in my chair and pouted. "You guys are going to make me fat."

Mikael smiled at me from the other side of the table. "You need to eat more if little Erykah is going to grow up to be a proper Viking."

I rolled my eyes at him, then placed a hand on my rapidly growing belly. Little Erykah, named after the woman who'd lost her life to the key, and who'd helped me learn how to defeat it, was currently jabbing my bladder.

Still, I smiled through the discomfort, overjoyed that she'd be born into a brave new world of our creation.

Three months had passed since we'd regrown Yggdrasil, and things were slowly beginning to change. Though we were yet to see signs of the old gods, we had little doubt they'd be coming. Strange magical occurrences were popping up all over the world. The humans still weren't aware of the cause. Many now believed the apocalypse was coming, and an alien invasion was heavy on conspiracy theorist minds.

It was all building toward something. We weren't sure what, but as long as it wasn't the key returning to destroy us all, we could handle it.

Mikael and I had gone ahead with our plan to rule as Co-Doyens. After the tree had been regrown, we'd realized that Estus had just transported us to a different place, not a different time.

It had taken us a few days, but we'd eventually made it back to the Salr in Washington to find it wasn't there. None of the Salr were. At first we'd been horrified that those within had disappeared along with the magical structure, but eventually we found them under the care of Silver. He'd had faith Mikael would return, and thus found residences for everyone using a huge chunk of the money Mikael had amassed over his long life. Mikael had been a little pissed, but was also glad his people were safe.

Since then we'd done the best we could to get everyone settled into life outside of the Salr. It was difficult to assimilate into human life when most of the Vaettir had no forms of ID, and little knowledge of modern technology, but we managed.

Estus/the key had lied when he said his people were all ready to assault humanity. A last ditch effort to get me to cooperate. I was glad, because if the Vaettir had started attacking humans, we'd be worrying about a lot more right now than making sure everyone had a place to stay.

For now, the humans were safe. The rest of us were preparing for the worst, while enjoying our freedom. The key's warning still hung heavy on my mind. Would the old gods want to kill me for being an abomination? We still didn't really know what I actually was, not really. Maybe if they didn't jump right to killing us, the old gods could answer some questions.

I would have liked to ask Marcos what Hecate thought, but he'd disappeared while we'd all been in awe of the newly grown tree. No one had seen him since, but I had little doubt he'd be popping up eventually. Whether he'd be popping up as friend or foe was anyone's guess. He'd claimed Hecate wanted to regrow Yggdrasil, but hadn't divulged *why*. I wasn't sure I really wanted to know.

For the time being, I was just going to enjoy my life with my odd little family. Erykah would be born into an environment filled with love, and would learn how to be a tough little spitfire from her aunties Sophie and Aila. Her uncle Mikael would probably try to teach her how to fight and drink whiskey, but I'd do my best to hold him off until she was a bit older. Uncle Faas would be there to make sure she got proper nutrition, if nothing else.

I leaned my head against Alaric's shoulder and smiled,

watching my family chat and eat, then Kira and Sivi walked into the room hand in hand.

Sivi was a different woman since getting her sister back. She'd lost her motivation to destroy to all humans, given that motivation had sprung from the death of her sister, which was a lie. She still scared the living bejeezus out of me, but as long as she wasn't killing anyone, I was happy to have her and Kira around.

I lifted my head from Alaric's shoulder and sipped my coffee. Sophie and Aila returned to the dining room with a fresh pot of coffee, chatting in cheerful tones neither of them ever directed at anyone besides each other.

I laughed to myself. Life was strange, but I wouldn't have it any other way. I might have spent most of my life without a family, but I had one now, and that was all that mattered.

Now one might ask, "Since when does death get a happy ending?"

The answer to that is quite simple.

Since death grew a heart.

NOTE FROM THE AUTHOR

I hope you've enjoyed the fourth installment in the Bitter Ashes Series. Please take the time to leave a review!

To be notified of new releases, please sign up for my mailing list by visiting:

www.saracroethle.com

Printed in Great
Britain
by Amazon

32152322R00190